THE
KAMIKAZE
LEGACY

Books by Jerry and Sharon Ahern

Miamigrad
Yakusa Tattoo
WerewolveSS
The Kamikaze Legacy
The Takers
River of Gold
Summon the Demon

THE
KAMIKAZE
LEGACY

Jerry and Sharon Ahern

SPEAKING VOLUMES, LLC

NAPLES, FLORIDA

2012

THE KAMIKAZE LEGACY

ISBN 978-1-61232-335-0

For lifetime Ahern pal Jerry Buergel, again, who knows that all this stuff really goes on in Chicago and that's why it's so neat to live there. Best of everything, buddy. . . .

Acknowledgments

Whenever we write a book that deals with anything underwater, we know the one man to whom to turn for assistance. His information is not only imaginative and accurate, but cheerfully given. That man is, of course, Jim Foley. Jim is Manager, Sales Administration, for Mares USA, a division of Head Sports, Inc.

An expert's expert, he is the author of the standard divers' navigation manual, *How to Find Your Way*. Ask anyone who knows his stuff in diving, and he'll know Jim Foley, too.

We've "found our way" through the diving sequences in *The Kamikaze Legacy* because of Jim, and thanks just really aren't enough.

Also, a special thanks to our friend and neighbor, Terry Bennett. Terry assisted us mightily (at six foot six, he does everything "mightily") in developing accurate Japanese names for our characters, which otherwise might have proved impossible. We wish to also thank Daichi Saito, a resident of Japan living in close proximity to the area mentioned in our story, for his additional input regarding traditional Japanese names.

Jerry Ahern and Sharon Ahern
Commerce, Georgia
1990

Contents

CONTENTS

Chapter One

Appearances

She looked both ways when she reached the corner, but not because she was a good little girl taking her mother's advice.

John Trench Osgood rubbed a fast-food restaurant napkin over the porthole-shaped window on the van's left side and watched the Eurasian woman intently through the borrowed 8 x 30s. She was too obvious and too tacky to be his type, but he was bored out of his mind, and she was, at least, diverting. He sent her a silent "thank you" across the cold night.

Straight, almost black hair cascaded to a waist tightly cinched into a maroon trench coat. The mist-slicked vinyl dramatically accentuated a tight-looking little rear end made more prominent by the impossibly high-heeled shoes she wore. Her calf muscles, bound within fishnet stockings, looked well developed. A jogger in her off hours, he conjectured.

Maybe eighteen, except for the heavily made-up eyes, which were well past oblivion.

1

She was not about to cross the street, as she'd set up shop there. The kind of traffic she was watching for wouldn't normally be vehicular, either. Smart ladies of the evening these days avoided jumping into passing cars, because they could get more than they'd bargained for—in spades.

Osgood looked away from the Eurasian with the steaming breath and steamier profession, put down the binoculars, and rubbed his eyes with balled-up fists. When he glanced back into the van, he thought about Nelson Eddy.

Sergeant Pierre Frontenac of the Royal Canadian Mounted Police sat calmly in front of three video monitors, headphones over thinning gray hair, with a cup of coffee and a glazed doughnut—Frontenac's third. He did not fit the dashing Mountie image. Pierre Frontenac riding at the center of a phalanx of red-coated heroes singing "Dead or Alive"? Or wooing Jeanette MacDonald with an Indian love call? Osgood doubted Pierre Frontenac could woo the Eurasian girl with anything but a gold card.

No, Frontenac was not the classic Mountie, but neither was Tom Hardington very much in the mold of James Arness, the quintessential marshal. Rather than a long-barreled Colt Single-Action Army slung to the hip of a near giant frame, the skinny, wiry-looking Hardington shoulder-holstered a German-made SIG-Sauer P-226. His United States Marshal's Service circled star wasn't pinned to a faded vest, but in the pocket of the parka he draped over the back of a folding chair as he sat down. Unless he'd moved the badge case.

Montreal, P.Q., Canada, was a long way, after all, from any frontier, really. It was as close to Europe as anything in the Americas could be. Images of heroic marshals and Mounties were equally alien here. And the Eurasian girl was neither a red-haired saloon proprietress with a heart of gold nor an operatic soprano in search of a wayward brother. She was just a hooker; and fantasies of any kind, rather than beginning with a girl like her, ended abruptly.

2

"Cold out there, guys. Wish these buttheads would've picked a warmer climate for this deal they're puttin' down."

"We're having a mild winter, fellows," Frontenac told Hardington almost absently through a mouthful of doughnut, as if his oath to defend Canada extended to the weather as well. "Usually a lot colder about now, really."

But both Frontenac and Hardington were good at their craft, however little they physically resembled the stereotype.

Osgood opened his silver cigarette case, lit a Pall Mall with his Dunhill lighter, and glanced at the face of his Rolex as the lighter flared. He was reminded suddenly of something told to him years ago by one of his instructors at the Farm in Virginia. He'd just been entering Central Intelligence, learning the basics of a trade he'd studied for in private ever since boyhood and plied ever since adulthood. "John, damn, but you really look like a secret agent, son. Tall, slim, kinda 'don't fuck with me' look in your eyes, athletic as hell. I mean, you're good! Languages, firearms, encryption and decryption techniques, analysis, electronics, sabotage, explosives, martial arts. If I've ever had a better student in 'spy school,' I'd be damn hard pressed to think of who the son of a bitch was. Learn to use that look, son. It'll inspire confidence, even if sometimes you just plain don't know what you're doin'. 'Cause you'll never know when that look you got can help you get the job done and still get home with all the major parts of your ass intact."

His ass, at the moment, was numb, but there wasn't room in the van to get up and move around much. On the plus side, however, his ass was intact. The search for Takeuchi Arisato, so far, was more challengingly boring than dangerous.

"So, Mr. Osgood, anybody in this video look like you think your man Takeuchi might look?" Frontenac asked through more doughnut.

Osgood hunched his shoulders into his black woolen

coat—he was a little cold just sitting here for three and a half hours—and leaned forward, staring over the Mountie's right shoulder. "The center screen?"

"Yes, sir, that one. The group of Japanese walking along into the cabaret there? Any likely prospects?"

The camera monitoring the front entrance to the Shamrock Pub was part of a window display in a women's clothing store across the street from the night spot, and every time a bus or car drove past at the right angle, the lens was temporarily blinded by the lights. Such was the case now, but after a moment the video was restored.

There was only a "profile" of Takeuchi Arisato, a physical description put together by computer analysis out of bits and pieces of fragmentary recollections culled from Takeuchi's victims in airports, on school buses, in churches and synagogues, and in semidemolished public buildings over the years. "I think when he shot that poor woman—my God—but he held the gun in his right hand." "He was tall, not like a Japanese at all, but definitely Japanese." "It sounded like he had a cold or something, because his voice was deep." "Big jaw, ya know, like his face was all kinda skinny." "Looked muscular under those black clothes, kind of athletic and powerful." John Osgood could close his eyes and hear the voices quite clearly, even now, and sometimes see the faces—pain and fear still in their eyes—which belonged to those voices.

The computer had dutifully generated a probable sketch of Takeuchi Arisato, if that was really the man's name. No one knew for sure. The face in the sketch was something like Arnold Schwarzenegger's countenance might appear if he were to go on a starvation diet and have his eyelids surgically altered to simulate epicanthic folds. That Takeuchi looked anything like the computer's handiwork was doubtful at best. Six Japanese, almost stereotypical businessmen, walked toward the club, eyeing the Eurasian girl fleetingly. They were laughing, talking, seemingly oblivious to the cold that gripped the city this night. All were

4

average height for Japanese, none of them large or physically powerful seeming.

None of them was a likely candidate to be Takeuchi Arisato.

"I don't know," Osgood said.

"Bring up the camera on the alley, Pierre," Tom Hardington suggested.

"Right." Frontenac pushed some buttons, and the far left monitor showed the alley. This camera was hidden in a utility pole array, and the image was crisp and clear, but the lighting was poor. Nothing was on the screen except the same slightly overflowing trashcans and slicked black pavement Osgood had seen the last time he looked.

"So much for that," Osgood commented. He flicked ashes from his cigarette into a Styrofoam cup half-filled with coffee and floating cigarette butts. As he looked back to the console, the third screen—the one on the far right—caught his eye. "You taping?"

"Yes, sir."

"Good. Play back the last sixty seconds of camera three."

"Yes, sir."

"Whatchya see, Mr. Osgood?"

Osgood didn't answer Hardington, but instead riveted his eyes to the screen. Flicker, static, picture. "Freeze it!" At a table in the far corner of the club, the clandestinely planted camera—which had taken them two weeks of planning and a four A.M. black bag job to plant behind an identical duplicate of the bar mirror—caught the florid, furtive-eyed face of Randy Bleeker.

"How the hell'd he get in there?"

This time Osgood answered Hardington. "I don't know." But he had a hunch that perhaps the Shamrock Pub had more than front and rear entrances, although architectural plans, building permits, and everything else imaginable they could dig out on the building housing the Shamrock Pub indicated there were none.

"If our Mr. Bleeker's inside, then Takeuchi's coming,"

Frontenac said, putting down his doughnut and lighting a cigarette, an air of finality about his words.

Osgood agreed. "I'm going in. Takeuchi shouldn't know my face. Try to keep an eye on me once I'm inside."

Frontenac nodded, exhaling. "Right you are, sir."

"Hey, why don't I go in there and back ya up?" Hardington suggested, a smile crossing his face, lighting his pale blue eyes.

"Keep a weather eye on that monitor and do what you think's best if anything happens, instead," Osgood suggested.

Hardington sighed, nodding. "Your play."

Osgood opened the rear door of the van and stepped out into the underground parking garage, his eyes moving toward the street corner a block away, fixing on the Eurasian girl. He snapped up the collar of his coat and began to walk—up the slight dip in the yellow-line-painted concrete, across the emptied parking spaces, and toward the sidewalk.

The girl was watching him now.

Osgood was tempted to wave. Instead, he shrugged his shoulders slightly inside his coat, to shift the weight of the Sam Andrews shoulder harness. Andrews was a custom holster maker of considerable skill and had hand-built the rig John Osgood had been wearing for the last year. On the left side, hanging diagonally, was his standard Walther P-38K, not the latest in multifeatured 9mm Parabellum fighting handguns to be sure, but his favorite for fifteen years. On the right side were two spare eight-round magazines and, diagonally behind these in a pull-through snap-closure removable sheath, butt downward, was one of the two knives he habitually carried these days. It was hand-made for him by knife maker Pat Crawford and called the Special Dart. The other knife was clipped into the breast pocket of the black shirt he wore, beside his Mont Blanc pen. That second knife was a B&D Grande folder.

The old George Lawrence #8 shoulder holster he'd worn for so many years was packed away in the bottom of the cedar chest in which he kept his woolen sweaters at home. The other Walther he'd always carried as a spare gun in his luggage—a standard postwar P-38 with full-length barrel— was secured in the safe at his home. Other items of value were in that safe, among them a gold Rolex President, the good silver service, family albums, and his most prized possession, love letters exchanged between him and his late wife. It was a fireproof safe of the finest quality available. The watch and the silver could be replaced and were insured. The photo albums would be sorely missed. But the letters . . .

He snapped away the butt of his cigarette. The voice of the Eurasian girl called after him, "Hey, mister?"

Osgood turned the corner, at last could see the green, neon-outlined sign: Shamrock Pub.

His hands dug into the pockets of the hip-length black jacket. His breath steaming, Osgood quickened his pace, the click of his shoes on the pavement the only sound he could hear except the distant acceleration of a bus.

At the pub door Osgood nudged with his shoulder, and the overly elaborate, yet still cheap-looking door—green, of course—opened. The atmosphere inside the pub was a shock to his lungs after the cold of the street. The Shamrock was warm, thick with gray trailers of cigarette and cheap cigar smoke, heady with the smell of beer and hard liquor.

The main portion of the floor was given over to small round tables, not much larger in diameter than the seat of a bar stool, yet three or four or five—in one case six—people crowded around each. At the far end was a six-foot-wide stage, with an acoustic guitar on a stand there beside the chrome shaft of a microphone. Overlarge disco speakers were set on either side of the stage.

To Osgood's left was the bar. It was segmented at the center, stopping dead from either end to allow for a dart board. No one was playing now, and the darts were on a small shelf below the pitted board. He wondered absently how the barman—correction, barmaid—made it from one

7

side of the bar to the other without being impaled while a heated game was in progress.

John Osgood started toward the bar now, threading his way through the interesting crowd. The mixture here would have gladdened the heart of the most wide-eyed liberal social planner, the attire ranging from evening dress to workman's clothes, with men and women of virtually every social strata imaginable. As Osgood gently shouldered his way to a position at the bar, he found himself between a blond-haired woman of about thirty-five dressed in a tailored suit and a man in worn blue jeans, a frayed peacoat, and navy blue watch cap.

The barmaid—a marvelously pretty brunette with pansy-blue eyes and an impossibly small waist—called over to him. "With ya in a minute, sir."

Osgood nodded, lit a cigarette from his case once he spotted an ashtray nearby, and swept his gaze over the far end of the floor. Sitting alone at a table, nursing a beer, was Randy Bleeker, the man who'd gotten inside, somehow, without detection.

"Whatchya have, sir?"

Osgood turned back toward the bar, startled at the barmaid's eyes so close to his. She smiled, evidently used to the reaction and liking it. "I'll have a Cutty, neat, please."

"Right you are," she said, and she was gone. Osgood could see Bleeker clearly in the wide mirror hung over the bar, and knew that Pierre Frontenac and Tom Hardington could see him through the lens of the video camera clandestinely installed behind it.

The door opened and a man and a woman in expensive business suits left, talking, laughing, arm-in-arm, and a tall, bony-featured man in work clothes entered. For an instant Osgood thought it might be Takeuchi, but the features were East Indian, Sikh to be precise, rather than Oriental.

"Here's your Cutty, sir," the barmaid said, putting Osgood's drink down in front of him. "Run you a tab?"

"No. I'm expecting a call on my pager."

"Four even, then. You don't look like a businessman, so you must be a doctor or somethin'."

"I'm a specialist, actually. Something might go critical at any moment."

"I can always pick 'em," she said, smiling back, making Osgood realize just then that he was smiling at her. The barmaid's speech, as well as that of quite a few of the patrons, was dotted with the antiquated French accent frequently spoken in the streets of Quebec.

"That man over there alone in the far corner. He looks familiar," Osgood told her.

"Him? Friend o' the boss, ya know, but a real nasty sort, really. Even uses the boss's private entrance."

"Well, he must be close with your boss, then. What's this private entrance?" Osgood pressed. "Back door or something?"

"No, the back door just opens up from the alley. It's through the office somewhere, but I've never seen it. They say this place was built when you Yanks had that Prohibition law, and the rum runners used to use it for their comin's and goin's."

"That's really fascinating," Osgood told her, sipping at his drink. "May I buy you a drink?"

"Can buy me a Diet Coke if ya like, but I don't touch none o' this stuff. Bad for the health and the figure," and as if to accentuate the latter she placed both hands on her waist and twirled around for him once. "See?"

"I see, indeed. A Diet Coke, then."

"Thanks." Her smile was genuine.

"You're welcome." He smiled back.

As she got herself the Diet Coke, Osgood looked into the mirror again, alternating his gaze from Randy Bleeker to the doorway at the end of the small hallway. There were rest rooms along the hallway, and the doorway at the far end was presumably the entrance to the office. It could be a storeroom, with the office beyond that.

As he sipped his Cutty, he heard some less than enthusiastic applause. He turned around from the bar and saw a girl with waist-length, very pretty brown hair come onto the small stage and pick up the guitar. Her hair was parted in the middle, and the look she conveyed—floral print skirt to her ankles, peasant blouse, an abundance of bracelets and necklaces and large earrings—was at once reminiscent of a 1960s flower child and a gypsy.

She strummed a little on the guitar, tuning it, and as she did so the noise level in the bar dropped by fifty percent.

When she began to sing—"Don't Weep After Me"—the room fell into a hush so total it was almost unnerving. Osgood stubbed out his cigarette. The lights were going down, and his eyes were focused on Randy Bleeker, because if anything was going to happen, it was going to happen now. Osgood's right hand rested on his right thigh, so he could reach for the Special Dart in a second.

The girl's voice was not only beautiful, but trained, without a hint of quiver in the higher range, nor a suggestion that it was forced as her voice lowered. Her breathing was even, her composure perfect, and her timing exquisite. Her guitar work was simple, but that was the nature of the song.

Randy Bleeker downed the remains of his beer, lit a cigarette, and stood up.

From behind Osgood the pretty barmaid asked, "Another drink, love?"

"Another time, love."

Bleeker moved along the wall, toward the little corridor. John Osgood took the last swallow of Cutty and stood up, his eyes moving about the room, looking for some sign that Bleeker had friends here. He saw no sign of that, then started through the crowd toward the corridor at the rear of the Shamrock Pub.

The corridor was in shadow, but the darkness was not so absolute that Osgood lost sight of him. Bleeker passed the doors on the right side of the corridor and walked toward the single door at the rear.

As Osgood neared the wall, he realized the man in the

worn jeans and peacoat was right behind him. Osgood turned toward the man quickly, looking down, and saw a switchblade knife flick open in the man's right hand.

Osgood reacted, and with his left hand grabbed up a mug of beer from the table nearest him, then smashed the mug down across the man's right wrist. Osgood's right hand snapped the knife from its inverted sheath. He drove the knife forward and upward under the rib cage to the left of the sternum and into his assailant's heart.

The peacoated man doubled forward, groaned, and started to collapse. His lids snapped wide open and his eyes stared. Osgood grabbed for him, twisting the knife to knot off as much blood flow as he could, but leaving the knife where it was. He raised his voice to shout, "Someone call a doctor! This man's had a heart attack!" It was the truth after all, because the knife Osgood used had penetrated the heart.

Other hands helped Osgood. There was a loud sound of flatulence and the smell of fecal material as the dead man's sphincter muscles relaxed. A puddle started on the floor at the apex of the dead man's legs. The long-haired girl's singing was drowned out under the growing noise from panicky bystanders. "Better cradle his head, there." Osgood kicked away the dead man's switchblade knife and pulled his own knife free of the body. Wiping the triangular blade along the lining of the dead man's peacoat, Osgood stood up and stepped back. "I'll get some water!" The knife was along the inside of Osgood's right forearm as he pushed through the crowd toward the corridor where the bathrooms were.

There was no sign of Bleeker now. "Damn."

Osgood quickened his pace. With the lights down would Frontenac and Hardington know what was going on? Would they act?

Osgood reached the corridor and resheathed his knife. His right hand glided beneath the left side of his coat and grasped the butt of the P-38K. He kicked open the door into the ladies' room, a sliding bolt lock shattering and skittering across the floor. A solitary woman of about thirty was standing in front of the mirror. She was pretty, and she turned around to look at him. "Hey!"

No hidden entrances or exits were in view, and no one else was in the small rectangular-shaped room. Both stall doors were open. There was an overpowering smell of disinfectant mingled with hairspray and perfume. "Some other time," Osgood said, and smiled at the woman.

John Osgood moved along the corridor, stopping next at the door to the men's room. Again, his hand on the butt of his gun, he kicked open the door. This time there was no lock. A solitary man knelt in front of the solitary booth, barfing into the toilet. No entrances, no exits, nowhere else someone could hide.

Osgood started back into the corridor when a burly man grabbed for him out of the shadows. "What the fuck you doin', man?"

The club bouncer? There was no time to find out. Osgood turned into the man, and sent his right knee smashing upward into the crotch, the middle knuckles of Osgood's left hand snapping out and back, striking against the windpipe, but not hard enough to kill. The burly man dropped to both knees, doubled forward, and rolled onto his right side into a fetal position, gasping for air, hugging his testicles with both hands, knees locked together.

"Breathe slowly, evenly, and you'll be all right," Osgood cautioned, already moving along the corridor. Osgood popped the thumb break on his shoulder holster and snapped the pistol out of the leather, still keeping the gun under his coat.

He stopped before the rear door, took a step back, and wheeled half right, his left foot snapping out against the door near where the lockplate met the frame.

The door sprung inward, parts of the lock flying across the room. Osgood dodged left as he came out of the kick. There was a sound like an automobile backfire, barely audible over the din of shouting customers beyond the mouth of the corridor. There was a metallic scraping sound, too, and a thud into the corridor wall near Osgood's right shoulder. All three sounds came in the same instant.

It was a suppressor-fitted pistol without a slide lock. Osgood's mind processed the data and printed out the conclusion without any conscious thought. Then Osgood was moving, snapping off two shots through the open doorway, high because he couldn't see a target, didn't want to kill an innocent, and was even less desirous of killing Bleeker or anyone who could lead him to Takeuchi Arisato.

There was a scream from beyond the doorway as Osgood flattened himself against the wall, the P-38K tight in his right fist. His thumb worked the decocking lever because he would be moving fast and didn't want a cocked pistol to worry about. His left hand groped into the pocket of his slacks and found a small handful of change. "Canadian money," Osgood thought, raising his eyebrows. He flicked the change through the doorway, then darted through, the pistol in his right 'hand tight against his right hip. Another shot was fired, suppressed like the last, the bullet tearing into the doorframe.

Osgood hit the floor and rolled behind a stack of packing crates. Another suppressed shot tore a chunk out of the crate nearest the level of his head.

Osgood threw his body weight tentatively against the crates, realized they'd move, then pushed hard. The crates tumbled onto the floor of the storeroom, the sound of glass shattering and the smell of whiskey instantly filling the air. Osgood moved right, his eyes nearly adjusted to the semi-darkness. There was another suppressor-modified shot, but he had the origin now—the packing crates to his far left.

Osgood pumped two shots as he ran, then dived behind another stack of crates. A split second later two more shots came toward him, the bullets burying themselves in the crates.

Osgood left the P-38K's hammer cocked, tried his weight against the crates, and realized they, too, would topple.

He tucked back, working the Walther's heel-of-the-butt

magazine release, withdrawing the partially spent magazine. He pocketed it and drew a fresh magazine from the carrier beneath his right arm. He thumped the magazine home, nine rounds loaded again.

Whoever was firing at him from the opposite corner of the storeroom was buying time, Osgood realized. He threw his full body weight against the stack, and the crates tumbled across the storeroom floor. Osgood ran right, made a right angle, charged against the crates behind which the gunman was sheltered, and rammed his body weight against them. He worried that these might be vastly heavier, filled with something other than liquor bottles, and that all he'd get for his trouble would be a broken shoulder.

But the crates tumbled back. Osgood caught himself, drawing back and right, the pistol tight beside his right hip again.

As the crates collapsed, a man dodged away from them. He held a pistol with a long suppressor fitted to the muzzle in both hands at maximum extension of his arms, like someone out of a TV show.

Osgood snapped the Walther's trigger back twice. The gunman's body slammed back into the storeroom wall, spun around, then slid down, a solitary shot coming from the weapon in the already dead man's hands.

Osgood was beside an open doorway. He looked to his right, grabbed two bottles of Scotch whiskey by their necks in his left hand, hurtled them through the doorway, then ran in after them. The whiskey bottles went right, Osgood went left.

No shots met him here. Under the smell of Scotch there was a heavy smell of dampness. Osgood edged along the wall, unable to make out any details of the dark chamber into which he'd come. "Bleeker!" Osgood shouted, dodging left and ducking down, the pistol in his hand ready to respond.

There was no answer, but the din from outside the storeroom was vastly reduced here, and as the echo of his own voice died, Osgood could faintly make out a thrumming somewhere in the darkness ahead of him, the sound of running footsteps.

Osgood's left hand moved to his outside jacket pocket. With his thumb, he pushed two hollow points one at a time from beneath the feedlips of the partially expended magazine and clutched them tight in his fist. Nearly to his knees, he removed the magazine from his pistol as quickly as he could and worked the two loose rounds into this magazine to replace those he'd fired. He slapped the spine of the magazine against his right thigh to seat the rounds, then put the magazine back up the butt of the pistol.

His gun fully loaded again, Osgood's left hand moved to the interior breast pocket of the jacket and found the flashlight clipped there. He twisted the head, but kept the lens beneath his coat, flush against his thigh. Edging a little right, he snapped his left hand up and outward, shining the beam forward into the darkness. No shots rang out toward him, and there was no sound of sudden movement.

There were two schools of thought when a flashlight was used in conjunction with a handgun. The modern idea was that the hand holding the light should support the hand holding the gun, so the bore of the handgun and the beam of the flashlight pointed in the same direction at all times.

Osgood had always seen that as a marvelous way to give an adversary an ideal target. It was the other school of tactics to which Osgood subscribed, less fashionable but, he felt, decidedly more practical in the real world. He kept the flashlight high and left of his body, his right hand holding the pistol close in against his body frame.

Holding gun and light this way, Osgood raised up from his crouch just inside the open doorway and started forward now.

The beam from the Mini Maglite revealed wall surfaces made of old, rough-hewn stone blocks in irregular shapes, patched together with flaking mortar, the seams sweating dampness in large, almost crystal-clear droplets.

Osgood began moving across the room, and the walls narrowed in the beam of his flash. Now they were little more than shoulder's width apart.

It was a tunnel.

Osgood quickened his pace, the beam from his flashlight zigzagging across the floor of the tunnel several feet ahead of him. He focused the light as pencil thin as he could make it and held the Walther tight in his right fist. The floor of the tunnel—slick under foot—angled slightly downward. He thought of the barmaid with the pretty blue eyes and the dark hair and her trim waist. It was a tunnel from the old days—Prohibition—when American gangsters came to Canada to arrange their shipments of illicit booze.

Where the tunnel originated was the question now. He had to catch up with Randy Bleeker before Bleeker reached that point of origin and escaped into the Montreal streets. Osgood assumed that the man who'd come after him with the knife had just been insurance for Bleeker, and had not been there specifically to foil this operation. Because if Bleeker had suspected a trap, why would he have come to the Shamrock Pub in the first place?

But now any hope of catching up with Takeuchi Arisato was essentially dashed.

Unless—John Osgood quickened his pace at the thought. What if Bleeker had been sent to meet Takeuchi here in the tunnel, and Takeuchi Arisato hadn't yet kept his appointment?

Then there was still a chance.

He kept running.

The tunnel leveled off, but the surface and the walls were slicker here. Large drops of water dripped down from the tunnel ceiling, more than could be accounted for by normal condensation from dampness. He ran on, and the tunnel began to rise sharply, making the surface beneath his feet much more treacherous.

Ahead of him, he heard a loud thudding noise, as if a door had been slammed.

As John Osgood rounded a bend in the tunnel, he stopped. There was a door just visible at the far end of the tunnel another two hundred yards ahead. If the door was secured so well that he could not pass, he would have no choice but to turn back, and Bleeker would be lost.

As he came closer to the tunnel door, he could see it better. The door was made of wood, four-inch-wide verticals bound at top and middle and bottom by four-inch-wide horizontal crosspieces, with no knob. A chain was visible where one might expect to find a handle.

Osgood slowed his pace, approaching the doorway with caution lest someone was listening from the other side of the door for his footfalls, ready to fire through it. Because of the configuration of the tunnel, there was no cover from gunfire.

Osgood stopped before the door. There was a different smell here—fresher air, but a fishy smell, too—as if the doorway led out onto a wharf or dock area. With the flashlight clamped between his teeth like a cigar, Osgood's left hand tugged at the cord. The door held fast, barely budging at all.

He stepped back, away from the door, and rubbed a spot on the stone floor as dry as he could with the sole of his left shoe. He balanced on his right foot and tried a kick against the door with his left.

The door vibrated under the impact of Osgood's foot. That seemed encouraging. There were hinges, seemingly well oiled, that were exposed at top and bottom. Osgood reached into the bottom of the jacket's inside breast pocket for the Leatherman Tool folded flat there. After extracting the tool from his pocket, he shifted his gun to his left hand and unfolded the tool with his right hand. It was a pair of full-sized pliers.

Osgood pocketed his pistol, put the pliers to the ball at the top of the lower hinge pin, and started to pull. The pin didn't budge. He closed the pliers and took out the stoutest of the screwdriver blades. He worked the blade against the juncture of the hinge pin ball and the hinge, pushing, twisting, eventually wedging the screwdriver in place, then twisting slightly to pry the hinge pin upward just a little.

Once the pin was slightly elevated, he found the last of his Canadian quarters and slid it into position beside the screwdriver blade. As he drew the blade away, he wedged the quarter in.

With the quarter beneath the hinge pin ball, Osgood tried the pliers again. The pin held for an instant, then moved upward. He caught the coin as it fell free.

Osgood repeated the process with the upper hinge, but the prying part wasn't necessary this time. He then pulled the lower pin all the way out.

Here was the critical part. Osgood grabbed at the rope handle and pulled back as rapidly and as sharply as he could.

The upper hinge began to separate, and Osgood used the pliers to pull the pieces further apart. He then pushed against the upper portion of the door, the pliers serving as a fulcrum, and the lower hinge separated slightly. Then he worked the lower hinge, pulling again on the rope handle.

Then the upper hinge again.

He gave a strong tug at the rope handle.

The door began to fall inward, and John Osgood stepped back, one-handing the tool closed, his left hand drawing the pistol from his coat pocket.

As the door collapsed toward him, then swung left on its lock, Osgood edged right, snatching the flashlight from his teeth.

Beyond the door was a room brightly lit by overhead fluorescent fixtures. The tunnel mouth was flooded in a shaft of yellow, and he squinted against it. It was another storeroom piled high with cardboard boxes, but the crates were not so neatly stacked as in the liquor storage room at the Shamrock Pub. As Osgood started across the room, a woman with pretty red hair and a hard, scowling face entered from another doorway on the opposite side of the room.

There was a crowbar in her hands, and she flung it toward him as she shrieked, "Eric!" She ran as the crowbar bounced off a stack of crates almost a yard from Osgood's right shoulder, and then she ran back through the doorway through which she'd come.

Who was Eric?

Osgood sprinted across the room, his pistol in his right hand.

Eric was tall, blond, almost muscular to the point of absurdity, wearing a tight-fitting black turtleneck. He filled the doorway, going into a full-flexing strong-man pose.

John Osgood gestured with the Walther in his hand, and said, "Gun?"

"No."

"Move it, then," Osgood ordered. Eric backed up, and Osgood advanced through the doorway, then stepped back quickly as a large claw hammer arced down toward his gun hand. Eric launched himself through the doorway, Osgood sidestepping. As Eric flung himself past, the butt of Osgood's gun impacted on Eric's skull behind the left ear.

The redhead threw herself toward Osgood, and Osgood shoved her away. As he started through the doorway again, she screamed, "You son of a bitch!" She was coming at him again, the crowbar she'd originally thrown at him back in her hand.

Osgood shook his head in disgust, then quickly looked over his shoulder to make sure that he wasn't walking into something worse. He slammed the door just as she came at him. Her body crashed into it, and the door snapped back toward him.

She collapsed in a heap at his feet.

He was inside a store that was considerably longer than it was wide. The floor was covered by a dark green carpet, and fishing nets hung from the walls. In lighted glass cases all about him were sculptured reproductions of every sort of sea creature imaginable, in all sizes and colors, some very faithful to real life, some imaginative things out of a childish fantasy or a nightmare. With a few of the pieces, possibly both.

Osgood ran toward the front of the store. There were keys hanging in a lock near the top of the door on his right. He reached for the door, tore it open toward him, and stepped out into the street. A strong, icy wind lashed across his face and hands, and the perspiration from the run through the tunnel dried on his skin, chilling him.

Stretching before John Osgood to the right and left was a narrow street. Across it, there were no buildings at all, but wooden docks fronting on the St. Lawrence River.

Osgood crossed the street. A motorboat was pulling away, fighting the wind-whipped swells rising in the river's current.

John Osgood could see its only possible destination, the larger of the two islands forming Terre des Hommes, or Man and His World, the one-time site of Expo '67.

There were a number of powerboats tied along the dock, and it took John Osgood only a few moments to hotwire the fastest of them.

He threw off the last line, backed the craft out of the slip, then cut the wheel hard to his left and toward open water, throttling up port and starboard engines. Out here on the river the air was even colder, and Osgood stabbed his right hand into his pocket, holding the wheel with only his left. There was no time for gloves. The glare from the streetlights near the dock subsided, and except for the running lights of the nearly identical vessel pulling in along the northwest shore of Ile Sainte-Helene, the river was in total darkness.

Lights shone from the exhibition area on the island, but they were only security lights, as the park had closed several hours ago. As the boat Randy Bleeker piloted swept toward the shore, John Osgood thought he caught sight of another craft. He throttled back as much as he could and still make way, hoping that the noise of the wind and water would drown out any sound from the boat. He cut the wheel hard to port, glancing over his left shoulder for one last look toward the docks.

Aiming the prow toward Pont Jacques-Cartier, a plan was already forming at the back of his mind. If what he had seen along the shore of Ile Sainte-Helene had been another powerboat, Terre des Hommes could have been the planned meeting site all along, and Randy Bleeker might just be desperate enough to try to get his money from Takeuchi Arisato anyway.

All Osgood could do was hope.

John Osgood crouched on a pylon beneath the bridge, well away from the stolen boat, which he had tied beneath the bridge.

He could hear the sounds of the river lapping against the hull of the powerboat, against the pylons, too. But that was all.

The lightweight cotton sweater Osgood wore beneath his jacket was white, the shirt beneath it the same color. Osgood buttoned the neck of his black coat, and turned the collar up. Because he would need to keep the coat closed, he had already transferred his handgun to the coat's right outside pocket. He carried the spike knife in his right hand as he moved away from the pylon, jumped the short distance to the gravelly shoreline, then started inland.

He navigated high, dead grass, and some patches of old snow as he moved toward the fence. He tested the high chain-link fence with a glove to confirm that it was not electrified. Then Osgood stuck the knife through an opening in the links, leaving it in the ground on the other side. He moved back, took a running start, and jumped onto the fence. The rattling noise it made was frustrating, but there was no other way to cross without clippers, which he did not possess.

At the top of the fence there were six strands of barbed wire, but Osgood cut through these with the pliers from his

21

Leatherman Tool, cutting each strand twice and discarding the cutaway portions so he wouldn't catch lothing or flesh on the ends.

Osgood continued crossing the fence, rolling over, then jumping clear. He retrieved his knife, then started deeper into the island. He crossed a tree-lined area that in spring and summer would be grassy, but now was covered with calf-deep snow. There was enough starlight so that he could tell that no feet had trod here recently.

Osgood's feet were cold in the low boots he wore, as he hadn't really planned for a walk in deep snow. Ahead of him was a circular walkway with a circular-shaped building set within it. As he drew closer, he saw another building beyond the walkway, part of it roughly silo-shaped. Gripping the knife tighter in his right fist, he moved through the plaza between the structures, toward the far building.

It was an aquarium. Osgood got a fleeting glimpse of a light from within it. He stood stock-still, let out his breath in a cloud of steam, then ran through the snow toward the side of the aquarium, well away from the doorway through which he had seen the light. Perhaps it was a flashlight, maybe even a cigarette lighter or match.

The profile on Takeuchi Arisato indicated that the man smoked a pipe. Bleeker was not known to smoke.

Just maybe, Takeuchi was inside.

John Osgood's eyes scanned the side of the building near which he stood. There had to be other doorways, but anything not already open might trigger an alarm.

Drawing the pistol from his pocket, the knife shifted to his left hand, he approached the main entrance. He stopped when he saw movement. Flattening himself against the wall, Osgood waited. His patience was rewarded. A man in dark clothes and hat stood beside the doorway, holding something in his right hand.

Osgood drew back, mentally ticking off options. If Takeuchi Arisato were inside, it stood to reason that

Takeuchi would have taken at least elementary security precautions. The Canadians had no particular reason to want him, but other nations did, and the Canadians wouldn't pass on the opportunity to arrest him for whatever charge they could come up with—weapons violations, even trespassing—until the right documents could be gathered to ship him to the United States or Germany or Norway or Italy or Israel or any number of other countries, although the U.S. or Great Britian would be tops on the list.

There was only one option, Osgood realized. Kill the man by the doorway.

John Osgood replaced the Walther in his coat pocket, shifted the spike knife back to his right hand, and started walking parallel to the building wall. He was careful of each footfall, for with each step came the sound of snow crunching under his boots. He was grateful for the wind, which masked some sound.

The man then did something terribly stupid, for which John Osgood was terribly grateful. The man placed the object from his right hand—clearly some sort of handgun—between his left arm and left side while he cupped his hands around a lighter to light a cigarette. John Osgood sprinted the last few yards. The man started to turn around, but Osgood's left hand grabbed for his face, and Osgood's right hand punched the Special Dart into the carotid artery beneath the man's right ear. The blade penetrated all the way out the windpipe as Osgood, supporting the man by the lower portion of his face, eased him down into the snow.

Osgood pulled his knife out and wiped the three-sided blade along the man's clothes to clean it. Quickly he picked up the gun, which had fallen into the snow. It was a Beretta 92F. A smile crossed Osgood's face. Ed Mulvaney carried one of these. He wondered for an instant what Mulvaney was doing tonight. Hopefully, nothing like this.

He made certain the Beretta's safety was on, then dropped the gun into his left outside pocket. There was no time for any further searching of the body, nor any point in dragging it somewhere, because the imprint of the body would be clearly marked in the snow.

So he left it, starting toward the aquarium entrance again.

Osgood stopped beside the doorway.

He could hear nothing, but he could see a faint wash of yellow light inside the building. Perhaps it was light from one of the aquariums. While still holding his knife, he approached the doors and tried one. It was unlocked.

Taking a deep breath, Osgood opened the door about eighteen inches.

Nothing happened.

He slid between the doors, pulled them closed behind him as soundlessly as he could, and moved quickly to the nearest wall, still holding his breath.

As he took a breath, the heat and humidity within the building nearly suffocated him. There was a smell which he instantly identified—it smelled like every other aquarium he'd ever visited throughout the world.

Osgood opened the top button of his coat and moved along the wall, further away from the door.

He thought he could hear someone coughing faintly at the far end of the building.

Opening his coat all the way now, Osgood paused for an instant to resheath the Crawford Special Dart and close the snap. With the Walther tight in his right fist, he started into the graying darkness toward the faint yellow light.

Again he heard what might have been a cough. And, barely discernible, he thought he smelled Captain Black pipe tobacco.

Years before, while recovering from an injury incurred during a particularly difficult field assignment, John Osgood had been assigned to desk duties in Covert Operations for a period of three months (which at the time had seemed like three lifetimes). The fellow in the next office cubicle had smoked a pipe. It was wintertime and the strong but pleasant smell of the man's tobacco came over the cubicle

24

wall. Osgood felt that even if all olfactory sense somehow abandoned him, he would still be able to identify Captain Black.

The fishy smell became stronger as well as, mothlike, Osgood moved toward the light. He realized that the entrance hall through which he moved housed no operational tanks. Hence the darkness.

As he approached the light, it grew decidedly stronger. It came from an open entryway to his far left. He stopped and heard the sound of a cigarette lighter clicking. He could hear voices, although it was impossible to discern their number or their exact nature.

His fingers moved on the butt of his pistol. He edged along a wall, and very gradually the voices grew in definition and the smell of Captain Black became stronger.

". . . is nothing wrong, but I just want my damn money so I can go. Maybe you got nothing better to do, but I got a warm bed to get to, Ari."

"Be patient."

"How long's it take your bloody guys to go through the crates?"

"We once purchased Soviet RPGs, but the supplier neglected to mention that in half of them the fuses were no good. One of those RPGs cost the life of a comrade who was like a brother to me. Count your money, if it will make you feel better, Bleeker."

There was a woman's voice, too, so low that Osgood could not make out the words. There was laughter, which matched the voice belonging to Ari. Takeuchi Arisato?

John Osgood got as near as he dared to the opening, and when he flattened himself against the wall, he could see through just enough to detect smoke rising against the yellow light from an enormous aquarium.

"Fine, Ari, the money's all here. Look, can you radio your guys down by the marina?"

"In due time we will hear. Why are you in such a terrible hurry, Bleeker?"

25

"You Japanese guys have enough patience for all of us."

"Maybe he was followed." It was the woman's voice.

Bleeker laughed, a little strained. "Your guys on the river would've spotted another boat."

"That did not answer the question put to you, Bleeker."

"What do you mean?"

"Were you followed, Bleeker?"

There was a long pause. "There was this guy earlier in the evening, at the place I hang out."

"Hang out?"

"The Shamrock Pub over in the city. The guy who owns it got him an armored car job he's planning, and he needed two M16s. When I got your stuff, I had a whole crate more than I needed, and his money's good. I brought him the two guns tonight and picked up the dough before I left to meet you, okay? And there was this guy in the club, maybe a cop or RCMP or somethin', but—"

"He followed you," the woman said. "And that is why you wish to hurry, Bleeker."

"Naw, he didn't. I know Elmo didn't nail him at the club, because there was some gunfire, and Elmo never carries a piece, just a blade. I figure Jeff—"

"Jeff?" The woman's voice again.

"The guy who owns the Shamrock. I figure he wasted the cop or whoever the fucker was."

It was now or never, Osgood decided.

Reflected in the glass of a second aquarium, its lights not on, he could just discern the positioning of the personnel on the other side of the opening. But he saw five figures rather than only those of the three speakers. Two of them had to belong to Takeuchi, likely the tallest of the five. The shortest figure would be the woman, but as to which of the other three was Randy Bleeker, Osgood was uncertain.

He reached into his left pocket, and checked the position of the extractor on the captured Beretta. It was distended slightly from the slide, indicating a loaded chamber. Under normal circumstances, he wouldn't have trusted a mechanical indicator and would have examined the pistol in greater detail. But that would have made noise.

With the pistol still in his pocket, he slowly rotated the safety tumbler upward into the firing position, hoping his coat pocket would mask any noise the safety might make.

He drew the Beretta from his left pocket. It felt fully loaded, but he wouldn't count on the number of shots being just as it should—sixteen, with the one in the chamber.

Holding a gun in each hand, John Osgood stepped away from the wall and stepped through the opening into the room.

"Hold it!"

Takeuchi Arisato did three things at once: He shouted, "Kill him!", shoved the girl toward Osgood, and started to draw a gun from under his coat. As the girl bumped against Osgood, Osgood sidestepped, firing toward the nearer of the two men with Takeuchi. Neither of them was Japanese, and both had M16 rifles with sawed-off barrels. Osgood fired two rounds from the P-38K, catching the first man both times in the chest. As the man fell backwards, his rifle discharged on full auto. The woman screamed as the long burst cut through her from her left hip to her right shoulder. Her body flopped to the floor.

Takeuchi fired and missed, his bullets striking the entry-way frame inches from Osgood's head. As Osgood returned fire, the second of the two men fired his M16, chunks of the floor and wall surface ripping up under the impact of the bursts.

Osgood jumped, stumbled over the dead woman, and fired the Beretta from his left hand as he fell back, emptying it into the torso of the second gunman.

The rifle, still on full auto, and still tight enough in the dead man's grip to fire, sprayed across the aquarium tank to Osgood's right. The glass shattered in huge shards, the tank exploded outward, and thousands of gallons of water gushed out.

Osgood tried to stand, but was swept from his feet.

27

He saw Bleeker.

Where was Takeuchi?

Bleeker had a .45 in his right hand, fired, missed, slipped in the water, and fell. Osgood got to his feet. Bleeker was grabbing for the .45 as Osgood kicked, his left foot catching Bleeker at the tip of the jaw, snapping Bleeker's head back. Bleeker's skull hit the floor with a loud crack.

Osgood threw the empty Beretta away and ran through ankle-deep water with fish flapping in it, dying. Glass crunched under his feet.

There was the sound of a door slamming shut, and in the next instant an alarm went off.

Osgood crossed the exhibit hall, spotting a door. He ran toward it, threw his weight against the panic bar, and tucked back, as bullets hit the interior of the door as it swung outward.

Osgood saw the origin of the shots. He fired two rounds, then another double tap. Osgood withdrew the partially spent magazine from the P-38K and pulled his second and last fully loaded spare from the Andrews rig's magazine dumps under his right arm.

Slamming the fresh magazine up the butt of the pistol, Osgood dived through the open doorway into the snow, coming up in a roll beside a low hedgerow.

Takeuchi was running east along the esplanade.

Osgood got to his feet and started running after him.

Takeuchi was fast for a big man. He was so tall and so broad-shouldered, Osgood told himself that Takeuchi could not be all Japanese, perhaps part Korean or Chinese. More likely the latter. As Takeuchi veered left off the esplanade and along the mall, Osgood tried to quicken his pace, but he realized he was no match for a man ten years his junior, and obviously a born distance runner. The cold was gripping Osgood's leg muscles like a vise, his trousers and shoes soaked with water from the aquarium. The wind seemed stronger and colder now.

John Osgood turned into the mall, with Takeuchi better

than a city block's length ahead of him. Osgood thought to try a shot, but his body shook with the cold and his breath control was totally gone. It would have been a waste of ammunition.

Osgood kept running, lungs aching now, shin muscles tightening with pain, calves stiffening.

In the conversation he'd overheard, Bleeker—probably still alive—had talked about an arms shipment and—

Could the boat they'd alluded to be in the little Port Sainte-Helene Marina on the far northeastern side of the island, near Le-Moyne Channel? Osgood tried to quicken his pace but couldn't. He could barely maintain his present pace. He'd always prided himself on being fit, always thought himself a good runner.

But this Japanese terrorist was phenomenal.

Takeuchi disappeared, running off at a tangent to the right.

Osgood kept running, trying once again to quicken the pace before Takeuchi disappeared. As he reached the point along the mall near the needle-shaped Spirale, the point where Takeuchi had veered right, Osgood stopped, still holding his gun. His hands went to his knees as he doubled forward, trying to breathe.

He had narrowed the gap, but not enough. Takeuchi was cutting across the slope leading down toward the beach and the first three of the eight boat slips.

Osgood shivered, half from the cold, half from exhaustion, then shook his head, telling himself, "If you haven't given yourself a heart attack yet . . ." He forced himself to start running again, his clothes soaked with sweat, his body trembling with the cold.

Ahead of him, Takeuchi was running effortlessly toward a power launch in the farthest right-hand slip, and for the first time Osgood noticed that Takeuchi carried a briefcase in his left hand.

Takeuchi had the money.

John Osgood reached the snow-covered grassy area behind the beach. The distance between himself and Takeuchi was in excess of two hundred yards, out of range of even the most skillful pistol shot not possessed of a rest, a scope, perfect wind, and a great deal of luck.

Osgood kept running as Takeuchi started clambering down into the power launch. The launch was parked stern in, and it started forward now.

John Osgood reached the beach, snow and ice-encrusted sand crackling under his feet.

He dropped to both knees, bringing the P-38K with its two-and-three-quarter-inch barrel into a solid two-hand hold. His hands were shaking.

Osgood just looked at his gun, then caved forward to breathe. Craning his neck upward, he watched the boat picking up speed, toward the little break between the club-shaped spit and the island itself.

Takeuchi was gone, into LeMoyne Channel, with the Saint Lawrence opening on either side of his craft, and all of Quebec, Ontario, upstate New York—even Vermont— open to him for escape.

As he tried to breathe, his lungs aching and cold, John Osgood cursed his luck; then he started wondering what he might be able to get out of Randy Bleeker.

That meant another run, back the way he'd come.

"Damn."

He got to his feet.

Chapter Two

Seven Guns,
Twenty-one Shots

In one respect only, Vicki was the ideal widow: She looked sensational in black.

Snow fell so heavily at times that Mulvaney could hardly see her standing beside him, let alone see to the other side of the open grave. There stood the precious few that he and Bill Grimshaw had survived Vietnam with.

The commander of the honor guard started his seven men firing their rifles. The priest made the sign of the cross over the coffin. Beside Mulvaney, one of Bill Grimshaw's two little girls hugged to her mother's skirts and visibly shivered with the cold wind against her bare legs.

Mulvaney let go of Andy Oakwood's right hand, then dropped to a crouch beside Bill Grimshaw's youngest daughter, Ginny. He folded her into his arms and into his coat with the same gesture. As she let go of her mother, she turned her head into his chest and wept, murmuring, "Uncle Ed."

Ed Mulvaney looked up from the little girl, stood, held her

31

in his arms, lied, and said to her, "Everything'll be okay, babes, honest." Her mother was selling Bill's executive protection service to a larger security company, which would fold it to eliminate a competitor. Every dime he'd planned to cut out of the Chicago P.D. with, like every dime the three survivors of the A-Team standing on the other side of the grave had been able to scrounge, had gone to pay Bill's hospital expenses, to keep the mortgage from being accelerated and foreclosed, to pay for the psychiatric counseling both little girls had needed when they'd learned their daddy was dying, and to keep the business going so Vicki and the little girls would have some kind of future. Mulvaney's eyes focused on the seven dress-uniformed riflemen and their weapons. For some reason—and he'd attended enough full military honors funerals to qualify for an opinion—M16s looked awfully tacky for a twenty-one-gun salute.

Two of the soldiers began to triangle the flag. In a moment they would present it to Vicki Grimshaw. Tammy, at nine (two years older than her sister), was crying now, too. Mulvaney could hear the sounds of her sobbing over the wind.

The little one in his arms just clung more tightly to him.

Under his breath, as they handed Vicki the flag, he said, "Fuck you, Agent Orange, fuck you."

And he rocked the little girl in his arms.

Mulvaney closed the limousine door with his left hand. Bill Grimshaw had lost a left hand in a bar in Saigon when the eight of them—Stan, Sid, Al, Chet, LeRoy, Herschel, Grimshaw, and Mulvaney—had been drinking it up a little and the V.C. decided this was the lucky place to receive a fragging. Bill got the grenade, in more ways than one. Eight lives versus one hand, four of those lives still living—Stan, Sid, LeRoy, and him. Mulvaney shook his head.

Mulvaney remembered the first time at the hospital when Bill had been awake enough to talk and not so doped up that he couldn't make sense of what Grimshaw said. "I don't mind so much about the damn hand, but that was a good Omega I just bought. Damned prettiest wristwatch I ever saw. Fuckin' Commie bastards."

"It was a fake. Counterfeit face and the wrong guts."

"Just like all of us, maybe," Bill said, lighting a cigarette.

Mulvaney hadn't stayed long. He found the men's room, found an empty stall, and closed the door. He sat there and just cried for a long time.

Through the back of the limousine window, now, Mulvaney watched the little one he'd been holding in his arms. She waved at him and he waved back.

Andy Oakwood, beside him, clutched at his arm, her hair cascading across his shoulder. "I'm so sorry."

From someone else the words would have been empty. He touched his lips to her forehead, nodded, and swallowed. Tears. They were usually a woman's prerogative. He wondered if that was why women lived longer.

"Mr. Mulvaney?"

He didn't recognize the voice. Years of surviving that sort of experience had taught him that prudence was a virtue. His hand went to the little revolver inside the pocket of his coat. It was the same gun he'd carried as a backup weapon in Vietnam and as a Chicago policeman. His right hand curled around the butt as he turned to face the voice. "I'm afraid I don't know you."

The man was tall, skinny, and balding. Where he had hair, it was almost black and slicked back. He had blue eyes against a pale skin, and a firm set to his mouth. He extended his hand, saying, "I'm Tom Peterson, Mr. Mulvaney."

Mulvaney left the gun in his pocket and took Peterson's handshake. The hand was cold like his own, but dry and firm, too. "I came across your name in Bill's stuff."

Peterson nodded slowly. "Yes, Mr. Mulvaney. Mr. Grimshaw took on a job for us just before he was stricken."

"He was stricken years ago and knew he was dying for a long time. But he hadda work." That would have been a good epitaph for most men, Mulvaney thought.

"We issued a twenty-five-thousand-dollar advance to Mr. Grimshaw for his services."

There was a sick feeling starting in the pit of Mulvaney's stomach now. "Everybody knew he was dying, but nobody figured he'd go so suddenly, Mr. Peterson. The doctors were telling him that the chemotherapy was working, and he might have a couple of years left and, ahh . . . about that—"

"I realize Mr. Grimshaw's condition deteriorated more rapidly than anticipated, Mr. Mulvaney."

"Maybe his body got tired of fighting another war nobody'd let him win," Andy said.

Peterson just looked at her.

Mulvaney cleared his throat. "Mr. Peterson, Miss Oakwood, my fiancée."

Peterson smiled thinly and nodded. "Miss Oakwood." Then his eyes came back to Mulvaney's eyes. The smile was gone. "The point isn't about the money, Mr. Mulvaney. The point is that my firm still needs to get the job done for which we'd originally hired Mr. Grimshaw. Bill Grimshaw earned his twenty-five thousand dollars. He located the item in question and the person in whose custody it now resides. But Bill Grimshaw died before he was able to undertake the second portion of the assignment."

Ed Mulvaney found his cigarettes, then lit one with the flame of his Zippo. "Bill Grimshaw's wife and kids have a paid-off mortgage, and most of the doctor bills are being taken care of. The funeral was pretty much paid for by Uncle Sam. They've got a little money coming from the sale of the business, but not enough to do a lot of good."

"You may be leading up to the same thing I'm thinking of, Mr. Mulvaney. I understand you're still a Chicago policeman, however."

"I'm on leave. I was going to take over Bill's business, but I guess I'm out of luck, too." Since Bill's condition started falling apart and Vicki announced her decision to sell the company, Mulvaney had thanked whatever Guardian Angel watched over fools, drunks, and Irishmen—he was always one, sometimes two, occasionally all three—that he hadn't just taken his money and run, quitting the cops, but listened to Andy and taken a leave instead. Maybe she was his Guardian Angel; at least, she looked pretty enough to be an angel of some kind.

"My company would be willing to pay generously—say a hundred thousand dollars plus expenses—if you would undertake to pick up where Mr. Grimshaw left off. We can pay the money to you or to his survivors, whatever you prefer."

Ed Mulvaney looked down at Andy.

She blinked, nodded, telling him silently that she knew already what he'd do and it was all right. But he said to her, "Bein' a cop's wife okay?"

"So long as you're the cop."

And he looked at Peterson. "Let's talk."

"Tonight? How about dinner, for you and the lady?"

Mulvaney nodded, saying, "Tell Andy when and where," and Mulvaney squeezed Andy Oakwood's hand and left her there in the roadway with Peterson. He started up the hillside, into the deeper snow, the insides of his shoes filling with snow again.

Mulvaney stopped beside Bill Grimshaw's grave. The diggers weren't filling it in yet, but the machine lowering the casket was running and it would only be a couple of minutes before the digging began. Already, the top of the gunmetal-gray casket was obscured with snow.

Ed Mulvaney picked up a handful of snow and dirt and threw it into the grave, over the coffin of his friend. "Don't you worry now, Bill. We got this knocked, Stan and Sid and LeRoy and me, okay? Vicki and the girls are gonna be fine. They're gonna miss ya, but, ahh . . . Anyway, God— God—"

He was cold, shaking, his throat so tight he felt he was going to choke.

Ed Mulvaney made the sign of the cross and let the tears come. The dead were the ones who had it easy.

He touched his lips to her eyelids and her eyelids moved. He touched his fingertips to her nipples, and they came erect, hardened as his flesh brushed against hers.

"Love me?" she asked, not as a question concerning affection, but as a request for physical activity. He folded Andy into his arms, arching her back upward so her abdomen pressed against him. He kissed her hard on the mouth as her hands touched his face.

Her hands were warm, but her feet were cold.

The winter was cold, cold as all northern winters seemed. When they'd returned from the cemetery to the small, modestly furnished apartment they had been renting by the month, she'd poured him a glass of Seagram's Seven. Still wearing his coat, Mulvaney sat down on the sofa, drinking his drink slowly, letting it warm him.

The northernmost corners of the windowpanes were frost-etched, looking like the shop windows downtown and in the malls, all ready for Christmas. The frost here was real, though, and despite the heat the apartment wasn't as warm as his house at the far western edge of Chicago, just on the border of Oak Park. It had to do with the insulation, he knew, because in the summertime, even with the air conditioning going full blast, the apartment was never perfectly comfortable.

They'd moved into this apartment in the late spring, after spending a week in a hotel while just trying to find a place that was affordable. After Christmas last year time had gone by interminably. Mulvaney at last had arranged his leave of absence from the Chicago Police Department and had finally convinced himself that Bill Grimshaw's business was growing at a rate that would be adequate to sustain himself and Andy Oakwood.. It never had a chance to happen.

"How are your feet?"

"Fine," Mulvaney answered.

Andy looked at him, shook her head as she slipped out of her coat, then dropped to her knees at his feet and started removing his shoes. His feet were cold, not as cold as they had gotten when he was a rookie working traffic in the Loop, but cold. And in those days he'd worn lined boots and two pairs of socks. This time, having to look all gentlemanly and civilized for the funeral of his friend, he'd worn low shoes and thin black socks.

She skinned off his socks, saying, "You're part Chinese."

"Why's that?" He lit a cigarette.

"Your feet are yellow."

"I got a touch of frostbite years back. My feet always go a little yellow when they're cold."

Andy lifted the front of her sweater and placed the soles of his feet against her bare abdomen, shivering as flesh touched flesh. He went to draw his feet back, but she held them there. "Are you going to do this thing for that guy Peterson?"

"What? Warm up his feet? I don't think so; he's not my type."

"No, silly. This job."

"Yeah, probably."

"I can help."

"Probably not."

"It's not as if I haven't been shot at before."

"That was different. We're gonna be married. And I probably won't get shot at anyway. This is just some industrial job. No big deal."

"That doesn't mean I can't do what I used to do, just because we're getting married."

"Yes, it does," Mulvaney told her.

"What'll I do when we go back to Chicago?"

"Get a nice sensible job, if you want, or just stay home and keep supper warm."

"I can get on the police department. I spent all those years in the MPs, and women get preferential minority status for slots, anyway."

"You're not getting on Chicago P.D., Andy. Too good a way to . . ." He didn't finish that.

"Maybe a suburb," she suggested.

He tried to lean forward, couldn't, leaned back, looked up at the ceiling, and then just closed his eyes. "You know what being a civilian cop is like? You take orders from a bunch of leadpipe buttheads, you treat the good guys who pay your salary like criminals, and the criminals get treated like damn prima donnas. And the thing that really sucks is it's the best you can do."

"Like bein' a cop in the military. Not much different. Anyway, Ed, if it's so bad, how can you go back? On the cops, I mean. Especially after what you did."

She cleared her throat. As he looked down at her, she looked away. He'd murdered a corrupt Chicago Police captain because that was the only way to nail the guy; and he'd gotten away with it. The case was closed, the gun was never found, and even if it did get found someday, there was no way to trace the gun back to him. He had a perfect alibi, ironclad like they said in the mysteries, from Andy, his old partner and buddy Lew Fields, and Fields's wife, who was a high school principal. And then Osgood showing up out of the blue with that pizza.

The only thing that bothered him about killing Hilliard then—and still bothered him—was that pulling the trigger on the rotten son of a bitch hadn't bothered him at all. For once in his life he'd gotten the good clean feeling inside of doing the right thing at the right time the right way.

A feeling like that was dangerous for a cop. "No, I don't want you being a cop. Get into security or something if you wanna stay in the business. I've got some friends in the northern suburbs in that racket. Hours are better and the money's good."

"Then—why don't you do it, Ed? Or why don't we start our own thing like Bill Grimshaw had? I've got some money."

" 'Cause," Mulvaney told her.

"Ohh." She kept holding his feet against her; and after a while she began to massage them. "You're stubborn, Ed."

"No shit." He laughed, pulling her up from her knees and onto his lap. His hands—still ice cold—went under her clothes.

She started to laugh.

She made them a late lunch while he dug through her purse, found the business card, and put in a call to Peterson to set up the dinner meeting. He took a hot shower, then went to bed with Andy, snuggling with her for a while under the covers. He slid down under the covers, enjoying how warm it was against her body, touching her, kissing her. And as Andy wrapped her legs around him when he slid between her thighs, his feet were warm, but the soles of her feet were cold as ice.

"I don't know if I can deal with it, Ed."

"Deal with what?"

"Us."

"I know."

"I love you. Shut me up, huh?"

And he shut her up, kissing her so hard on the mouth she couldn't have talked if she'd tried.

Ed Mulvaney didn't know if he could deal with it, either—being married, making do on a cop's salary, building a life on a cop's hours, and wondering if someday they would find out who'd offed Captain Hilliard. They made it through the thing in Japan, where they'd first met, fell in love, and nearly died. Made it through coming back to Chicago and knowing what had to be done. Then they'd lied to themselves and each other that everything bad was behind them. Cops' marriages sometimes turned to shit. He'd already had one of those, and the smell of it still lingered. He stopped thinking about it. Mulvaney edged up tighter to her, and her hands brought him into her. Andy sucked in her breath and held him tighter. She kissed his chest, his shoulder, his cheek. Mulvaney turned her face toward his.

39

The dead ones were the ones who had it easy.

He kissed her hard on the mouth again and thrust himself into her still deeper. He'd read once they called this the little death anyway.

"It's called a 486 SX chip."

"That's nice," Mulvaney said.

"It makes any computer work like a Cray Supercomputer, and makes a Cray work like nothing we can even dream of."

"A cray?"

"The supercomputer's supercomputer, okay? It can do two hundred and fifty million computations per second just as it is. Take the Cray Y-MP. There's been a big competition going on between the United States and Japan, and the Japanese are pushing ahead with their single processor machines over the eight processor tandem setup of the Cray Y-MP. This is all because the Japanese hold the lead in semiconductor technology."

"What's this 486 SX chip?"

"You don't know much about computers, right?"

"Right." Mulvaney speared a shrimp on the tines of the little silver cocktail fork and dipped it into the cocktail sauce.

"All right. Basically," Peterson explained, "the chip is sort of like the carburetion system in an engine. You said you owned an old bathtub Porsche, right?"

"Right." The restaurant was stiff city, Mulvaney thought, but the shrimp cocktail was okay. A busboy who looked like the kind of guy who dropped his soap in public showers in order to make new friends came over and topped off their water glasses. They hadn't been touched since the last time he'd minced over. The blond-haired harpist in the long black velvet dress had a smile on her face which looked painted. The chandeliers overhead probably were crystal. Peterson was paying, so Mulvaney didn't worry what dinner was costing; besides, there weren't any prices printed on the menu.

40

"So some cars have bigger engines than a Porsche, but they don't fly down the road as fast, right? It's the components that make the car do its thing. The 486 SX chip is a component. Think of it as the top-of-the-line carburetor. You put it into an existing engine—this carburetor—and tune up this and that and wham, you got yourself a car that's going a lot faster than before. The 486 SX works like the world's best carburetor, but on a computer. Design recently has been going toward developing the Flash Chip. You can put as many as sixty-four million bytes into one of these Flash Chips. The 486 SX is a chip that is vastly more advanced than these Flash Chips, although a lot of the technology involved is similar. Put the 486 SX into your average computer, and you can make the computer work like the Cray. Put it into a Cray, and nobody has any idea what you can do with it yet. And we probably won't for years.

Peterson paused. It was obvious just watching his blue eyes light up when he talked that he was getting into something he enjoyed. "The National Science Foundation realized that not everybody who needed a Cray could afford one, right? So they started NSFNET, which is merely a networking system allowing access to the supercomputers. The 486 SX will mean computations will get done faster, more information can be stored or retrieved, anything you want. Or if you had the 486 SX and you could get into NSFNET or any of the other networks, even the most classified systems in the world, you could raid the network's total contents in a matter of seconds, faster than anybody could cut you off."

"You make this thing?"

"I represent people who make this thing."

"Your company."

"My company."

"Why don't you get the company to get it back for you?"

"Because the man who stole it has very strong ties to the Eastern Bloc, and the United States government wants this to look like something it isn't. Anyway, we got our tit caught in the wringer, Mr. Mulvaney. If we go broadcasting this thing all over the place, even in the Intelligence community, we're just as screwed from a profitability standpoint as we are with the chip stolen. We invested more millions than you could imagine."

"I've got a pretty good imagination, Mr. Peterson."

"We need it back to succeed as a commercial endeavor."

"Can you make another one?"

"It's the technology, not the artifact, Mr. Mulvaney. We need it back before it can be copied."

"So the perpetrator is giving it to the Commies?"

"No. We're more afraid he'll sell it to the Japanese. The Russians don't have the technology to use it, let alone make it. And this Ladislaw Gorchek wouldn't give his mother spit if she was dying of thirst."

"Ladislaw Gorchek," Mulvaney said thoughtfully. "Neat name. Have you guys tried buying it back from him?"

"He's going to put it up for auction, Mr. Mulvaney. The Japanese could outbid us."

"Wouldn't it be cheaper for 'em to let your people get in the low bid, then just buy your company?"

Peterson laughed. "We're a diversified firm, Mr. Mulvaney. They can't buy us because of our involvement in electronic media, and a lot of the development money we utilized came from the U.S. government. You see, the defense applications are enormous, as you might surmise."

"So you want me to steal it back."

"That's it, Mr. Mulvaney. Either that, or destroy it."

Mulvaney submerged a shrimp in the sauce and listened to the harp music, hoping the instrument wasn't an omen. . . .

There wasn't any harp music as Ed Mulvaney broke the surface and spit away the mouthpiece of his regulator. He half-crawled along the sand and rocks because the incoming white-edged surf was high enough and strong enough to knock him down and drag him out to sea. Finally he was able to rise into a crouch. He broke the seal on the padded flotation bag, pulling the little suppressor-fitted Heckler & Koch submachine gun from it, then racked the bolt.

He stood.

He ran.

With his left hand Mulvaney snapped away his mask. He made his way diagonally up the beach, looking for any sign that he'd been spotted, knowing full well that if he'd been detected electronically, he'd never know it until it was too late.

A high wind tore over the island, screeching with heightening intensity. The waves were building with the wind, maybe high enough to cover over everything on the island and wash it away, into the ocean forever. Then nobody would have to worry about a chip.

The storm had moved up his timetable, which was why he was alone here tonight instead of here seventy-two hours from now with his three ex–Special Forces buddies from the funeral. They'd all agreed to do this for Bill's widow and kids. When he'd told Andy about hitting Gorchek's island, she'd just kissed him and called him an asshole.

Maybe she was right.

Mulvaney waited in concealment within high, smooth rocks that looked black in the moonless night, like giant precious pearls, slick to look at and to touch. Waves crashed over them as the tide surged violently around them. He was nearly out of his wet suit.

The swim had been the toughest one of his life, harder even than the swim to the island off the northern coast of Japan with John Osgood and Nobunaga and his men. Mulvaney closed his eyes and shook his head. "John Trench Osgood." He laughed, saying the name almost aloud under his breath. "Wonder what old Ozzie's doin' tonight?" Mulvaney imagined Osgood eating hundred-dollar-an-

43

ounce caviar, drinking Dom Pérignon, and getting ready to spend the night happily screwing some knockout defecting from the KGB, all to make the world safe for democracy.

Mulvaney shook his head again, ran his fingers back through his hair. On the streets of Chicago his watch commander would have told him to get a haircut, regardless of trying to look like a street hood for his Tac Squad work. He'd always hated haircuts. As opposed to Chicago, the worst that could happen on this little island off the South Carolina coast was that somebody would kill him.

Mulvaney slipped into the backpack in which all his electronic marvels were carried, and secured its strap around his abdomen. He took the Beretta out of its plastic bag, slid it into the waistband of his black Levi's, and pulled his black knit shirt over it.

He felt better now.

It took the better part of an hour to make his way from the south side of the island to the north. Away from the beach, the island lost its wild, tropical feel and was replaced by an atmosphere more reminiscent of ordinary woods at night. But even in the deepest portion of the pine forest that dominated the central highlands of the island, he could hear the ocean slamming away at the shore, as if sea and land were bitter enemies engaged in some primordial fight to the death.

As Mulvaney broke from the trees, lightning crackled white over the west end of the island.

The ground rose as he moved eastward. The house for which he'd studied aerial photographs and computer-enhanced partial architectural plans over the last two weeks appeared at the end of a long runway-shaped summit. It seemed to extend over the edge of the rock itself, to float serenely above the churning chaos below. As Mulvaney drew nearer, he could detect lights through some of the windows in the upper floor. Hiding in a nest of convenient rocks, Mulvaney used his binoculars, starlight 8 x 50s, and began, methodically, to familiarize himself with the real physical counterpart of the materials he had studied. What he'd thought to be a bedroom seemed to be some sort of second-floor library or sitting room. The fence surrounding the house was, indeed, electrified, but his entire plan of entry was predicated on that.

Mulvaney glanced at his watch.

There was time yet. The wind was blowing in the right direction. He could risk a cigarette if he stayed low. With the Pall Mall cupped in his hands, Mulvaney fired the cigarette. He pocketed the lighter, holding the smoke of the first drag in his lungs, then exhaling.

The wind was still increasing, but he told himself it wasn't hurricane season.

As he smoked, he checked the equipment in his backpack. The backpack was actually two units, zipped and Velcro-locked together like two halves of a sandwich. The outer portion's contents held what he needed to get onto the grounds, the inner portion's contents what he needed to get into the safe where—as best he and Peterson could estimate —the 486 SX chip was being kept.

The materials in his pack unit were just as they should be, and he'd rehearsed their use several times.

As the days had gone by while planning this assault on Gorchek's island base off the Carolina coast, Mulvaney had become convinced that Peterson was CIA or NSA, or that Peterson's company was a prime contractor to the U.S. Intelligence establishment. The high-altitude aerial photos, the taciturn crew of the fishing boat that had brought him to within a mile from the island—all those little details bespoke money and professionalism.

One of the potential uses for the 486 SX would doubtless be ELINT, Electronic Intelligence. With the general warming trend in East-West relations, human intelligence gathering would become more and more potentially embarrassing, yet satellite, high-altitude overflight, and other forms of electronic spying would be even more necessary. Each side wanted to be certain the other side wasn't speaking out of both sides of its mouth concerning nuclear arsenals and deployment of conventional forces.

With the 486 SX, ELINT evaluations would be faster, more precise, and more accurate as aids in strategic and diplomatic planning.

As he smoked, Mulvaney reviewed the facts he'd been given by Peterson, facts that Andy, through painstaking research, had confirmed. Ladislaw Gorchek (which was not the man's real name but had been an adopted alias for so long that his real name could not be discovered) had been in charge of internal security field operations for the Rumanian Secret Police. Three years ago, perhaps seeing some handwriting on the wall that the cruel dictatorship which he served was destined for oblivion, Gorchek left Rumania with a wealth of contacts and considerable financial resources.

Having often served the KGB's interests in international arms smuggling, Gorchek already knew the business that he entered. Utilizing the same techniques of brutality that had kept him in power in the secret police, he was able to eliminate competition and soon became known within the international arms trade as someone never to cross and never to trust. Many of the big arms traders had some noticeable political affiliation that could not be violated.

But Gorchek's only requirement was money.

Andy had discovered something through her former colleagues in the Criminal Investigations Division, the Army's counterpart to the FBI. Her CID contacts recounted a rumor that the Soviet Union had very quietly placed a death sentence on Gorchek a year ago and that the KGB was still interested in carrying it out.

All things considered, why was Ladislaw Gorchek living on an island off the coast of the United States? The possible answers to that question were more than tantalizing. Was he being given a place to stay in exchange for information? Or did the government know Gorchek existed here? It was even possible that Peterson's company had been in some sort of deal with Gorchek—the deal itself going sour—with Gorchek gaining the means to steal the chip. If the latter was true, then the reasons why no one from the U.S. Marshals Service or the CIA had been dispatched to arrest or kill Gorchek were obvious. The publicity couldn't be risked. Whatever Gorchek had been involved with in association with Peterson's company could potentially damage relations between the United States and Eastern Europe.

Mulvaney wasn't much for literary quotations, but as a kid in school he'd memorized Tennyson's "The Charge of the Light Brigade." *Theirs not to reason why, theirs but to do and die.* Mulvaney looked over the rock fortress toward the house with its big electrified fence, thinking. *Into the valley of Death rode the six hundred.*

He stubbed out his cigarette and grabbed his pack. Too bad the other five hundred ninety-nine guys couldn't make it. He set out from his rock shelter, moving at an easy pace along a ridge through the sand and scrubby brush, the Beretta 92F 9mm tight in his right fist. The gun was only there for the most dire of emergencies when no other alternatives were available. Invading private property—even Gorchek's private property—in order to steal back a computer chip with national defense applications from a known arms smuggler with Eastern Bloc connections was something Mulvaney could talk his way out of, especially if he actually got the chip back. Once he started littering the island with dead bodies, that would be another matter entirely.

Mulvaney reached the edge of the ridge, then started down a narrow defile. At the base of the defile he was parallel to the runwaylike spit. At the other end lay the house. By keeping close against the spit, he was able to avoid the windblown surf. The tide was already invading the treeline.

Mulvaney kept moving. The wind howled more viciously, and he was actually cold.

The baseline of the fence rose up ahead of him. He found

a reasonably dry spot, dropped to his knees, and began to remove the outermost portion of the modular backpack from the rest of the unit. He slipped the harness for the remaining pack element back onto his shoulders, then began to open the first element.

It was a large, oddly shaped battery—the like of which he'd never seen before—until Peterson had given him the device as a means of dealing with Gorchek's security fence. "The fence is electrified," Peterson had told him, "and the same system that powers the fence seems to power the entire house. Because the island is so far off the coast, no electrical cables were ever run to it from the mainland. Gorchek generates his own power out there, mostly from solar cells." Peterson had pointed out the solar cells in several of the high-altitude photographs of the island. "But he'd have a backup unit, too, of course. If you just killed the power connection to the fence, you'd still have to deal with the backup generator kicking on. There might not be enough time to get over the fence before you were fried. We're talking seventeen thousand volts."

"How do you know it's seventeen thousand and not ten thousand or twenty thousand?" There was a pause, and before Peterson came up with an answer, Mulvaney told him not to bother.

Instead, Peterson picked up where Mulvaney had interrupted. "Besides, even if you got over the fence, there'd still be current to the house, and you'd have alarm systems and everything else to worry about. There's a storm brewing—a big one—well west of the Cape Verde Islands. When it comes up the U.S. coast, that's when you should hit. The storm could knock out the power in the fence, so Gorchek's security people won't know they have an intruder. They'll probably go into a heightened defensive posture, though."

"What if the storm craps out?"

"It's not supposed to. If it does, you use explosives and blow the fence, which will kill all power as well. Your three buddies cause a diversion, you go in and steal the chip back, and Gorchek's people deal with the diversion. The storm makes it a lot cleaner."

As if on cue, there was an earsplitting crack, lightning striking a half-submerged pine tree not fifty feet from Mulvaney's position.

Mulvaney pulled on gloves that went past his elbows and were so heavily insulated that he could barely move the fingers. He found the lowest of the powered lines in the fence and attached one of the alligator clips to the line. There was a small shower of sparks, and if the security people Gorchek used were any good, they'd already be getting out of their chairs. But there was no surveillance camera in sight, and he'd stayed low along the fence line. He hoped he'd be in a blind spot even if there was a camera he couldn't see.

The next part of the operation was tricky, and it had to be fast. Once he attached the second alligator clip, he'd bridge current through the battery and fry it, temporarily shorting out the fence. So he had to actuate the power charge in the battery—it would be a four-second pulse—just as he attached the clip.

Mulvaney armed the battery so only one switch had to be flipped. He took a heavy, rubberized square of cloth with the Bianchi clip at one corner and attached it to his belt. His left index finger was over the switch, his right hand gripping the second alligator clip.

His mouth was dry. His palms sweated inside the heavy rubber gloves.

Mulvaney counted. "One . . . two . . . *three!*" As he closed the second clip on the line, he flipped the switch and jumped back. Current arced through the battery, and a shower of sparks flew all around him. Mulvaney ran back, knowing what was supposed to happen next wouldn't be a good thing to be near.

As he threw himself to the wet ground, gloved hands going over his head, there was an explosion.

Mulvaney rolled over onto his side and looked toward the fence. There was a small pile of smoldering rubble where the battery had been, and the grounds beyond the fence (and the house itself) were in total darkness.

Ed Mulvaney pushed himself to his feet, stripped away the gloves as he ran toward the fence, and jumped, grabbing on to the chain links halfway up. As he neared the barbed wire at the top, he hung by his right hand, removed the square of heavy insulated cloth from his belt, and dropped it over the barbed wire.

Mulvaney swung upward, rolling over the cloth-covered barbed wire, grabbed the fence on the other side, and stopped himself from falling to the ground. He yanked the cloth he'd used as a shield against the barbs, tore it free, and jumped the last six feet, the fence rattling maddeningly. He picked up the square of cloth and ran from the fence, dropping to his knees beside the north wall of an equipment shed twenty yards from the fence line.

He breathed.

No alarm had sounded. As yet, there were no human shouts, and no barking dogs. Although no dogs had been detected in the aerial photos, he couldn't believe that none were present. There had been far too many stores in Charleston and its suburbs to check for dog food purchases.

Mulvaney shrugged off his pack, replaced the cloth in it, then pulled the harness back on. As he started to move, he heard the crunch of gravel and he drew back. A voice some distance away said, "There's somethin' wrong with the fence, Hassim. Looks like lightnin' struck it, way it's all smolderin' and ever' thin'."

Mulvaney looked heavenward and smiled.

Then he reached into his right hip pocket for the time-honored Chicago policeman's friend, his blackjack. It was an old Smith & Wesson leather-covered medium-sized flat sap which he kept in good condition. The snap that closed the strap handle to the sap body was already popped open, so if he needed it there would be no betraying sound.

Mulvaney closed his fist around the shaft of the blackjack and pulled back flat against the wall of the shed, waiting.

The gravel crunching became louder. He could hear the man who'd spoken cursing softly under his breath about the "damn storm, the fuckin' lightnin', and the piss-poor island."

Mulvaney crouched, weight slightly forward, waiting.

When he saw the man, he was taken aback by the fellow's sheer size: six and a half feet, and broad in shoulders and back. The man carried an Uzi in his five-pound ham-sized right hand, but it wasn't in any sort of ready position. Giant, spatulate fingers wrapped around the front handguard and over the barrel. The butt of the weapon and the magazine which extended from it was pitched downward, with the sling swinging free.

Mulvaney reminded himself of the old aphorism, "The bigger they are, the harder they fall," and hoped it was operable tonight.

As the man walked past, Mulvaney shot a quick glance toward the house, saw no one who could observe him, then stepped out behind the man. Mulvaney's right arm hauled back and arced forward and downward with a snap, the widest portion of the blackjack impacting the big man behind the left ear.

As Mulvaney drew the sap back for a second strike, the big man caved in and fell to the gravel, out cold.

Mulvaney looked around again. There was no sign that he'd been observed. He bent over the unconscious man. Mulvaney's pistol was in his left hand, ready in case the man was faking, but he wasn't.

Mulvaney pocketed the blackjack and took the Uzi—with some difficulty—from the man's grip. The Uzi's condition of readiness made Mulvaney feel better. The bolt was closed and the submachine gun could only be fired out of an open bolt. The lightning-striking-the-fence theory seemed to have more credence. Mulvaney rolled the man over onto his back, grabbed the man's ankles, and started to pull, falling on his butt when he lost his balance against the man's considerable weight. Finally Mulvaney got him beside the outbuilding wall.

Mulvaney took the man's wallet, the spare twenty-round magazine for the Uzi, a well-worn Colt Detective Special .38, a half dozen rounds of .38 Special ammunition, and a very attractive looking switchblade knife. Mulvaney had planned ahead for the possibility of leaving men behind him, bringing several sets of disposable plastic restraints with him as well as a roll of adhesive tape. He rolled the man over onto his face, turning the head to the side so the man wouldn't choke on his saliva, then caught both wrists behind the man and wrapped one of the red plastic restraints around them. He used another of these around the man's ankles, then placed a wide strip of the tape over the man's mouth.

Mulvaney unloaded the bad guy's revolver, taking the loose ammo with him, as well as the knife, the Uzi, and the spare magazine.

He started for the house, too much time already wasted. . . .

There was still no power in the house, so Mulvaney opened the second-story window, closed it, then re-enabled the alarm trigger on the lock. There was no need to risk a flashlight, because his eyes were accustomed to the darkness. There were also a sufficient number of lightning flashes to see by. He'd scaled a trellis (which any decent security man would have gotten rid of) and made it to the overhanging roof fronting the rooms on the seaside of the house. It was almost too easy.

When he passed through the doorway into the upstairs hallway, it was even darker. Still having no wish to use his flashlight, he hugged the hallway wall instead, moving as silently as he could toward the room at the far end of the hallway.

If this wasn't the room housing the safe, he was in for a difficult time, but estimates indicated that it should be here.

When he reached the end of the hallway, he looked down the circular stairwell. There were faintly audible voices, but still no sign of alarm. He saw a flashlight beam from below and held his breath, but the beam of light passed by the base of the stairs and vanished.

Mulvaney tried the door.

It was locked.

That was a good sign.

Peterson had arranged for Mulvaney to spend several hours with a housebreaker who had been recommended by a friend in law enforcement, and the reformed burglar had given Mulvaney a quick course in lockpicking. Mulvaney didn't mention to Peterson (or the helpful ex-burglar) that he was already pretty good with pics (another skill he'd picked up as a policeman), but he learned a few techniques he hadn't already known.

From his left front pants pocket he took the PCS lockpick set, selected what he hoped was the right pick, then set to work on the old-fashioned skeleton-key lock. He had it opened in under thirty seconds. He replaced the pick in its case, then tried the door.

It opened easily, but there was a soft click. He realized he'd triggered another alarm. He closed the door, re-enabling the alarm as he did so. Had he left the window alarm and this door alarm disconnected, any alarm that had been actuated would go off when power returned.

The room, which was a library/gun room, had several windows looking out on the sea. The curtains were drawn back wide, and as he crossed the room looking for some sign of a safe, lightning flashes guided his way.

After several minutes he found the safe—in the obvious place where he should have looked first. It was behind a painting on the wall between two glass-fronted gun cabinets. Mulvaney stripped off his pack, reslung the Uzi crossbody, then pushed it behind him on its sling. He opened the second element of the pack, removed the device inside, and set it on the floor under the wall safe.

It was a computerized safecracker's friend (as Peterson had described it) and simplicity itself to use. He merely attached one of the suction cups to the dial, moving the other one from one place to another over the safe door, then twirled the locking knob until the readout on the tiny monitoring screen showed him numbers. He had to move the second lead several times until he had it positioned properly.

Mulvaney held the computer terminal in his right hand, then flipped the switch to actuate the lead placed over the dial. A second number appeared on his screen. He began moving the dial back and forth. When he had a number match, he had one element of the combination. The computer logged each new number, and once he had the final combination number, the computer would automatically show him the entire combination, in order.

There was a slightly larger version, Peterson had told him, which actually turned the dial for the operator.

Mulvaney had the first number, thirty-six.

The second number took a long time, at least a minute, but he got it: fourteen.

He got the third number quickly. It was eighty-one.

The numbers and sequence of turns were displayed on the screen. Mulvaney cleared the safe's dial as he'd been taught to do, then started the fresh combination.

He worked slowly, so he could read the numbers off the computer screen instead of using a flashlight to read the numbers off the dial.

When he had the last number, he set down the computer, pulled the leads, and stepped back in the event there might be some sort of gas device set to explode when the safe was opened, then threw open the door.

Every light in the room came on.

Behind him, his eyes squinting against the sudden brightness, he heard a submachine gun bolt snap back. A Slavic-accented voice said, "If you move, you die."

Ed Mulvaney stood there, evaluating his options. He could barely see, didn't have his hand on a gun, and knew there was a submachine gun behind him.

Mulvaney said, "I'll just bet you don't think I have a good explanation for being here, right?"

He did, but this guy wasn't going to like it.

Chapter Three

Cornered

He counted seven more submachine guns.

Ed Mulvaney looked over his shoulder. "Hi!" he said cheerily. He would have recognized Ladislaw Gorchek even if he hadn't memorized the guy's picture. With thinning blond hair on his bullet-shaped head, beady eyes, a leering grin, a thick neck over narrow shoulders, and a huge gut, Gorchek looked like the villain from a rip-off of a James Bond movie. Behind Gorchek were twelve men, eight with submachine guns and four in wet suits with large-capacity 9mm pistols in their hands.

Gorchek himself held a pistol, either a Czech CZ-75 or one of the Swiss or Italian clones, its muzzle drooping with casual disinterest. "Now disarm him, but do not harm him."

"When it comes to the arts, I always liked ballet more than poetry, but you have a natural talent, sir," Mulvaney told him, smiling over his shoulder at him.

Two of the men in wet suits came forward, relieving him

of the switchblade knife he'd taken from the man on the beach quite systematically, professionally, without any unnecessary roughness. They also took the Uzi, the spare magazine for it, his Beretta, the two spare twenty-round magazines, and the Cold Steel Tanto he'd strapped to his right leg under his trousers.

"Now that everything has been found, feel free to turn around," Gorchek said.

Mulvaney laughed as he turned around, telling Gorchek, "That poetry stuff. Gotta cut that out, man."

Gorchek snapped his fingers. The two men who'd disarmed Mulvaney walked out of the room and returned after a second or so with a woman.

When Mulvaney saw her, he started toward Gorchek, but the muzzle of one of the eight Uzi submachine guns was suddenly less than three inches from his right eye. Mulvaney stepped back. There wasn't much left of the woman's clothing, just blood-stained tatters of a bra and panties. She was in her twenties and might have been pretty once, but her face was so bruised and puffed up and burned that one of her eyes was closed and her nose was almost flat against her right cheek. Her left ear was partially ripped away along with most of the blond hair on the left side of her head.

She just stood there, her almost bare body trembling, shoulders and head bowed, as if waiting inevitably for more punishment.

"You know a man named Peterson," Gorchek told Mulvaney. "Your name is Edgar Patrick Mulvaney. You are a Chicago policeman on leave from your department. Peterson, whose 486 SX chip you evidently wished to remove from my wall safe, sent you here. This filthy bitch supplied Peterson with the information concerning the location of my safe and even informed him that I still had the 486 SX in my possession. She told him that the fence and the house and all the alarm systems were on the same circuits."

"You're wrong, man. I never heard of her. No shit."

Gorchek laughed. "Perhaps you did not, but that matters little to me. I believe she first began to dislike me when she realized that my taste for pleasures of the flesh was considerably more varied than she was used to." He was fondling the switchblade Mulvaney had taken off the guy he'd cold-cocked with the blackjack.

Mulvaney licked his lips, saying, "Look, you're right that I came for the chip. Peterson hired me, sure. But it's nothin' to do with this dame or any other one."

"You have balls, as they say, Officer Mulvaney. But soon we'll cut them off and stuff them down your throat to choke on. You will not die quickly, although you'll ask for that."

"Listen, motherfucker, I told you Peterson hired me. I told you I never heard anything about this woman or any other woman helping out. We had high-altitude photos, computer imaging, shit like that. I took over the job because the guy who was gonna do it died before he could finish it. That's why I'm here. So you know what you wanna know."

"What do you expect me to do, Mulvaney?" Gorchek smiled, the beady black eyes flickering back and forth between Mulvaney and the woman. "Let you go? Hardly. Call the South Carolina State Police? Or the FBI? The computer chip was not mine to start with, so I can hardly have someone arrested for attempting to steal it from me. And, anyway, I enjoy hurting people. See?"

The windows rattled. Mulvaney had forgotten about the storm for a moment. Lightning crackled. The lights flickered, but did not go out.

The switchblade flicked open in Gorchek's right hand, and he turned toward the girl.

"Hey, no, man!" Mulvaney shouted, pushing past the nearest of the submachine guns aimed at him, trying to grab Gorchek, but something hammered down across his back, dropping him to his knees.

He looked up as the girl screamed. The knife in Gorchek's hand raked across her throat, and the scream died. Blood sprayed out in a cloud from the front of her neck, and her knees buckled.

Mulvaney rammed his left elbow into the crotch of the wet-suited man standing beside him, threw himself to his feet and toward Gorchek, reaching for him.

The butt of one of the submachine guns slammed against the left side of Mulvaney's head, and he fell right, a green-tinged gold washing over his eyes, the thunder in his head louder than anything the storm could have come up with. He was on his knees at Gorchek's feet, both hands clasped to his head. Gorchek's voice rolled over him. "Take him downstairs. Have him carry this trash out with him, then strip him and get him ready for me."

"Yes, sir," one of the twelve men around Mulvaney said.

Mulvaney opened his eyes. The dead woman's open eye stared at him. Mulvaney said, "Gimme one more poem to remember you by, Gorchek."

He knelt there, looking at the dead girl.

Gorchek laughed a little, then said, "You will have much to remember me by, when you beg and plead with me so you can die."

"It doesn't scan," Mulvaney said, looking up at him.

Gorchek turned around, walking away. Mulvaney's eyes followed him. As Gorchek reached the door, he stopped, saying over his shoulder, "Close the safe," and then went out.

There was a clap of thunder almost as loud as the noise still going on in Mulvaney's head. The lights flickered.

Hands hauled Mulvaney to his feet, and the thunder in his head was even louder than before. He swayed on his feet for a moment, eyes shut against the pain. "Pick her up, asshole." Mulvaney opened his eyes and looked at the face belonging to the voice. The face was unique, like every human face. But the eyes were eyes he'd seen before—in Vietnam, on the West Side of Chicago. The eyes—a washed-out brown—sparkled a little, and there were tiny smile lines around them. Here was a man who enjoyed his work. The man had a submachine gun slung at his side and Mulvaney's Beretta in his left hand. "Pick her up with both hands, or we smash up one of 'em and you carry her with one hand."

Mulvaney didn't say anything. He bent down to pick her up, half-expecting a blow from a gunbutt as he did, but evidently the guys were eager to get on with the evening. The four in wet suits left. Mulvaney started to take the dead woman up into his arms.

There were old bruises all over her body, badly healed scars and welts that looked like they'd been made with a belt or a whip. There were burn marks, too, a lot on her face. The panties she wore—what was left of them—were stiff with dried blood, and there was a strong, bleachy smell of semen on her. Evidently Gorchek liked to share his fun with his friends.

Mulvaney had her in his arms. The man holding Mulvaney's gun told two of the other men to "Go look for Harry. When you find him, give 'im his knife back. Shove it up his ass. Tell Hassim I wanna see him in the playroom."

"Right, Mr. Teller," one of the two said as they left.

Mulvaney looked at the man. "Teller?"

"Shut the fuck up." He looked away from Mulvaney and nodded toward the remaining three men, saying, "Get 'im outa here. I'll join yas in a coupla minutes."

"What's the playroom, Teller?" Mulvaney asked, still holding the dead woman in his arms.

Teller smiled. "You're gonna find out, cop. But you won't like it."

"That's what I thought it was," Mulvaney told him, forcing a grin.

The three men delegated to get him to the playroom formed up around him, and Mulvaney started toward the door. As he looked back over his shoulder—his head hurt when he turned it—he saw Teller go to the safe and close it. There was a clap of thunder louder than any before and the lights flickered again, but they didn't go out. Mulvaney turned sideways to get through the open doorway with the dead girl in his arms.

The three men with submachine guns were behind him, and the two men who'd just left—also armed with submachine guns—were nearly to the bottom of the circular staircase. No one was in evidence along the entire length of the upstairs hallway.

Ed Mulvaney shrugged his shoulders, whispered, "Sorry," to the dead girl, then hurled her body like a battering ram back through the doorway and into the nearest of the three men with submachine guns just coming through behind him.

Mulvaney ran for the staircase as the first shots came from behind him, vaulted onto the railing, and rode it down, his hands skidding over the smooth wood. More gunfire came from behind him now. Mulvaney slid around the circle in the staircase; he launched himself from the railing as one of the two men near the base of the staircase wheeled toward him. Mulvaney's body crashed into him as the submachine gun came up, knocking the man back into the other man a tread or two below. Mulvaney's body and the bodies of the two men were a twisted mass of arms and legs as they rolled down the staircase. Bullets tore into the black and white tiles of the floor. Mulvaney grabbed one of the two men by the front of the face and slammed the man's head into the floor as hard as he could. Mulvaney grabbed the submachine gun, and racked the bolt.

The second man was already up, his submachine gun coming forward, his left hand working the bolt.

Mulvaney was on his knees. He told the second man, "Go for the closed-bolt design in your next life, pal." Mulvaney put a burst of five or six shots into the man's chest. Gunfire rippled across the tiles near Mulvaney's feet, and Mulvaney sprayed out a few bursts toward the head of the staircase, driving the men there back into the room he'd just left.

Mulvaney reached down to the dead man, grabbed up his submachine gun, tore the sling free, then snatched the spare magazine from the man's belt.

And Ed Mulvaney ran for his life.

There was a double doorway at the far end of the front hall, with elaborate stained-glass panels set into the doors. Mulvaney emptied the first submachine gun through the doors, and the glass disintegrated. He threw the empty submachine gun to the floor, then rammed his body weight against the doors. The right door snapped outward off its hinges. Mulvaney was outside.

The two men sent to return Harry's knife were running back toward the house now. Mulvaney jumped the three steps from the doorway to the ground, the bolt of the Uzi already racked. He fired, cutting down one of the two men, then the other, the second man's submachine gun discharging into the ground as he fell.

Mulvaney was up, running again. Hassim, whoever the hell he was, was out here on the grounds. The four guys in wet suits were around somewhere, and there was still Teller and three other guys upstairs. They were probably downstairs by now.

Mulvaney reached the two dead men, dropped to one knee between them, and grabbed the Uzi that wasn't half shot out. He rolled over both bodies and grabbed two more twenty-round magazines.

He saw his blackjack stuffed into one of the dead men's belts. "Hey, thanks a lot, pal." Mulvaney grabbed it, snapped it across the dead man's face, then ran.

Thunder rumbled over the ocean, and suddenly the rain fell in torrents all around him, drenching him to the skin and freezing him.

He kept running.

They'd figure he would go for the fence and try to get across somehow.

He wanted them to think that.

When he reached the fence, Mulvaney punched one of the

Uzis forward and fired it out, pulling the muzzle upward and right in an arc, then down again toward the ground as he emptied the magazine. He finished the job with the first Uzi, the one that was already partially emptied into the two guys he'd just killed. As the last round fired, a section of the chain link fell through, outward, big enough for him to get through and out. Mulvaney took one of the empty Uzis and pitched it through the fence, then ran for the cover of the outbuilding. As he slammed against the wall, he saw Teller and three other men coming through what was left of the house's main entrance.

Mulvaney put one of his two remaining full magazines up the well of the Uzi and edged along the wall of the outbuilding, away from the main entrance to the house.

He could hear them running across the gravel when the thunder didn't drown out the sounds of their feet and voices as Teller cursed them out.

They reached the fence.

Mulvaney could have opened fire on them, but four to one with submachine guns didn't count up to odds he liked. He pulled back closer to the wall. The rain pouring off the roof of the outbuilding soaked him even more than the rain which blew across the grounds in sheets.

He could hear Teller shouting, "You cocksuckin' idiots! He blew his way through the fuckin' fence! Get him! Get him! I'm gettin' Mr. Gorchek the hell outta here. Get Mulvaney!"

Ed Mulvaney smiled.

The basement was smaller than a good-sized kitchen. But he found the circuit-breaker box and the auxiliary generator unit.

He pulled the main breaker off, then snapped the butt of the Uzi against the breaker panel a few times, smashing as much as he could. He went to the generator. He was no expert on the things, but everything that looked important he beat into junk.

When he went out through the basement doorway again, there were no lights in the house, except for on the second floor, where he saw a flashlight beam.

He started toward the house, but then pulled back into the basement doorway again. The four guys in wet suits came out and formed a half circle, M16 rifles in their hands. Then Mulvaney saw Teller and Gorchek.

If Gorchek was leaving, he had to have the chip. And if he was leaving by anything short of a time machine tonight with the high seas and the rain and the high winds, he had to think this place had suddenly become too dangerous for him.

Gorchek was right about that.

Chapter Four

Good-bye, Mr. Chip

Mulvaney found Hassim. Hassim was about five feet nine, stockily built, or at least looked that way in his yellow slicker and big-brimmed yellow rain hat. Maybe the guy did television commercials for fishsticks on the side. Hassim moved along the deck of the yacht Mulvaney had seen in aerial photographs of the island. Peterson had told Mulvaney that first time, "From the photos, she looks seaworthy. Yar, huh?"

"Yar?"

"Yeah, yar."

"Yar . . . ?"

"Nice-looking, all right?"

The yacht looked pretty yar up close, too, Mulvaney thought. He skidded on his butt half the distance to the boat dock along a defile that the downpouring rain had turned into a raging torrent of mud. Going the hard way had gotten him here about two minutes ahead of the bad guys, he figured. That gave him about one minute to polish off

Hassim and get into Hassim's rain gear. He'd have to keep his shoulders hunched to hide the height difference. It was the only chance he had to get Gorchek—the hell with the computer chip. There were already enough bodies around the island so he didn't worry about leaving some more, but Mulvaney's best bet was to stow away on the yacht, and, once it was out to sea in this storm and everybody had their hands full just staying alive, to kill them.

The thought had crossed his mind that once he killed everybody who was running the boat, he'd be stuck in the middle of a large storm in the middle of a larger ocean, but there had to be life rafts. He was a strong swimmer. Anyway, Gorchek had to be killed for what he'd done to the woman.

That was a given.

Mulvaney started forward along the boat dock, ducking from bitt to bollard, then made a last, long dash to the edge of the dock. He took a running jump and crashed down onto the yacht's deck, slipping and falling flat.

Hassim couldn't have heard him over the roar of the waves, the thunder, and the constant hammering of the rain, but Hassim turned around anyway. There was a knife in Hassim's hand. Mulvaney reasoned that firing the Uzi would attract the attention of Gorchek, Teller, and the four other men. So Mulvaney got to his feet, shouted to Hassim, "Drop the friggin' knife, asshole!"

Hassim didn't drop the knife. He charged toward Mulvaney instead. Mulvaney sidestepped against the rail and swung the Uzi, folding stock extended. The buttplate caught Hassim in the middle of the face. Mulvaney's right foot hammered down on Hassim's right wrist. Hassim's bloody mouth opened for a scream as his wrist broke. Mulvaney hammered the buttplate of the Uzi down a second time, this time smashing the base of the nose and breaking it, driving the bone up and through the ethmoid bone, into the brain.

Hassim stared wide-eyed into the rain. Mulvaney

dropped to his knees and started stripping the man of his rain gear.

Mulvaney inverted the hat, letting it start to fill up with rainwater. He'd caught head lice once in Vietnam and had no desire to catch them again. When he got Hassim's body clear of the slicker, Mulvaney took the pistol from Hassim's belt—one of the really expensive Walther P-88 9mms—and shoved it into his own belt. There wasn't any time to search for spare magazines, and barely enough to check that the one in the pistol was loaded. It was, and a quick press check confirmed that the chamber was loaded as well. Mulvaney rolled the body close to the rail, then rolled it over the side.

Mulvaney pulled on the yellow slicker, inverted the hat, shook it, then put it on, pulling the strap down under his chin. He looked at the Uzi, snarled under his breath, and tossed it over the side.

He picked up Hassim's knife and started forward, trying to figure out what to do so nobody would notice he was doing the wrong thing. . . .

He knew about motorboats from his service in Vietnam and he'd gone out on Lake Michigan with girls who had their own. Without her sails up, the yacht was just a big motorboat.

Without a word to him except "Be ready to put out to sea, Hassim!" from Gorchek, Teller's four M16 armed men had set to work at once, casting off lines. Mulvaney set to work trying to figure how to start the engines. The things on the right were throttles for the port and starboard engine, the things on the left clutches to facilitate gear changes. That much he had figured out. Once the last of the lines was cleared, he advanced the starboard engine, and the yacht started moving away from the dock. So far, Mulvaney figured, so good. As they rolled over the first of the enormous, deck-washing breakers, Mulvaney advanced speed on the starboard engine and initiated the portside engine. The yacht seemed to lurch ahead. He consoled himself with the fact that the ride tonight would be bumpy no matter how good or bad the man at the helm was because the sea was beyond choppy. It was dangerous.

As he throttled out the port engine, turning the wheel hard to starboard over the swell, he looked behind him. Gorchek had disappeared below decks, two of the other four men were well aft (guarding against the terrible Mulvaney), and the other two crouched by the prow near the rail, just a few yards ahead of the pilothouse.

Ed Mulvaney wanted a smoke. Two things mitigated against that. His cigarettes were soaked to the point of brown-paper mush, and he had no way of telling whether or not Hassim had smoked. He forced the idea from his mind, concentrating instead on how to kill the four men on deck so he could go below decks and kill Teller and Gorchek. Maybe he could even grab the 486 SX chip. Four assault rifles versus one handgun was even poorer odds than four submachine guns against one of the same.

The windshield wipers on the pilot's cabin windscreen were working furiously and, largely, fruitlessly. But when the windshield cleared for a split second, Mulvaney saw the rocks ahead, well to his left. A clear channel out to sea on his right.

The two men in the prow would spot what he was doing first, of course, but they would be the two easiest to kill if he had to because they were the closest of the four armed men on deck.

An enormous wave crashed over the yacht amidships along the starboard side and Mulvaney steered out of it to port. He was already heading the vessel toward the rocks, his decision all but made for him by the forces of nature.

Mulvaney felt along the underside of the control console and found a stout cord that was attached to a grommet beneath the console. It was fitted with a Velcro fixture at the other end. He was familiar with the idea such a thing represented. One lashed the wheel with it, to keep the wheel

68

from moving when there was clear sailing ahead and man's full attention wasn't needed. The first cruise control, Mulvaney thought, smiling.

He cut the wheel hard to port, turning the bow of the vessel full on toward the rocks, the incoming breakers now crashing with terrible ferocity across the starboard side of the hull, the deck fully awash. Mulvaney pulled the cord up, put one of the Velcro strips through the wheel, and mated the Velcro together when he had the right tension to keep the wheel from moving, locking the boat on course.

And then he reached under the closed slicker and drew the Walther P-88 from his sodden trouser band. Looking over his shoulder once, he started out of the pilothouse to work his way forward just enough to take care of the two men there before they took care of him.

As he pushed open the pilothouse door, another wave, so violent it slammed against the doorframe and smashed the window nearest his head, crashed over the deck in a broad roll. The weight of the water was so great that the deck sank from beneath his feet. Mulvaney fell to the deck. He was showered with shards of flying glass. "Unbreakable my ass," Mulvaney snarled, spitting water.

He pulled himself to his feet, his hands against the doorjamb, his eyes blinking. Sucking in breath, Mulvaney started forward, losing his balance as the vessel caught a swell and rolled. His hands were on the rail, gripping it white-knuckled as he edged forward. Spray washed over him and for an instant he couldn't see. As he regained his sight, he realized one of the two men crouched in the wedge formed at the base of the bow pulpit was turning toward him. A wave crashed across the cabin roof, slamming Mulvaney against the rail.

As Mulvaney looked forward again, rubbing his right hand across his eyes to clear them, the man who'd been looking at him was moving his mouth, shouting something to the second man. The second man was trying to raise his M16.

Mulvaney dropped to his knees beside the cabin roof. He twisted his left wrist into a line and held the Walther P-88 in his right fist. The first man was bringing the muzzle of his M16 on line with Mulvaney's body. A wave broke across the starboard bow, engulfing them all.

A burst of automatic weapons fire cut across the cabin roof, one bullet hitting a cleat and spraying sparks. Mulvaney stabbed the P-88 toward the bow pulpit, his eyes still blurred from the last wave, firing double taps as he turreted the pistol left and right. As he blinked his eyes clear, one of the two men was down and the other was firing. Mulvaney swung back against the tension of the rope as the deck rolled beneath him. Gunfire rippled over the cabin roof. Mulvaney fired two shots, then two more. The second man's body slammed back into the rail, his assault rifle firing into the air as he tumbled over the side.

Mulvaney had six shots left. He twisted right, pointing the pistol aft as the two men there—they had heard the shots, despite the roar of wind and water—started forward. Mulvaney fired, using up four of the remaining rounds, catching the nearer of the two in the face. A wave crested, crashing down across the starboard side. The blood that had appeared in the man's cheeks and forehead disappeared. The dead eyes just stared blankly, then the body was swept over the side.

Mulvaney pulled himself back to his knees. The fourth man edged back and fired a burst which cut across the deck, missing Mulvaney by inches.

Mulvaney let go of the rope, dived forward around the corner of the cabin roof, and another burst of gunfire riddled the cabin roof.

Mulvaney crawled on knees and elbows toward the dead man still remaining in the bow pulpit. The sling from the M16 rifle was entwined around the dead man's right arm.

The deck lurched violently beneath Mulvaney. Mulvaney slid toward the portside rail, and caught himself. His eyes, as soon as he blinked them clear enough to see, focused on the dead man and the rifle. The body had also been caught by the wave and now lay perilously close to the portside rail. The rifle hung over the side. The next wave would wash man and gun into the sea.

More shots cracked from Mulvaney's right, and as he threw himself to the cover of the cabin roof, he saw Teller and Gorchek huddled aft with the other gunman. With the high volume of fire the cabin roof disintegrated in huge chunks. Mulvaney snapped off his last two shots and tossed the Walther over the side. Mulvaney skidded across the water-slicked deck toward the dead man. He clawed at the body. Mulvaney's left hand at last grasped the rifle by the pistol grip.

Mulvaney tore the sling clear of the dead man's arm. The deck shifted again, and Mulvaney slid hard into a bow rail stanchion. Gunfire rippled over the deck toward him. The M16's weight felt all right, and there was no choice but to hope the magazine was at least partially loaded. Mulvaney triggered a burst as the last remaining man from the original four on the deck came toward him along the portside of the cabin roof.

Mulvaney's bullets caught the man at waist level. The burst stitched its way upward along the abdomen and chest and into the neck. The gunman's body spun wildly and careened over the portside rail amidships and into the sea.

For a split second, Mulvaney caught a clear glimpse of Gorchek's face. He saw panic there. Mulvaney looked back, across the bow and toward the rocks. The vessel was nearly on them. The rocks were larger and more deadly now, water-slicked, black, and jagged.

Mulvaney pushed himself out of the bow and toward the cabin profile, the M16 in his right fist. Gunfire tore into the bulkhead beside him and across the cabin roof again, but it was pistol fire—Teller. Mulvaney pulled out the M16's magazine. "Dammit!" The magazine was empty, meaning the one round he had in the rifle's chamber was it.

He risked a peek around the side of the cabin.

Teller was moving toward the wheelhouse. Gorchek had a pistol in his hand.

Mulvaney fired the last round from the M16, pointing the rifle toward Gorchek. A wave washed across the deck over the starboard side just as Mulvaney triggered the shot. Gorchek was hit, falling away down through the open companionway door. If Teller could somehow save the ship, he might save Gorchek and the 486 SX chip, too.

Mulvaney lurched aft along the rail and toward the wheelhouse, the empty rifle still in his right hand. Teller wouldn't know it was empty, and Mulvaney could still use it as a club.

Mulvaney looked over his shoulder. Although the vessel was almost on the rocks, he could feel it coming about to starboard, veering away. Mulvaney reached the shattered wheelhouse door and saw Teller at the helm, fighting the wheel. Mulvaney threw the door open, shouted, "Teller!" then threw himself toward the man, hitting Teller's body. A wave broke diagonally over the starboard side well forward and crashed along over the cabin and the wheelhouse. What remained of the glass exploded inward, showering them both as they fell to the floor.

Mulvaney's Beretta was in Teller's right hand, and Mulvaney still held the empty M16. Mulvaney crashed the rifle's butt downward, just missing Teller's face as a knee caught Mulvaney in the left thigh, just nicking his testicles but sending him rolling away.

Teller was up, lurched against the control panel, one hand on the wheel, the other still gripping Mulvaney's gun.

Ed Mulvaney, on his knees, rammed the rifle upward toward Teller's face. The flash hider struck Teller's right cheek, scraped away skin, and buried itself in Teller's right eye as the Beretta discharged into the deck beside Mulvaney. But Mulvaney was already moving. As Teller screamed, Mulvaney bent low and threw his full body weight against Teller's midsection. Mulvaney's right fist hammered Teller's testicles, and Mulvaney's left elbow struck upward into Teller's thorax.

Mulvaney threw Teller to the deck, Mulvaney's left foot coming down hard over the inside of Teller's gun-hand wrist. Mulvaney kicked with his right foot, catching Teller at the base of the nose, snapping his head back and breaking his neck.

Mulvaney looked forward over the wildly spinning wheel.

The rocks towered over him, even higher, it seemed, than the main mast.

Mulvaney reached to the deck, pried his pistol from Teller's fingers, threw himself through the open doorway, and ran for the portside rail.

There was a sound like a tree falling, then a loud snap.

Mulvaney looked right.

The main mast was tumbling toward him, and the prow of the ship was driving upward into the rocks.

Mulvaney vaulted over the railing and into the raging sea.

Chapter Five

Goddess

John Osgood squinted through his sunglasses.

There was a look of determination in her dark eyes, her face like something crafted under the hands of a sculptor. She ran toward him, stopped, swatted the ball with a kind of natural, animal ferocity. She skimmed over the sun-bleached sand but didn't quite touch it. As she wheeled away, the ball popped upward over the net, then dropped like a rock inches away from the hands of her nearest opponent.

Twenty-one for her team. Game point.

She jumped up and down shrieking with glee, hugging the other girls, all of them almost as long-legged and as darkly tanned, but none so savagely beautiful as she.

Her sweat-glistening buttocks jiggled, but only a little. The two cheeks rose up on either side, the crack between them starting subtly, disappearing beneath the almond-colored fabric almost as soon as it began, a dark line of sweat following its course for several more inches. She turned around suddenly, staring at him. She spoke in Portuguese, which he understood sufficiently but had never spoken well. But he did not respond, because Randy Bleeker didn't know any Portuguese at all. Her English had a slight Germanic flavor to it as she tried again. "You are staring at me?"

"You are very beautiful; yes, I was staring at you."

As she turned fully around, bending over to brush sand from her bronzed legs, there was a wonderful view, surpassing even that of Sugarloaf just beyond the crescent of beach and across Guanabara Bay. The string bikini's top covered her nipples. And that was essentially all. "Thank you," she said and she smiled at him.

"I think you're expecting me, if you're Miss Reimann."

"Am I expecting you?"

Apparently she wanted the code phrase they'd gotten out of Bleeker in Montreal after all those hours of questioning. Osgood gave it, and under the circumstances, looking at her, it wasn't inappropriate. "I am humbled by the beauty of nature."

She seemed to think about what he said for a moment, then cast her gaze downward over her own body, then looked up into his eyes. As she tossed back her long, wet, honey-blond hair, she laughed. The sound of her voice was like the soft melody of an Antonio Carlos Jobim samba. She extended her right hand to him. "I am Magda Reimann. My brother, Artur, waits for us on the Island of Love."

John Osgood took her hand in his. Her pink nails were perfect but almost as short as a man's. Her fingers were long but her small hand showed strength and almost disarming honesty in her grip.

Osgood slipped his cane under his arm and lit a cigarette. An island of love would, indeed, be delightful to visit with this marvelous-looking girl. He wondered, though, if her neo-Nazi brother, an international arms smuggler like Randy Bleeker, had ever heard the old expression about three being a crowd?

"I have a car."

75

"That's great, because I came by taxi."

She smiled again. Her teeth were also perfect, and so white they positively gleamed. "May I have a cigarette, too?" Magda Reimann asked, pushing her hair back with both hands, looking very provocative as she did it.

"Yes, certainly, Miss Reimann," and Osgood fished his case out of his right hip pocket again. She started walking in long, healthy barefoot strides toward a towel and a large straw handbag several yards away. "I have your cigarette."

"Light it for me? And, please, call me Magda. Randy, are you?"

He didn't want to answer that. But he lit her cigarette. She stopped beside the beach towel, folded it back, and revealed a pair of straw sandals. After brushing her feet a little on the towel she stepped into these, then took the cigarette from him. "Umm—I like American cigarettes."

"Yes, so do I. Sometimes hard to find my brand, though, in Canada."

"I've never met a Canadian before," she told him, smiling. "Take my cigarette?"

He took it from her as she pulled several yards of floral print fabric from inside her handbag, shook it, then started wrapping it around her waist to form an ankle-length skirt. "I hate it when a woman has a cigarette hanging out of her lips, don't you?"

"Oh, yes, indeed." He smoked his own cigarette, noting as he held hers that there wasn't any lipstick on it.

"It looks so cheap." She jackknifed her body forward, as if starting some sort of aerobic workout, but instead began wrapping a scarf that matched the skirt around her hair. She stood upright, tying the scarf—which now looked more like a turban—and saying, "Have you met Artur before?"

"No, I'm afraid our paths hadn't crossed till now. Do you work with your brother?"

She laughed, putting on a pair of sunglasses. "No, Artur doesn't think women should work. So I play." She slipped her left arm through the handles of her bag, letting it hang from the crook of her elbow. "I'll take back my cigarette now."

He returned it to her. As he did, he noticed her eyes were on his cane. "Did you hurt your leg? I should not pry. Artur always tells me that." She laughed.

He lied. "My knee goes out on me once in a while. Right knee. It's been acting up a bit—I guess it's the humidity— so I thought it might be prudent to bring it along."

"That is an English word I don't know. *Prudent?*" Magda repeated carefully. "You should tell me what it means while we walk to my car."

They began to walk, Osgood feeling light-hearted in her company, despite their destination. *"Prudent* means 'careful,' but with forethought, planning ahead for some contingency or another."

"Oh." She nodded. As they left the sand, it was as if they had crossed some invisible barrier. The breeze suddenly died and it was hot. She stopped before a Ferrari—candy-apple red with tan leather interior—and started fishing in her purse, presumably for her keys. Osgood looked up and down the strand. Volkswagens were the most numerous of the assortment of cars parked here and along the opposite side of the six-lane boulevard. Many of them were wonderful old Beetles. "There. For a moment I thought I'd lost them. Would you like to drive?"

John Osgood hated passing up the opportunity, since Ferraris were among his favorite things in the world, but he told her, "I really don't know Rio well. I wish you'd drive."

"All right. I like a man who isn't afraid to let a woman drive."

"Thank you. I like you," he said honestly, without thinking.

"Thank you." He held her door for her. The wrap that was her skirt shot up to her thighs as she dropped in behind the wheel.

Osgood walked around the front of the car, twirling his cane, his mind definitely not on his work.

They took the public ferryboat to Paqueta, the Island of Love—one square kilometer of paradise unmolested by the twentieth century. She stood in the prow of the ferry with him. The scarf was gone from her hair, and her hair and skirt caught in the wind. Her sensuality was something Osgood could not blot from his mind. Takeuchi Arisato's whereabouts was what he should be thinking about.

Artur Reimann's principal allegiance was to money, of course, but his philosophical bent—if such a bastardized collection of prejudices could be called philosophy—was national socialism. Reimann and this fantastically lovely girl were the offspring, supposedly, of a Nazi war criminal who fled Germany to Argentina, then came to Brazil. As Osgood watched the girl, it was hard to think of her as anything but a charming, perhaps slightly weird, goddess.

He turned his attention to the cane in his hands, feeling its weight. Magda's voice startled him, seeming to invade his thoughts. "I know why you carry that cane." He leaned back from the railing, looking at her intently and saying nothing. "Everybody who comes to see my brother carries some kind of a weapon. I'm used to it. Is it one of those canes that turns into a gun?"

He truthfully told her, "No." The cane guns, from England oddly enough, had been popping up lately in the south Florida drug trade. There'd be no reason to suppose the things wouldn't be encountered here. "No, but I know the sort of cane you're thinking of."

"Then why is it metal?"

"Well, I sometimes carry a lot of money, and in Canada I'd be making more headaches for myself than you might imagine if I were caught carrying a gun. This cane's like a piece of pipe. One could use it as a weapon if needed."

"You sell guns. I don't like guns, but I like you."

"I'm very glad you like me, but you shouldn't dislike

guns," Osgood told her. "Guns are only tools, like this ferryboat or your Ferrari, a hairbrush, anything. If you had a child, say a daughter, and your child were very well behaved, very ladylike, very polite, but you beat her with that hairbrush, then the hairbrush would be an instrument of evil. But if, instead, you were a kind and loving mother and you used that same hairbrush to groom the little girl's hair, to help you put pretty ribbons in it, to glorify her prettiness, then the hairbrush would be an instrument of good, wouldn't it?"

"I suppose so. You are a very odd man, Randy Bleeker."

Osgood suddenly felt very dirty inside lying to this girl. He asked her, "Do you take after your mother? If you do, she must have been exquisite."

She hugged her arms about herself and laughed. "I don't know."

"What?" He was prying, but prying was part of his job description.

"I was adopted. My real parents—well, I don't know who they were. The woman I called my mother, Artur's mother, she was very beautiful."

John Osgood took her into his arms without even thinking, then stepped back. She looked up at him oddly. "Why did you do that?"

"Did you like it?"

"Yes."

"Then, that's why I did it."

John Osgood took her hand and said nothing more.

Chapter Six

The Island of Love

A man of about sixty who appeared part black and part Indian drove the team of matched bays. They pulled the large surrey along the tree-shaded lane away from the pink and white gingerbread structures on the near side of the Island of Love. The tinkle of harness was punctuated by the occasional ringing of a bicycle bell. The cyclists—many of them—outdistanced the horses but still moved at a comparatively leisurely pace.

John Osgood and Magda Reimann sat side by side, facing forward. As the buildings disappeared behind them, palm trees began to rise along the boundary between the roadway and the beach. A skiff, prow high and dry, lay just out of reach of the surf in the shade of some of the higher vegetation, its red paint faded from times when it had not been shielded from the sun.

Beneath the white fringed canopy of the surrey, there was a cool breeze. Magda's hand touched at his thigh, found his hand, and drew it toward her, both their hands coming to rest on her lap. "You and my brother—when your business is completed, will you be leaving Rio?"

"Not instantly, of course, but soon, yes."

"In Canada there is snow on the ground, isn't there?"

"Yes. There's a great deal of snow in some places, and it's cold everywhere, not like here. This is like living in paradise." And Osgood watched her face, the corners of her full lips turning down slightly, a momentary sadness passing over her eyes. And then she smiled again, holding his hand more tightly. "Is there something wrong?" Osgood asked her.

"You should tell the driver to stop, and we will walk back. Then you should leave Rio at once."

"Why?"

She drew her hand away, hugged her bare arms over her breasts. "I do not know who you are, but Artur is not waiting alone. There are three Japanese with him."

"There are many Japanese in Brazil. Brazil has the largest Japanese population anywhere in the world outside of Japan, if memory serves."

"No," Magda hissed through her teeth, shaking her head. "Have the driver stop the carriage now. These men work with one of my brother's customers. They are bad men."

"Then, all the more reason I have to see them, Magda."

"No!" She screamed the word. The carriage driver stopped his horses and looked down from his seat and back at them. Magda lowered her voice. "They know you are not Bleeker. One of the Japanese I overheard said that you are very dangerous to them. They wait to kill you."

"Where?"

"When we stop at the little marina on the other side of the island. They will be waiting."

"How many? The three Japanese, your brother, and how many others?"

"Hans and Peter. They are very deadly men." She looked at him. "Who are you?"

"John Osgood." And Osgood told the carriage driver,

"Sempre a direito, por favor." And once more the carriage was on its way. . . .

Sometimes, there was no choice but to trust someone. Sometimes, too, after making that choice one was not lucky enough to live even to regret it. But Osgood made the decision to trust Magda, promising her he would do nothing to harm her brother if at all possible. And then she told him something that unnerved him. "My brother is a killer, John. Once he almost killed me. If that would make me free of him, then—"

With that thought still in his brain, John Osgood crept over the rocks that formed the rough, narrow border between the high shade trees on this far-reaching salient of the island's shoreline and the ocean itself. He reached the halfway point. The ocean here was calm, a bright azure almost the same shade as the sky, the horizon line so indistinct that one had the impression of being inside some vast surrealistic painting, the island being the only thing which was real.

But no Dali-esque giraffes with flaming necks moved along the land. Instead, about a hundred yards down from where the white sand again resumed, there was a motorized rubber raft, an Avon Inflatable. The only grotesques about were two large-looking blond-haired, deeply tanned men, one on either side of the craft.

Lying well out to sea, listing slightly on its leeward anchor, was a small yacht.

The scenario was simple and obvious. "Randy Bleeker" is met by the two men, "taken for a ride" to the yacht where Artur is waiting to talk about the arms deal for the Libyans, the proposed object of the meeting.

Surprise!

Three Japanese killers in the likely employ of Takeuchi Arisato attack and kill, aided, if need be, by the aforementioned Aryan supermen. Up anchor, out a few miles to sea, a few coils of anchor chain, and the irritation goes over the side.

John Osgood smiled.

He didn't have a gun, but he had his cane. . . .

Stripped to his khaki trousers and the underpants he wore beneath them, John Osgood swam beneath the surface, toward the yacht. The guts of the cane were clutched in his left hand, the head and the rubber-tipped buttcap in his pockets. The tube of the cane itself he used like the sheath of a Ninja Katana, as a breathing tube.

He reached the near anchor chain and grabbed hold, breaking the surface slowly. The inflatable with racially superior Hans and Peter was still on the shore. There was a ladder down the portside amidships, and Osgood went below the surface again and began swimming toward it. A rung of the ladder extended below the waterline, and Osgood steadied himself with it as he took his last breath through the tube. He surfaced, the little hermetically sealed packet and the blade tight between his left biceps and his rib cage.

There was no one that he could see on deck, perhaps because the sun was close to overhead and very hot now. Osgood squinted against its reflection on the water as he blew outward through the tube. He rested the packet on a rung just above the waterline and opened it, extracting one of the darts. They were very much like ordinary nails with orange plastic cups at one end. But the points were sharpened to an exacting degree. Osgood placed the dart over the mouthpiece, then screwed the mouthpiece in place, careful to keep the tube at a slightly upward angle relating to the muzzle.

He closed the packet, then placed it in a trouser pocket. The blade in his right hand, the tube in his left, Osgood started up the ladder, giving a glance forward and toward the shore. He could not see the spot on the beach where the

Avon Inflatable was, and logic dictated that anyone standing near the boat could not see him.

Osgood reached the top of the ladder, slipped through the gap in the rail, and huddled against the main cabin bulwark. He looked fore and aft. The yacht, single-masted, was fully rigged, but all sail was furled. He could see the edge of a canopy that was erected over the cockpit well aft of his position and assumed that someone would be seated there, "standing" deck watch.

Osgood slowly, silently, brought the shaft of the cane together against the blade, so he could use one hand to hold both. Moving quickly on his bare feet, but in a low crouch, he started aft.

As he neared the canopy, he stopped. He heard a voice, speaking in German-accented English. Another voice, the English very good but clearly flavored by Japanese.

Two, and one of them Artur. The other two Japanese would be below deck.

He wanted Artur alive, but not because of his promise. Clearly, if Magda had not betrayed him yet, and had meant what she said, then she was afraid of Artur and would be well rid of him. But Artur, more likely than any of the Japanese, would tell him something that would set him on the trail of Takeuchi Arisato again.

Takeuchi's right-wing terrorist underground had been quiet for too long, but it was known that Takeuchi was buying arms and equipment, not all of it military. And not all of it was purchased. Nearly six months ago there was a theft in Tokyo of an upgraded Japanese counterpart of a Cray computer, faster than anything the United States would be able to place on the market for another few years. The loss of the computer was merely an inconvenience to the Japanese, as another prototype was easy enough to build, albeit costly.

But why had Takeuchi wanted it, if indeed Takeuchi had taken it?

John Osgood crept forward again. By the time he reached

the open companionway hatch just fore of the cockpit, he had his plan.

The voices were more easily understood now, and he crouched there a few seconds, listening.

". . . it begins, I already have all the sources I need to supply what he will require. You must remember, Tsutomu, that it will not matter to my associates that Takeuchi-san strikes from the right. The disruption this will cause the global economy is the important factor. Right and left are, sadly, coming to lose their meaning. But gold, on the other hand, that is always important. The economic chaos Takeuchi promises will triple the value of gold."

There was the click of a cigarette lighter, and the Japanese spoke. "Reimann-san, you must be very careful of this Osgood. He has pursued my master for some time, and nearly caused my master to be killed in Montreal." John Osgood felt strangely gratified that he'd become such a thorn in Takeuchi Arisato's side. And he would have loved to have listened to more of the conversation, but he was already pushing his luck. As a brief gust of wind passed, Osgood could smell cigarette smoke.

"In my father's day, Tsutomu, things were different. But, at least, men such as Takeuchi-san and I are still allies. Some things never change."

John Osgood stood. The shaft of his cane snapped up, and his lips pursed to form the proper embouchure. He exhaled. And as the Japanese called Tsutomu turned toward him, the dart punctured the carotid artery. The dart was tipped with a synthetic equivalent of the poison used by one of the species of Pacific sea snake. There was no antidote for the poison, which attacked the central nervous system so quickly that whoever was bitten died in under a minute. There was no antidote because there would never be the chance to use it.

Osgood jumped over the body as it fell. Artur was drawing a gun as the shaft of the blow gun-cane crashed down over Artur's right wrist. Osgood put the point of the spike-shaped rapier that was the blade of the Crawford sword cane-blow gun against Artur's throat. Artur had half risen from his chair.

"Ver' stehen Sie, Herr Reimann?"

Reimann had none of his adopted sister's good looks. He was fat jowled and flaccid lipped, and his tongue flicked nervously over his lips now. "Nehmen Sie Platz, bitte."

Reimann sat down.

"Nur keine Aufregung, Reimann." Osgood reached down, released the shaft of his cane onto the deck, and started to pick up the gun, a Walther P-5 9mm. As Osgood drew back, the gun in his left hand, the rapier blade in his right, he gestured to Reimann to stand. "Nicht so schnell, Reimann!" Reimann slowed. Osgood turned the gun so he could hook his thumb through the trigger guard, then closed the four fingers of his left hand over the slide, drawing it back just enough to verify the chamber was loaded. He got a real grip on the gun, then, and gestured Reimann toward the companionway steps, then told him, "Halten Sie hier." Then Osgood raised his voice, shouting down the companionway steps. Two Japanese stood at their base. Osgood called to them, saying, "Konichi wa! Masugu!" Osgood jerked with the rapier up the stairwell. Neither man had yet drawn a weapon.

Both now raised their hands. "Hayaku!" Osgood urged. The two Japanese moved more rapidly up the companionway steps as Osgood kept the muzzle of the P-5 less than an inch away from Reimann's head. As the two men reached the level of the cockpit, Osgood drew back against the stern rail beside the wheel, with Reimann in front of him as a shield. "Koko de . . . uh . . . stop-o!" The two Japanese stopped in their tracks.

Osgood moved the rapier forward in his left hand, slipping the tip under the windbreaker of the nearest of the two men. There was a shoulder holster Osgood had already spotted profiled under the coat with a pistol in it. Osgood gestured with the rapier, and the Japanese started to with-

86

draw the gun from the holster. *"Muskoshi yukuri!"* Osgood cautioned, the man moving his hand more slowly now. The Japanese held the gun—a SIG-Sauer P-230 .380—by the butt between two fingers. Osgood put the tip of the rapier through the trigger guard, drew back, the gun sliding along the length of the blade, stopping against Osgood's hand.

The second man's gun was under the Hawaiian Aloha shirt's left front, and Osgood pushed back the fabric with the tip of his rapier. The man very slowly withdrew the gun from his trouser band—another P-230—and placed it over the tip of the rapier. "Arigatō." Osgood smiled.

But as Osgood raised the Crawford rapier to allow the gun to slide back toward him, the Japanese in the Aloha shirt shouted something incomprehensible and threw himself forward, impaling himself over the point at the chest.

Osgood stumbled as the body lurched toward him, Artur grabbing for Osgood's gun-hand wrist, shouting, "Get him, Ken!" Osgood let go of the rapier, the heel of his left hand connecting with Artur's temple. Artur's head snapped away, and the pressure from Artur's hands on Osgood's gun-hand wrist vanished.

The other Japanese, a knife in his right hand, lunged toward Osgood. But Osgood's hand was free now, and Osgood took a step back and left, firing Artur's pistol twice—point blank—into his attacker's chest.

The Japanese fell at Osgood's feet.

Hans and Peter would be doing one of two things by now, fleeing or coming to the yacht to investigate. Osgood bet on the latter.

Artur was standing, telling Osgood in English, "You will never escape Rio!"

"Who's to tell your people to kill me, Reimann? You?" And Osgood moved closer to Reimann. Perspiration was beading under Reimann's black eyes. Osgood brought the muzzle of the pistol to the tip of Reimann's nose. "What if you aren't alive to do it?"

Reimann began breathing rapidly and tried to edge back.

As Reimann moved, Osgood moved the pistol until Reimann stopped moving at all. "Please, Osgood. I was only following orders from Takeuchi. It is Takeuchi who wants you dead."

"What is he planning and where is he? What about gold tripling in value?"

Reimann threw up. Osgood stepped back just in time, then shoved Reimann toward the rail, keeping the gun against Reimann's heaving rib cage. "Tell me! I despise Nazis and I'd just as soon kill you. Tell me!"

Reimann turned around, both elbows on the rail, leaning heavily against it, face white as the dead. "Then he will kill me, Osgood."

"Takeuchi will kill you later. I'll kill you in the next ten seconds. Choose quickly." Hans and Peter would be coming alongside at any moment now, if they were coming at all. There was very little time.

Reimann looked about to vomit again, but Osgood gestured once more with the pistol. And Reimann nodded. "All I know," he began, "is that Takeuchi has something planned which will destroy diplomatic and economic relations between Japan and the United States. He foresees a general uprising from the right after that, and will require arms. It has something to do with Ladislaw Gorchek, the Communist pig." Reimann tried to spit over the rail, but couldn't.

"Where is Takeuchi now?"

Reimann's complexion was going from white to green as he said, "Takeshima. In Japan."

Something clicked in John Osgood's memory, and suddenly it was all there in front of him—the computer theft, the economic and diplomatic chaos, and the political upheaval from Japan's latent right wing.

Osgood took a step back. If he shot Artur Reimann, he'd be doing the world, as well as Reimann's adopted sister, Magda, a favor.

But it would be murder, the sort of thing men like Reimann paid others to do for them.

Reimann threw himself away from the rail and toward the rapier. Both pistols Osgood had taken from the Japanese men who had been below decks were there beside it. As Reimann's right hand closed on the butt of the nearer of the two semiautomatics, John Osgood's moral dilemma was solved.

Osgood fired twice into Reimann's head, then looked round the side of the canopied cockpit. Hans and Peter were about twenty-five yards off and closing quickly now.

John Osgood grabbed up the shaft from his cane and the rapier, twisted off the mouthpiece from the shaft, and dropped that into his pocket. The Walther pistol was in the waistband of his sodden trousers. As Osgood stepped over the aft rail, careful to avoid the puddling blood from Reimann's head, he flipped the pistol away into the sea.

And jumped.

Chapter Seven

The Grind

"Every night my wife and I get down on our knees and clasp our hands together and pray to the Lord Almighty that someday we won't find out you're part black."

"What?"

"You heard me, fool! All we need to pull our people down is to find out you're black. Look at you! Them raggedy clothes, that long hippie haircut. You lose your razor or somethin'?"

"I—"

"Yeah? Don't lay none of that shit on me you give the watch commander this morning. Andy should be ashamed of you."

"I got a skin irritation."

"Skin irritation my ass, Mulvaney. You just fuckin' lazy. Why don't you admit it? I'm the one's got me a skin irritation. Your white skin. It's irritatin' the hell outta me."

Ed Mulvaney started to laugh.

"And what's your silly white ass up to now, man?"

The car was swerving side to side a little, but it was still in the lane, Mulvaney reasoned. And the South Lake Shore Drive traffic was light this time of day. So long as he didn't hit too big a pothole, there was just enough friction between his right knee and the bottom of the steering wheel to keep things under control. And the temperature was above freezing, too.

"What are you doin'?"

"I'm gettin' a smoke, all right, Lew? I got the car under control."

"You sittin' on your cigarettes?"

"No. I know where the cigarettes are. I'm goin' after the lighter."

"Stupid white motherfucker," Lew Fields remarked. "Not bad enough you gotta kill yourself smokin', but you gotta kill us both crashin' while you're smokin'. Stop making the damn car weave!"

"Almost got it."

"All I know, Mulvaney, is gettin' pulled over by some rookie kid in his blue and white for us drunk drivin's gonna really suck! You just lose me my pension, you silly son of a bitch! Go ahead! I wanna see you get your ass taxed outta existence supportin' me and my wife on welfare!"

Mulvaney had his lighter.

Lew Fields said, "And my wife says Andy's too good for you, too."

Mulvaney almost dropped the lighter as he lit it. "She did not! Stop comin' up with this shit, man. You wanna say somethin' about me, then say it to my face, man. Don't go tellin' me your wife said it!"

"Hey, Ed, I ever lie to you?"

"Constantly, Lew."

And Lew Fields started laughing. Mulvaney lit his cigarette and had the wheel back in his hands again. Fields said, "Seriously, Ed, how's it going with you and Andy?"

Mulvaney shrugged his shoulders. Llewellyn Fields was

one of the two best friends he had left in the world, not counting Andy. Andy made three. "We're cool."

"Stop givin' me this black kid shit, like 'We're cool.' How you doin'?"

Mulvaney shrugged again."It's the money thing."

"You're not telling me Andy's worried about money?"

"No. I am. She's got a job with that P.I. outfit over in Downers Grove. We're makin' it fine. But, hell, I don't want my wife working."

"My wife works. Being a high school principal's a pretty good job. Beats bein' a cop, 'cept you can't carry a gun legally."

Mulvaney laughed, saying, "That doesn't stop her, though."

"Better to be judged by twelve than carried by six, like they say. What's the real problem?"

Mulvaney took his eyes off the road, looked at Lew Fields. "I don't want her doing something dangerous. And, anyway, what happens if she's pregnant and I get killed or something? She's not gonna get too far on a widow's pension, not these days. Every dime I had, except for the house, every lousy damn dime's gone."

"You still got that Porsche. Goin' on twenty years old, isn't it?"

"Get serious, man."

Mulvaney looked at his friend again. Fields was serious, saying, "All I know is you and Andy are in love. People are in love, they should get married. The rest of the problems sort of iron out after a while, or else if they don't, at least you can face 'em together. Anyway, somethin' happen to you, as long as my wife and I are alive, you know Andy or any kids you guys would have would be looked after. It's not like with you and Stella, Ed. Is that what's bothering you?"

Stella. Ed Mulvaney groaned at the mention of the name. "No. Andy isn't anything like Stella, Lew. That's not it. Stella was a vicious bitch. Andy's the neatest lady in the world. It's the money thing. It's not like if you never had it, you know?"

The sun was trying to make it through the clouds. It wasn't having much success.

"Do you regret helping your friend's wife and family?"

Mulvaney looked at Lew Fields for a second, then looked back at the traffic. A *Tribune* delivery truck was slowing things up, and Mulvaney started changing lanes. "No. He'd have done the same for me."

"I don't think so. No offense, but he would have told himself he had a wife and kids of his own, and he wouldn't have. Grimshaw was more than a buddy to you."

"Bargain-basement psychology?"

"He was a symbol to you, of your youth and of your future. Trying to keep things going for him was a way of ensuring the memory of the past wouldn't die and that you had a future. You helped his wife and kids just because you're a good guy. Don't go kicking yourself for doing that. Because you'd do it again. You're a softy, man, always were."

"Bullshit."

Fields laughed, "Well, you say what you want, but you can't change the way you are. Men are supposed to have a lot of bluster, keeps making us think we're macho. You'll work things out, whether it's stayin' on the cops or getting your own private security firm. Whatever it is, you and Andy'll make it happen. I got faith in ya."

Mulvaney looked at his friend and started to say something. He looked out at the traffic instead and started to laugh.

The radio in a police car is sort of like a fly buzzing outside a window screen. After you notice it the first time, the sound is still there but you ignore it, only noticing it if somehow the fly finds its way in through a hole in the screen and starts buzzing your head. But with a police radio there are several holes, things like "Officer down," "Two-eleven in progress," "All cars in the vicinity of . . ." or something that involves someone you know. As Mulvaney started to say something to Fields, several flies found their way through holes in the screen all at once. A silent alarm sounded at Hansel & Grits, on 79th and Jeffrey, about three minutes from their present location if you drove at a normal rate of speed, and a suspected 211 in progress and an officer down call came, all cars in the vicinity to respond.

As Lew Fields said, "Hit it, Ed," Mulvaney had the siren switch flipped and the Mars light stuck on the roof.

Hansel & Grits was one of those odd places Chicago seemed to have in abundance. It was run by a guy named Dave Strauss, just a kid in World War II when, as an American of German extraction, he fought Germans trying to take over the world. He had been a ballplayer and a pretty good one with a contract for a White Sox farm club. The Sox would have honored the contract after he got back from doing his bit, but the trouble was that the arm he'd pitched with wasn't there anymore. Dave married, but never had any children. In the sixties he and his wife—since dead— adopted Darnell Jefferson, the Down's syndrome son of the guy who'd swept up Dave's old restaurant near 47th and Ashland. Darnell's father and mother were killed in a car crash.

Dave sent Darnell through as much school as practical. Retired from the restaurant business, but not well off enough to know that Darnell would be looked after for the rest of his life, Dave set up a small corporation and went back into the restaurant business with Darnell as his "part-ner." But the thing was that Darnell had this latent ability, discovered wholly by accident. Aside from the fact that everybody liked him and he had a genuinely good sense of humor, he turned out to be a terrific cook. He became as intrinsic to the restaurant's success as Dave's years of experience.

A German and a black, Hansel & Grits.

94

Mulvaney got out of the car. Three blue and whites were cordoning off the street on either side of the restaurant, a fourth one parked in front of the place. A patrol wagon, an ambulance, two television news trucks, and about a hundred citizens, most of them black and female, were already there across the street and down the block. Police lines held them back. A second ambulance was pulling away slowly. Amos Browne sat on the passenger side of one of the blue and whites, his hat off and his face in his hands.

Mulvaney stared after the ambulance.

Fields said, "Dammit."

Lieutenant Ramon Diaz, his uniform hat in his hands, a grim look in his eyes, walked up and said, "Mildred Jones died before the medics got to her. Amos Browne pulled her out of the restaurant there, but Jones was probably dead already." Diaz had small black eyes and slick black hair and spoke in a monotone; Mulvaney had never liked him, chiefly because Diaz was so promotion conscious. Diaz did everything by the book. "You Tactical guys aren't needed here, but thanks for responding."

"You call the SWAT team?" Fields asked.

"That won't be necessary."

"Oh," Mulvaney said. "Why not?"

"There's a hostage negotiation team on the way, be here in about fifteen minutes, half hour at the most. We have the situation contained. Until then, we hold the line."

Mulvaney looked at Diaz. Fields asked Diaz, "How many and who's in there?"

"I told you guys; it's not your problem."

Mulvaney lit a cigarette, then exhaled as he said, "How many and who's in there?"

Diaz shrugged his shoulders. "Maybe a half-dozen customers this time of day, and the people who work there. Some retarded guy."

"He's one of the owners," Lew Fields supplied.

Diaz shrugged again. "Best Browne knows is that there were four guys with sawed-off shotguns, but we think he's probably exaggerating. His judgment couldn't have been correct. Heat of the moment thing, you know. Browne and Jones were starting through the doorway on a break, and somebody inside opened up on them—"

Mulvaney was already walking away, Fields falling in beside him.

Mulvaney stopped about a yard away from Amos Browne. "Amos? What happened?" The sun hadn't made it out, and Mulvaney hunched his shoulders inside the old olive drab M-65 Field Jacket he wore. He exhaled smoke from his cigarette. On the back of his neck he could feel the cold wind rising, "The Hawk," as they called it.

Amos Browne looked up from his hands. "Four guys, Sergeant. Diaz's full o' shit. Four guys, maybe more, all of 'em with sawed-off pumps. Millie took two in the chest. Blew her left tit all to—" And then Amos Browne started crying.

Lew Fields dropped into a crouch beside Browne, put his arm around Browne's shoulders. "Hey, man, it's all right—"

"I got my gun out, but they had a shotgun on Darnell's head. They woulda blown his brains out, ya know?"

"I know, man," Lew Fields told Browne in a fatherly way. "You did your best. And you got Millie Jones out, which was the important thing under the circumstances. Isn't your fault she's dead."

"She was a woman, see, so I let her go through the door first. Woulda been me, but—"

Edgar Patrick Mulvaney lit another cigarette with the one half burned out in his hand and gave it to Browne, not knowing if the younger man smoked or not. Browne took it, inhaled, coughed, but kept it. "What's the layout in there, Amos? They got Darnell by the counter or the salad bar or what?"

"Salad bar, I think. Yeah. Salad bar. I didn't see Dave, but Millie and me came up the alley, and we saw Dave's Lincoln out back, so he's gotta be there 'less they shot him."

"How many customers, other employees?"

"I dunno. Maybe a half-dozen customers. Probably some employees, but I didn't see any. Could have 'em in the kitchen."

"Which'd mean more guys keepin' them there, maybe," Mulvaney said, thinking out loud.

"Where were the other guys you saw, Amos?" Fields asked Browne, his voice low, easy.

"One sittin' on the counter. He's the one shot Millie. Black, about fourteen or fifteen, just hair on the top of his head, ya know? Shaved all around the sides." He dropped the cigarette, stepped on it. "Other two were over on the right as you come in, near the cash register."

"Four guys with sawed-offs for one restaurant? Sounds like more than an armed robbery, Amos. This is your beat. What do you think?"

"The Storms, probably them. They run protection around here, and most of the merchants pay up, won't file any complaints. I don't think Dave was the kinda guy who'd pay."

"Don't say *was*, Amos," Mulvaney cautioned. Mulvaney snapped away the butt of his cigarette. "Anyway, not yet." Mulvaney looked at Fields, and Fields shrugged his shoulders, then gestured with a nod toward where they'd left Diaz. Mulvaney walked away, approaching Diaz. "We think we can take care of this ourselves, Lieutenant."

"Fuck off, Mulvaney."

"Is that an order? I mean, to 'fuck off'?"

Diaz just looked at him strangely. "Hostage negotiation team will be on the scene as quickly as possible. I'm not getting more officers killed for something like this."

"Something like what?"

Diaz looked uncomfortable, then did that shoulder shrug again. "This is a black thing, Mulvaney. You're white. I'm brown. We get into it, God knows what sort of thing might start up around here. We wait for the negotiating team. The perpetrators are black, as far as we know, and so are most or all of the patrons and employees. I don't feel like sending this neighborhood up in flames because we made a tactical misstep. The chief negotiator is also black. We'll wait."

"I didn't think we were supposed to think like that anymore, Diaz, all this black and white and magenta shit." Some people never had thought that way, but Mulvaney suddenly doubted Diaz was aware of that.

"You wanna survive, you consider the results of every action before you take an action. You're what? Five, six years older than I am? You're a sergeant, I'm a lieutenant. There's your answer. Get with the program or get passed over," sneered Diaz.

"I thought a citizen was a citizen and a bad guy was a bad guy and we were supposed to protect the good guys and nail the bad guys."

Diaz smiled indulgently. "When you reach the higher echelons of command, if you ever do, Mulvaney, you'll realize that such a simplistic viewpoint is as outdated as—as—" And Diaz smiled. "As smoking."

Mulvaney lit a cigarette.

Diaz merely shook his head, as if exasperated but trying to be patient. "The impact on the societal infrastructure has to be considered before alternatives can be properly evaluated. You can't just run in there and shoot the perpetrators anymore. Even discounting the welfare of the persons who are being held hostage, killing or injuring the perpetrators might have unforeseen repercussions within the community. A rash moment can result in litiginous action which may take years to resolve. By the time the hostage negotiating team arrives, we may have a clearer insight into the demands of the suspected perpetrators."

"Demands?"

"Of course! They've demanded two cars and safe conduct in exchange for the release of the hostages once they feel it is safe for them to do so. I've told them that their demands will be presented to the proper authorities."

"Aren't we the proper authorities?"

Diaz shook his head again. "You can't give those men a police car, and neither can I."

"I wouldn't give them a police car; trust me on that."

Diaz went on, saying, "We haven't just been standing around idly, Mulvaney. There's no reason I have to tell you this, but the perpetrators announced they'd start killing hostages if we don't accede to their demands. But I've told them that if they do, they could very well jeopardize any possible chance for meaningful negotiation. That was as strongly as I felt I should put it, under the circumstances. Evidently they realized I wasn't lying to them. Trust. Once there's an atmosphere of trust, violence is really unnecessary to resolve a crisis situation. We don't want bloodshed on either side."

"You really care if the bad guys live or die?" Mulvaney asked him.

"Obviously. You mean to say—"

Mulvaney looked down at his shoes, puffed on his cigarette, and looked at Diaz. "I mean, I don't go outta my way to kill anybody, but I really don't give a flyin' fuck if a hood gets nailed."

Diaz closed his eyes and kept them closed as he spoke. "You and Fields clear out. That's the picture."

"What about Officer Jones?"

Diaz smiled patronizingly. "Those kids in there have records, certainly, and the restaurant will be full of fingerprints. We'll get them, but without any bloodshed. And, who knows, the negotiator may be able to talk them out without giving in."

"Gee! Really?"

"He's a good man. We went to the academy together."

"When do we learn if the 'kids' are going to wait for the negotiator or just start killing people?"

"We have it under control. Thanks for chatting with Officer Browne. Have a report on my desk, through your chain of command, of course, by this evening concerning anything he said."

"Fields and I can do this thing, Diaz."

"I wasted my breath, didn't I?"

Mulvaney stubbed out the old cigarette, intentionally lit a new one, and inhaled deeply. He stared hard at Diaz. "Fields and I eat in that place a lot. We know it like the back of your wife's ass. Or maybe it was her face. I can't remember 'cause they look so much alike."

Diaz sprang a half step toward Mulvaney, shoulders down, the tendons in his neck twitching, eyes hard. "All right, cocksucker! Get the hell outta here or you're up on charges. Now!"

"Kiss my ass," Mulvaney said, smiling.

Diaz stammered, started to speak.

The three sounds came almost at once—a woman screaming, a shotgun discharging, and a plate-glass window breaking. Mulvaney shoved past Diaz, his guns coming into his hands. The window on the left side of the restaurant front was shattered. A woman's body lay on the sidewalk, covered in glass. A voice, hard to hear, came from inside the restaurant. "You fuckin' pigs got us the damn cars yet? We don't see no car, they all go like the fat bitch!"

The dead woman wore an institutional gray dress that was bunched up to her hips and a long white bib front apron that was smeared red with her blood.

Some of the women on the street behind the police lines were screaming, little children were crying.

"Gee whiz, Diaz. She was black," Mulvaney said, not looking at Diaz, but looking at the dead woman. "Might have repercussions within the community. What do you think? And she looks like a senior citizen. Could get the old folks pissed, too." Mulvaney looked at Lew Fields and Fields nodded. Mulvaney looked over at Diaz and said, "Your way didn't work. Lew and I are gonna do something, or otherwise they'll all be dead. You wanna stop us, fine. Tell your guys to shoot us and see if they do it, Diaz." Mulvaney looked at the guns in his hands. It was time to get to work. . . .

The thing Mulvaney was relying on was that to be a member of the Storms (a street gang nobody had heard of two years ago, but which in the last year had come to dominate the Southside along the Lake Shore), you had to possess two essential qualities: ruthlessness and stupidity.

Ruthlessness: The Storms dealt hard drugs on an organized basis to schoolchildren all over the area; the Storms had what they called "Nights of Rage," when they would pick private residences, apartment structures and businesses (apparently at random), and simply do all that was possible to destroy them, from spray painting to smashing windows to arson; the Storms—whose signature weapon was the sawed-off shotgun—had never once had a member indicted for violation of the Gangster Weapons Act of the 1930s, sold sawed-off shotguns to every street punk who had the money to buy one (while honest citizens of Chicago were all but prohibited from legally having something as relatively modest as a handgun for protection); the Storms ran a protection racket that was backed by enough bloodshed to disgust the most hardened enforcers of the Chicago Crime Syndicate; the Storms ran prostitutes, but again not in the usual way—the hookers the Storms used were almost always under the age of sixteen and retired from service (when required) by murder; and the members of the Storms who were designated to commit such violent acts as might be necessary to keep business running smoothly were invariably under the age of sixteen, so the courts would consider them juveniles on those rare occasions when an arrest didn't end in a plea bargain.

Stupidity: The average high school or even college student these days knew next to nothing about geography, history, or much of anything else, and the Storms were dropouts, which meant they were dumber still. Add to that that the Storms became Storms in the first place, and it was a wonder they were bright enough to load their shotguns (the few Storms weapons Mulvaney had seen in property inventory were ill-maintained and covered with a fine layer of rust).

The Stupidity part was the important thing here.

He was counting on a poor tactical sense as, Lew Fields beside him, they reached the edge of the roof. The roof of the building where Hansel & Grits occupied the first floor was about seven feet of open airspace away, the ground about forty feet down.

"You're crazy."

"You got a better idea for getting into that place without getting up close and personal with a shotgun?" Mulvaney asked Lew Fields.

Fields shook his head. "No, but that doesn't mean I like this one. Who jumps first?"

"Well, you are older."

Fields shook his head, muttering under his breath, then said, "I'll show you how a real man does this." Lew Fields clutched the Remington 870 police shotgun at high port, jogged back several feet from the roofline, threw his shoulders back, and started running.

Mulvaney dodged in front of him, shouting, "Boo!"

Fields stopped dead in his tracks, dropped to his knees, started laughing. "You shit!"

Mulvaney took a few paces back, drew the Beretta from the waistband of his trousers, then threw himself into a dead run for the edge of the roof, past Fields, jumping, hitting the other roof running, slowing down. He just stood there and waved at Fields.

Fields tossed Mulvaney the shotgun, was moving again, ran, jumped, shouted, "Aww, damn!"

As Fields neared the roofline, Mulvaney reached, grabbing at him, Fields half falling into him. "Here's your shotgun."

Fields licked his lips, exhaling. "This is ridiculous," he said.

But Mulvaney was already moving, the Beretta tight in his right fist as he started for the roof service door. Fields was right behind him. . . .

The little Model 60 Smith & Wesson he'd carried ever

since Vietnam was in the Bianchi black fabric holster on his left ankle, but the full-sized Smith was in his right hand. The revolver was the discontinued L-Frame Model 681, stainless steel. The gun was action-tuned smooth as cream. The Beretta 92F 9mm military pistol, an Italian one instead of the identical pistol made in the USA, was in his left, safety off.

Mulvaney moved down the stairwell, knowing that Lew Fields was on the landing just above. At last Mulvaney reached the first floor. He moved along the wall toward the alley. When he found a relatively secure spot—under the stairwell beside the stairs leading down into the basement—he stopped, a pistol ready in each hand.

There was a creak from the stairs above his head, and he knew that Lew Fields had started down. . . .

They stood beside the rear wall of the building, Fields on the right side of the door and Mulvaney on the left.

The door lock had been shot away. As Mulvaney crouched he could look into the small yard behind the restaurant and the parking area just beyond.

The backyards and both ends of the alley would be bristling with cops by now, but to their credit, Mulvaney couldn't see any. What he did see, crouched inside Dave Strauss's Continental, was a guy in his late teens, with something carved in his hair—very little in area but of considerable depth, and standing straight up several inches from the top of the head.

Mulvaney drew back and closed his eyes.

To get inside the restaurant he and Lew Fields had to cross the yard and the parking area. Haircut would see them, and there'd be shots fired. Haircut would be dead, but the noise might start the other Storms inside the restaurant killing all the civilians.

Mulvaney looked at Lew Fields, but thought of John Osgood.

Mulvaney's blackjack, reconditioned good as new after its dousing in the ocean several weeks before, was in his hip pocket. But with a blackjack, even in experienced hands, there was always the possibility of a stray sound.

He thought of John Osgood again, the things they'd done together in Japan, and knives. And, at last, how he— Mulvaney—had had to use an edged weapon or die, and let others die, too.

Since that time Mulvaney had carried a knife.

The Cold Steel Tanto he'd bought just after returning from Japan nearly a year ago had been lost at the same time his blackjack had gotten a dousing in saltwater.

But there was a new one, identical to the first one, on the inside of his right leg.

The Storms didn't take any sort of decent care of their weapons, and their shotguns might not be something he'd want to count on, but he wouldn't take any chances with them anyway.

Mulvaney returned the .357 Magnum revolver to the shoulder holster under his left arm, safed the Beretta 9mm, and stuffed the pistol in his trousers butt outward beside his right kidney. He pulled up his right trouser leg and withdrew the Tanto.

Lew Fields just looked at him like he was crazy.

Mulvaney shook his head, hissed through his teeth as low as he could, "It's the only way."

Fields looked away, looked back, nodded, his eyes dark pinpoints of light.

Ed Mulvaney dropped down into a crouch again, looked through the hole in the door where the lock used to be. There was no way to tell from this vantage point if anyone else might be in the yard, but Mulvaney somehow doubted it. He redrew the Beretta just in case, offed the safety, and kept the pistol tight in his right fist.

Mulvaney gestured toward the door, and Fields nodded, putting the 870's action slide in his left hand so he could snap it to chamber a round. Only amateurs or idiots ever chambered a pump shotgun before absolutely necessary, not only for the sake of safety but because sometimes the psychological effect of the action going *chunk-chunk* could be a fight stopper without any shooting. Fields leaned out with his right hand, his coat falling open, the gleaming stainless steel of his Detonics ScoreMaster .45 visible in his waistband just over his navel.

Mulvaney nodded.

Lew Fields nodded, and slowly pulled open the door.

Ed Mulvaney went out fast and low, the Beretta now in his right hand, the blade of the Tanto—he'd washed it and sterilized it—clamped tight in his teeth.

He hit the snow and edged into a bank of melting, dirty slush and stayed there.

No one shot him, or shot at him, so he figured: so far, so good.

He safed the Beretta again, shoved it into the waistband of his blue jeans, and started moving along the low hillock of snow. The knees and elbows of his clothes were soaked through with slush before he'd gone ten feet.

But he reached a pile of trash cans, which made up the informal border between the building's backyard and the parking spaces beside it. Peering between two of the trash cans, he could see Dave Strauss's Lincoln, the doors closed and the windows down in front. And, peeking up above the level of the dashboard, Mulvaney could just see the muzzle of a sawed-off shotgun.

For a moment Mulvaney wished he were Phillip Michael Thomas's character on "Miami Vice," and all he'd have to do would be reach under his natty suit and pull out a witness protection shotgun and be equally well-armed as the bad guy. Mulvaney mentally shrugged. Under the circumstances the knife that was still in his teeth would be the only way.

Mulvaney moved along toward the farthest edge of the row of garbage cans. The temperature was still low enough so that what was inside, and dripping over the outsides, of the cans didn't smell.

At the end of the garbage can row, Mulvaney checked everywhere that he could see, looking for any sign that another of the Storms was in the yard or the lot. If any cops saw him, hopefully they'd recognize him, or notice the badge that hung around his neck in open view.

He shrugged that off, too. There was no way to predict what some rookie might do if he saw a scruffy-looking guy with a blade the size of a butcher knife lurking around.

Mulvaney started from the garbage cans, running in a fast, low crouch toward the Lincoln. Dave was well along in years and hadn't tried backing into the spot, so the front of the car was toward the building.

Mulvaney stopped by the rear passenger side door, sneaking a peak upward. The lock buttons were up. As Mulvaney took the knife from between his teeth, a smile crossed his lips. He wondered how many times this teenage mutant butthead in the front seat had seen safety advertisements warning people to lock their cars? Lucky some people never learned.

Mulvaney started to edge forward, the Tanto held edge up in his left hand in a saber hold, his right hand ready to throw open the front door on the passenger side. He heard a sound and froze, then almost laughed. The shotgun wielding killer in the front seat had just farted.

Mulvaney was beside the door now, the fingers of his right hand flexing as he put them on the door handle. He could smell what the Storm had done now, crinkling his nose up against it. Normally he would have taken a deep breath, to draw strength into his inner center and to steady his hand. But under the circumstances, he decided to forgo that.

Mulvaney tore open the door and rose half out of the crouch in one motion. The kid with the shotgun turned toward him, opening his mouth at the same time as he raised the muzzle of the sawed-off. Mulvaney launched himself through the doorway and across the front seat, his knife going first as he fell on the Storm. Mulvaney's right hand swept the muzzle of the shotgun away toward the dashboard.

Mulvaney's knife hammered into the Storm's chest.

106

Mulvaney wrenched it out as his knee smashed upward into the Storm's testicles. Now Mulvaney's full body weight was over the shotgun, blocking any movement of the muzzle. The heel of Mulvaney's right hand hit the Storm at the base of the jaw, rocking the head back as Mulvaney's left hand moved up with the knife. The Tanto's point went through the Storm's voice box, impaling him through the throat to the seat of the car.

Mulvaney left his knife where it was. The evidence people would need it anyway, and these days it wasn't smart to go messing around with people's blood. He pulled Dave's keys from the ignition, pocketing them.

Mulvaney took the shotgun as he slid down between the front passenger seat and the firewall, out of sight of the building. The shotgun had once been a well-crafted Mossberg 500 pump. But the barrel had been sawn away to the front of the magazine cap, and the buttstock had been cut away to a few inches behind the receiver, then wrapped with electrical tape. The metal was rusted badly in spots, and there was a good-sized ding halfway along the twelve inches or so of pipe that had once been a barrel.

Mulvaney pushed the next shell inward, then worked the slide release, ejecting the chambered round, then inverted the weapon and mass unloaded the magazine. He dropped the shells in his pocket, taking the shotgun with him as he slid out into the parking slot again. Mulvaney slipped the shotgun under the Lincoln and left it there. Evidence tech people wouldn't have liked him to be using it, and what had once been one of the finest practical pump shotguns was now a piece of bastardized junk and probably unreliable.

Lew Fields was coming through the doorway, hugging along the building wall. Mulvaney's Beretta was already in hand as he took the opposite side of the restaurant's back door. Flanking the door, Mulvaney nodded and Lew Fields took the radio from his belt, whispering into it, "This is Fields. Make some noise."

Fields pouched the radio.

Mulvaney drew the .357 Magnum revolver from the X-15 shoulder holster under his left arm, the Beretta in his left hand.

The door might be locked, but Lew Fields would fix that.

Then the noise began, sirens wailing, horns honking on the street out front.

Mulvaney looked at Fields. Fields gave him a thumbs-up and racked the 870 Remington pump, then stepped back from the door and put a slug load through the lockplate. Mulvaney threw his full body weight against the door and rolled through as it sprang inward, tearing through the screen door that collapsed around him. Mulvaney went flat to the floor and right as Fields put a load of buckshot into the kitchen ceiling (all the rest of the building had been evacuated, but Mulvaney and Fields had checked each floor as they'd gone down, just in case).

One of the Storms, light-skinned, dripping with leather, studs, and gold jewelry, threw a dark-skinned woman—maybe the dishwasher or a cook—toward Mulvaney and fired as Mulvaney fired both his handguns. The woman screamed and fell to the floor, the shotgun blast tearing up chunks of floor tile in a spray toward Mulvaney's face. Mulvaney was up and threw himself over the woman's body. She screamed again. The Storm's abdomen was bleeding and part of his right cheek was missing. He shrieked like a wildman as he tromboned his pump shotgun for the second shot. But Lew Fields fired his shotgun first, killing him.

Mulvaney pushed up from the floor. "You okay lady?"

"He—he—"

Mulvaney was already running, just behind Lew Fields, toward the double swinging doors from the kitchen to the restaurant floor. He shouted back to her, guessing she was okay, "Get everybody outta here through the back door and run down the alley!"

Lew Fields was through the doors, and there was an exchange of shotgun fire. Mulvaney launched himself against the double doors and came out onto the restaurant floor in a roll just like in the movies.

Mulvaney saw it all in the blink of an eye.

Lew was on both knees, holding his guts in with both hands.

One of the Storms was dead on the floor with the upper part of his chest and most of his face blown away.

Mulvaney already had both handguns punching toward the salad bar where one of the Storms had Darnell. Tears streamed down Darnell's face. Darnell pushed a bowl of lettuce toward the Storm with the shotgun on him, and Mulvaney fired both his handguns from shoulder height, slamming the kid's body back against the side of a booth.

Instinct.

Mulvaney rolled left. The floor where he'd been a split second earlier took a shotgun blast as Mulvaney came up out of the roll. The Storm who'd killed Mildred Jones was sliding off the counter. Mulvaney was already firing, and the mirror behind the counter shattered.

The Storm went through the double doors toward the kitchen as Mulvaney emptied the .357, missing, but blowing out one of the porthole-shaped pieces of glass in the right-hand door.

Mulvaney shouted to Fields, "Lew?!"

"Get the motherfucker!"

"Darnell! Take care of Lew!" Mulvaney was running again, the revolver stuffed into his belt. He threw himself through the double doors, remembering they swung both ways, hit the kitchen floor and came up beside a work counter as a blast from the Storm's shotgun tore into the stove about three feet away.

There was a flash of movement, and the Storm was out the back door.

Mulvaney went after him, catching the little Model 60 Smith from his ankle holster as he got up.

With a gun in each hand again, Mulvaney ran across the kitchen floor, almost tripping in the wreckage of the screen door, through the open outside door, and into the little parking lot.

The Storm was running, and Mulvaney fired two shots from his Beretta, missing. The Storm crossed behind a garage and turned into the alley.

Mulvaney ran after him, then skidded to a halt by the corner of the garage wall. The Model 60 revolver dropped into his coat pocket for a second as he grabbed a trash can lid and launched it Frisbee-like into the alley. Another blast from the Storm's shotgun followed. Mulvaney didn't wait for him to pump and ran into the alley, the revolver back in his left hand.

Mulvaney had hit the Storm at least once, maybe more than that. The Storm just stood there, blood dripping from his left side into a puddle in the slushy alley rut beside his foot. The busboy—a black kid named Tommy Livingstone—was in front of him as a shield. The screaming woman and two more of the restaurant staff were a few yards farther up the alley, just standing there.

Mulvaney stopped, both handguns up.

The Storm shouted, "What you gonna do now, motherfucker?"

Mulvaney considered that for a moment, put the little revolver into his pocket, and put both hands on his Beretta. "I'm figuring you didn't rack your shotgun again, shitbrain. So either drop it or I'll drop you." Mulvaney had the Beretta to eye level now, looking at the Storm across his sight, calling to the other restaurant personnel. "Back away to the side of the alley, to my left. Your right." They started edging back.

"I'll waste him, man!"

Mulvaney settled the Beretta on the bridge of the Storm's nose, saying in a loud voice, "If you had that shotgun ready to go, you woulda shot him or me already. Put it down or die, damn it. I don't care which."

The Storm's entire body seemed to shake, but not as badly as Tommy Livingstone was shaking. "Mr. Mulvaney—"

"Just close your eyes, Tommy, so you don't get any blood in them, and you'll be fine."

"You're shitting me, motherfucker!"

Mulvaney shrugged his shoulders, took a nice normal breath, released about half of it, and started his trigger squeeze.

"You're—"

The Beretta bucked once, gently.

The Storm fell down into the ruts.

Tommy took two steps and dropped to his knees, making the sign of the cross. Mulvaney ran forward, calling to Tommy as he passed him, "Lucky for you you're an altar boy!" Mulvaney picked up the shotgun. The previous owner was dead.

The shotgun's chamber was empty, but fortunately (it wasn't like the movies; shootings had to be explained) the magazine wasn't empty. Taking the shotgun with him, Mulvaney ran back, calling over his shoulder, "Tommy! Keep everybody together and get down to the end of the alley!"

Mulvaney sprinted back through the yard, slipping on the kitchen floor, then into the restaurant.

Diaz's uniformed guys were starting through the front door with shotguns.

Darnell knelt behind the counter, beside Dave Strauss, who was very dead.

And Lew Fields looked pretty dead, too.

Mulvaney got on his knees beside his friend and, still holding his guns, took Lew's head into his lap. "Don't be dead, okay?"

Chapter Eight

The Wages of Virtue

John Osgood recognized Lew Fields's wife. She sat hunched over on a blue vinyl-covered, disgustingly modern-looking sofa at the far end of the bland waiting room. Andy Oakwood, wearing a huge woolen poncho, sat beside her.

Osgood didn't go in, but walked along the corridor instead, lighting a cigarette from his case as he went.

There was a second waiting room at the far end, and as he approached it, Osgood heard the strains of Tchaikovsky. He stepped into the open doorway.

A cloud of cigarette smoke encircled Ed Mulvaney's head. Mulvaney stared toward a television screen. Obviously, it was Chicago's PBS affiliate, WTTW.

Swan Lake was being danced. Not a devotee of ballet, as Mulvaney oddly was, Osgood saw no familiar faces among the dancers, but it was well done.

It was time to break whatever spell Mulvaney might be under. "Ed?"

Mulvaney stood up, didn't turn around. "John."

"I'm sorry about your partner."

"You know anything I don't?"

"When I checked, they told me his prognosis was in doubt, that he was in critical condition and still under the knife."

"You show 'em your 'get outta jail free card' or something?"

"When I travel in the United States, I carry my U.S. Marshals Service badge; I'm a legal deputy. Saves a great deal of inconvenience in some places."

"I bet it does. What brings you to town?"

"You," Osgood told him.

"That a fact?" Mulvaney turned around, and Osgood stared at him. Mulvaney looked—well, like Mulvaney. His hair was well over his collar. He had the brown, curly sort of look women found attractive. But with his knowledge of Mulvaney, Osgood knew it was not a look Mulvaney cultivated. He just didn't get his hair cut that often, and when he did, Mulvaney's sister—who was a beautician—did it for him. The curls were natural, not courtesy of Mulvaney's beautician sister.

Taller than Osgood by two inches, Mulvaney looked as lean and fit as ever. Unlike the first time he'd seen him, almost a year ago to the day, instead of a disheveled peacoat that was too short for his long arms, Mulvaney wore a mud-stained, tattered M-65 Field Jacket. Mulvaney's name was emblazoned on the chest, as was 'U.S. Army.' Like the peacoat, the sleeves were still too short.

The knees of Mulvaney's blue jeans were worn almost white, but most of that was obscured with mud. "Time has been kind to you, Ed."

"Yeah, you, too."

"I'd come to Chicago to speak with you concerning a matter of considerable urgency, Ed. But when I learned Lew Fields had been shot, well, I felt that could wait a bit."

"It's not like Lew's dead, John."

"No. This is a marvelous hospital. You hear about hospitals in my line of work"—Osgood smiled—"and I've never heard anything but praise for this one."

"Yeah. They're real good here."

Osgood nodded. "I also understand your watch commander . . ." Osgood searched for the right word.

"He's pissed with me because of the asshole lieutenant I disobeyed."

"But you got the job done. None of the hostages who hadn't already been killed were even injured."

"This one lady, she was talkin about suin' the department because we scared her."

Osgood shrugged his shoulders and took off his trenchcoat. It was warm in this room, and the antiseptic smell of hospitals never sat well with his stomach. "Very unfortunate about the death of the proprietor. I understand his adopted son is retarded?"

"Down's syndrome. But Darnell does okay. Used to, anyway."

"And the purpose of the assault was merely to force extortion payments from the restaurant? Despicable."

"Yeah, what you said." Mulvaney nodded, stubbing out his cigarette. Edgar Patrick Mulvaney, a graduate of De Paul University (Dean's List nine times), B.A. in history, former officer in U.S. Special Forces, belied his education with every word he uttered. Sometimes Osgood wondered if that was some sort of defense against the world around him. Then Mulvaney said, "What did you want—I mean, before you heard about Lew?"

"Under the circumstances, as I indicated, Ed, regardless of the gravity of the matter—"

"No. Tell me."

It was as if Mulvaney were reaching for something, a life preserver. Did he—John Osgood—have that for him now?

"Perhaps I have an opportunity for you which might seem attractive."

"Maybe. Wanna go across the street to the bar?"

"That would be excellent." Osgood folded his coat neatly

over his left arm and flicked ashes from his cigarette into the pedestal ashtray. "I'm sure things will work out for Lew Fields."

"Why?"

"Why?" Osgood repeated.

"Yeah. Why? When do things work out for people, John? I never heard of it happening yet."

"I, uh—"

"When your wife and kids were killed by that drunk driver, how'd you feel then?"

Elizabeth had been on her way home from another Easter Sunday dinner with relatives without her husband, and a man had driven into them, killing Elizabeth instantly. John Junior and Natalie never made it to the hospital in time. "Why did you mention that, Ed?"

"Ever feel your whole world was caving in and you couldn't do shit about it, John?"

John Osgood stubbed out his cigarette, took a few steps toward Mulvaney, and extended his right hand.

Ed Mulvaney took it.

Chapter Nine

Divine Wind

"Bill Grimshaw was a good guy. 'nough said," Ed Mulvaney declared, taking a long pull on his drink. "God forbid I'm sayin' that about Lew after tonight."

"Andy will call us if there's the slightest change."

Mulvaney only nodded.

Osgood sipped at his drink, took a Pall Mall from his silver cigarette case after first offering one to Mulvaney—they shared the same brand—which Mulvaney accepted. Then Osgood lit both their cigarettes with his Dunhill. "Actually, your friend Bill Grimshaw has a great deal to do with what we're about to discuss, Ed."

Mulvaney just looked at him, then after a beat said, "What do you mean?"

"I mean, well—it was wonderful what you and your friends did for the Grimshaw family, exhausting some financial resources in the process, no doubt."

"You know damn well what I spent, don't you?"

"All the money you walked away with after you got back

from Japan, and then some. Yes. And it was no mean feat taking on Ladislaw Gorchek and his personal assistants, either."

Mulvaney laughed. "Personal assistants? Talk about your euphemisms, John. God Almighty. His personal assistants were—well, they were." And there was a little twinkle in Mulvaney's dark eyes.

"Yes. You may be under the impression that Gorchek died during the boating incident, but he did not."

"He was—"

"Then it's the most remarkable recovery since Lazarus, because he is alive and more or less well. The 486 SX chip was lost to Gorchek, of course, which was more important than Gorchek's life, anyway."

"Was that whole thing with Peterson and his 'company' some kind of intell op or what?"

Osgood let himself smile and shrugged his eyebrows. "I really don't know. And you know that's probably true, because matters such as these are on a need-to-know basis only. I would theorize, from what I've heard of the episode, that indeed one agency or another, possibly at the same time, had a hand in things. Why Gorchek was allowed to live on that island in the first place is a mystery to me, but there are some possible explanations, of course."

"Of course, golly whiz. So you guys want to proposition me to find Gorchek and finish the job? I might do that for free."

Osgood smiled again as he sculpted the tip of his cigarette against the lip of the ashtray. "You were a history man. How much do you know about Kubla Khan?"

"He wasn't a nice man. And some English guy wrote a poem about him."

Osgood was sipping at his drink again and nearly choked on it. His eyes began tearing, and Mulvaney smiled, evidently enjoying the reaction.

Mulvaney said, "It was U.S. History, with a side order of

117

Latin America. Closest I got to the Orient was a class on Russian history once."

Osgood stubbed out his cigarette.

There were two women up at the bar, secretary types, and the bartender himself. Otherwise, they were alone. "In the year 1281—and don't ask if that was before I was born, because it was—in 1281 Kubla Khan dispatched four thousand ships against Japan. These four thousand ships carried one hundred thousand men."

"Twenty-five guys each. Like amphibious landers, huh?"

"Cut it out, Mulvaney. This isn't an episode of 'G.I. Joe' or something."

"Hey, Ozzie, you watch 'G.I. Joe,' too?"

Osgood closed his eyes, reminded himself he genuinely liked Ed Mulvaney, that Mulvaney was under a great deal of stress, and that Mulvaney covered stressful situations with puerile humor at times. "Have you ever heard of the Friedman-Naguchi Expedition?"

Mulvaney seemed to think about that, and Osgood tried to avoid comparing the look on Mulvaney's face with that of a lowland gorilla contemplating a banana. At last Mulvaney said, "I seem to recall something about it on some science special on TV. I turned it off."

Osgood looked down at his hands, lit a cigarette. So much for cutting down. "Ladislaw Gorchek is a silent backer for the Friedman-Naguchi Expedition."

"What are they expeditioning for, exactly?"

"They're expeditioning for—" Osgood closed his eyes again, reminded himself of everything he'd reminded himself about before, then opened his eyes and said, "The purpose of the Friedman-Naguchi Expedition—ostensibly, at least—concerns my earlier reference to Kubla Khan. The four thousand ships of the Khan and his invading army of one hundred thousand men went down. The Khan was almost pathologically intent, so it seems, on the conquest of Japan. They were lost, every man and every ship as far as

118

history relates, near Takashima, in the Straits of Tsushima, when almost magically a storm of heroic proportions appeared.

"The invasion fleet and its armies were lost," Osgood went on, "and Japan was saved. Hence, the origin of the term *Divine Wind,* or *Kamikaze,* after which, seeing themselves as the saviors of Japan during World War Two, the suicide pilots who flew fighters packed with high explosives and only enough fuel to get them to their target took their name.

"At the close of the Russo-Japanese War of 1905, President Theodore Roosevelt—"

"Brian Keith in that Sean Connery movie."

"Ed. Please? You could probably tell me about Roosevelt's role in mediating the peace agreement."

"The Japanese felt that even though they had won the war, the American government had given away their victory because it favored Russia."

"Exactly." Osgood beamed. "And that feeling, of course, was the seed around which much of the anti-American sentiment that eventually manifested itself in World War Two was to grow. During the war—the Russo-Japanese War—you may recall that Admiral Rozhdestvenski's fleet was defeated by Admiral Togo."

"In the Straits of Tsushima, right?"

"Right. Japan, in fact, was never invaded until 1945, after the United States utilized two nuclear devices, in essence preventing actual invasion in the classic military sense. When Japan was forced to sue for peace, Japan was instead merely occupied. But in the Straits of Tsushima, there are more than four thousand wrecked ships, most of them dating from Kubla Khan's abortive invasion, but a good many others from as recently as Togo's defeat of Rozhdestvenski in 1905.

"The Friedman-Naguchi Expedition," Osgood continued, stubbing out his cigarette, then taking another sip of his drink, "is the most well-funded and technologically able marine archeological expedition ever mounted to attack the vast treasure of ships lying in the straits. The finest equipment, the most qualified personnel. Nothing but the best. That is why Dr. Edith Blandish will be contacting the Chicago Police Department tomorrow morning about the possibility of getting released from duty one Sergeant Edgar Patrick Mulvaney, on behalf of the Friedman-Naguchi Expedition as chief of security."

Mulvaney was very quick. "What happened to the last guy?"

"There was an accident."

"Was the last guy yours, too?"

"As a matter of fact, I don't really know anything about him. Dr. Blandish knows all about your background, because the Friedman-Naguchi Expedition has some very highly placed friends."

"The same people maybe who let Ladislaw Gorchek use that island off the Carolinas?"

Osgood smiled. "Possibly. She knows about your SF tours in Vietnam, your record with the Chicago P.D., and even the sub rosa job you and I were involved with in Japan last year. Your lack of language abilities—"

"It's not as if I don't speak English, John."

"I meant Japanese, of course. But your lack of Japanese is of no consequence."

"Why me?"

This was the part John Osgood genuinely hated, because he liked Mulvaney, and more important, respected him. But if the Friedman-Naguchi Expedition was nowhere near finding what it really searched for, Ed Mulvaney had no need to know. So he began spinning the carefully fabricated lie, but not without regrets. "When the Nationalist Chinese Regime under Generalissimo Chiang Kai-shek was breathing its last few gasps under the continued assault of the forces of Mao Tse-tung, United States Intelligence contacted a number of anti-Communist American business-men. The purpose was to raise a rather large amount of gold to prop up the Nationalist Chinese Regime. Despite prohibitions on private ownership of gold by American citizens, which was then in effect, it was well known that there were certain persons who hoarded large quantities of gold. At today's prices the amount collected would equal half a billion dollars. The gold was converted to diamonds, much more portable, of course, and more easily moved. The diamonds were to be sent to the generalissimo, perhaps even with the idea of buying off Mao Tse-tung. The diamonds left Japan aboard a World War Two vintage B-29 bomber. The aircraft was lost in a storm over the Straits of Tsushima, joining the four thousand ships of the Khan and the more luckless vessels of Admiral Rozhdestvenski's fleet of 1905.

"Gorchek, who is an anonymously involved backer of the Freidman-Naguchi Expedition, is seriously involved with pro-Communist terrorists in Japan. He's using the Freidman-Naguchi Expedition as a cover to locate the missing aircraft and secure the diamonds. Several members of the expedition's crew are in Gorchek's employ, and perhaps they are responsible for the death of the man who filled the position Dr. Blandish wants you to take. If he succeeds, Gorchek will become one of the richest and most powerful men in the world. The terrorist group he supports in Japan will be so well funded as to be nearly impossible to defeat.

"And," Osgood went on, "with the diamonds were certain documents. If the documents are recovered sufficiently intact, relations between the United States and Communist China—already a little strained—would be set back irreparably. The balance of world power—"

"Let me guess. It might shift? There'd be dogs and cats living together, an end to civilization as we know it, and they'd stop making Coca-Cola."

John Osgood smiled, saying, "Something like that.

121

There's a finder's fee for this property of the United States," Osgood told him, and that part was true. "It could go as high as a quarter of a million dollars. But even if the missing property is never recovered, there's a rather handsome salary that goes with the position of security chief for the Friedman-Naguchi Expedition. You'll be able to assist Japanese authorities in nailing this terrorist group, as well as possibly netting the elusive and hard-to-kill Mr. Gorchek."

"You're bullshitting me, Osgood."

Osgood smiled.

"Tell me the truth."

"There's a valuable prize beneath the waters of the Straits of Tsushima, and if you can prevent its recovery by Ladislaw Gorchek's people and its being utilized to the benefit of the terrorist group he supports, you'll be doing your country and the world a favor of enormous proportions, not to mention aiding your current financial crunch and facilitating your marriage to Andrea Oakwood, Ed."

"Gorchek murdered a woman right in front of me. Cut her throat open because he enjoyed it, the son of a bitch. Whatever the hell it is, there's really a chance to get Gorchek?"

"Yes."

"What about Lieutenant Diaz?"

"I can fix that with a phone call, Ed. And I will regardless."

"This business about the diamonds . . . for real?"

John Osgood had spun a story to Ed Mulvaney, but they'd gone through too much against the Yakusa in Japan a year ago for an outright lie. So he merely said, "If we don't find what went down in that aircraft, Ed, and Gorchek's people do find it, there's more trouble, more destruction, and more horror than you can possibly imagine."

"If Gorchek's running this thing, he sent this Dr. Blandish lady after me because he wants me out there, right?"

"Right."

"A lot of trouble to go to in order to kill me."

"Evidently," Osgood said truthfully, "he thinks you're worth it."

"You going to be covering me?"

"I'll be covering you all the way, except when you're out on the water. That I cannot do, but I'll be working from the other end, looking for Gorchek and his terrorist connection."

"No guns, right, because the Japanese don't like guns."

"I can't get you aboard the *Archimedes*—"

"The what?"

"That's the name of the headquarters vessel for the expedition, the *Archimedes.* I can't get you aboard her with a gun, but in terms of an edged weapon, of course that's a tool for you to use if you elect to carry out your security functions below the surface as well as above."

John Osgood silently wondered if it was all starting to sound the same to Ed Mulvaney. The last time Mulvaney had been lied to. The last time Mulvaney had been forced by circumstance to violate a long-standing self-prohibition. The last time both of them had nearly died.

"A good buck doin' this?"

"Yes, Ed. And the satisfaction of knowing you're serving the best interests of your nation and the world community."

The bartender called out, "One of you guys named Mulvaney?"

John Osgood watched Ed Mulvaney's eyes go dead, then closed his own. . . .

Mulvaney held Andy Oakwood tight in his arms.

Then he let her go and walked over to Lew's wife, took her in his arms, and touched his lips to her forehead.

"Ed?"

"Yeah?"

"Why?"

"Why what?"

"Why do you guys do what you do?"

"Somebody's gotta do it, right? Can't let the bad guys win. And they would. They would if we didn't."

"There's no sense to it, Ed."

"I know."

She looked up into his face. "But why you guys?"

"Maybe—hell—" There were a lot of things he could have told her, that despite the bullshit from above and the apathy from all around and the evil below, some people still believed that there was a clear line of demarcation between right and wrong.

But he'd learned philosophy didn't really count for much, learned that in Vietnam, because the philosophy of the good guys was clearly right and the philosophy of the bad guys was clearly wrong. But the governments involved didn't care, and it was easier to be safe than right, easier to be alive than honest.

From behind them Mulvaney heard a woman's voice. He assumed the voice belonged to a nurse, but these days it could have belonged to a doctor. "You can see Detective Fields now."

Ed Mulvaney looked down into Lew's wife's eyes. "You go see him. If he's awake, you tell him we got the bad guys, and don't tell him about Dave Strauss."

Lew's wife only nodded, sniffed back a tear, then leaned up and kissed Mulvaney on the cheek.

Ed Mulvaney walked over to the waiting room window. Behind his own dark reflection he could see Andy. And past his reflection Ed Mulvaney saw Chicago.

When he'd joined the cops, he realized now, he'd thought of himself as some sort of "Divine Wind," that just by being who he was and doing what he did he could change things, turn everything around and make it better.

One time, over a couple of drinks, Lew told him, "You should never have become a cop."

"Why, man?"

"Because you care."

"You care, Lew."

"I know, but we're not talkin' about me. We're talkin' about you, Ed."

"If you don't care, why bother doing it all, Lew? Why bother doing it at all?"

"I hope to God you never get an answer to that question, Ed."

Chapter Ten

Dreamer

Osgood ran, his chest aching, his shins tightening to the point that he could no longer properly move his feet. But he ran anyway.

The BMW was going very slowly along the road, and if he could just keep running, everything would be all right.

He kept running, but in the distance he saw the full-sized Pontiac. Oddly enough, the way the headlamps were set in the grille, the lights looked like eyes. And the bumper somehow resembled a mouth, its corners drawn down, lips drawn back, evil, ready to strike.

He kept running.

The BMW—it was a very pretty car, but he'd selected it because BMWs had an outstanding safety record and were easy for even the most inexperienced driver to handle—was keeping an even speed.

Elizabeth was a good driver, so the ease with which she would be able to handle the BMW would be even greater. Its responsiveness would be better under her hands than under average hands.

He reminded himself to tell her, however, that she should not let young John and Natalie stick their heads and arms out the windows. It was nice that they were waving to him, but a thoroughly unsafe practice.

And now Elizabeth was doing it.

John Osgood waved toward her, trying to signal her to stop, but she evidently didn't understand him. There was a smile on her pretty face, and her almost black hair blew in the slipstream surrounding the vehicle.

She'd never gone in for hairsprays or anything that detracted from her hair's natural softness, its own natural perfume.

He couldn't stop running. His breathing was so labored now he thought he would die, and his legs ached so badly he thought he would fall. But, somehow, he had sufficient breath to shout to her, "Elizabeth!"

"John. You've come for Easter dinner, haven't you, but Easter dinner is all over. The children were very good, John, but they always are."

"I didn't come for Easter dinner, Elizabeth. I came to warn you about that car coming toward you."

"What car?"

"Turn around and look at it, Elizabeth! See the way it's looking at you? It wants to hurt you and the children, Elizabeth. You must turn away from it."

"Easter dinner was very good, John."

Evidently Elizabeth could not hear him properly. Perhaps the throb of the BMW's motor with the windows down and open drowned him out, or perhaps her mind was on other things. He did not know. "Just stop driving and pull the car over onto the side of the road so I can catch up with you and then I can drive. I should be driving. You know that. I'm the one who should be behind the wheel."

"But it doesn't matter, because I love you! Children, wave to your father."

Young John and Natalie, who looked just like Elizabeth, were already waving, but they waved harder.

John Osgood ran faster.

Then the Pontiac hit the BMW and there was fire everywhere and John Osgood tried to shout to Elizabeth, to John, to Natalie, "I love you and always will!" But no matter how he tried forming the words in his mind, there was not enough wind in his lungs to make the words come out, and when he looked away from the burning wreckage, tears streaming down his cheeks, John Osgood saw that he'd been running on a treadmill.

That was when he opened his eyes and when, every time he'd had the dream, he always opened his eyes.

And he just lay there in the darkness, naked and sweating under the covers, not wanting to close his eyes again.

Chapter Eleven

Arrangements

His helicopter now flew over the Eastern Channel from Takashima where it had set down to pick up some replacement parts for electronic equipment aboard the *Archimedes*. They were well west of the Island of Iki and north toward the eastern coast of Tsushima Island, where the small fleet of ships surrounding the *Archimedes* lay at anchor.

The open sea below him masked centuries of a violent past, and he was well aware of that. Despite his pursuit of American history during his university days so long ago, Ed Mulvaney considered himself far from ignorant of the unique character of this boundary between the Sea of Japan and the East China Sea. Certainly he was not so ignorant as he had deliberately caused himself to appear when John Osgood proposed the idea.

When he'd at last gotten home from the hospital that evening now some five days ago, knowing that Lew would live and was not likely to suffer any permanent disability from his injuries, Mulvaney already knew what his decision would be. He didn't want Andy crying over him someday. Andy was exhausted, as was Mulvaney. He'd poured them each a drink and started hitting the books. Andy was soon asleep on the sofa, but Mulvaney kept reading, everything from the Encyclopedia Britannica to *National Geographic*, and the next morning on his way to work, rather than taking the Lake Street El downtown or getting a ride from somebody, he went across the border to Oak Park and to the excellent main library there.

He'd thought there had been an earlier invasion than the famous one of 1281, and he was right. In 1274 Kubla Khan, descendant of Genghis, had made his first attempt, but with a vastly smaller fleet and concurrently smaller army. It met almost the same fate, all but annihilated by a sudden storm after indecisive land battles with the Japanese. During the first invasion, the Japanese learned bitterly that the tactics of individual combat were no match for the Mongols. When the second invasion came, both the Japanese forces and the forces of nature delivered the Sunday punch.

Try as Mulvaney might, he could find nothing to indicate that any truly serious attempt had been made to make a full-scale investigation of the area near the island of Tsushima, where, doubtlessly, many of the ships from both lost Mongol invasion fleets had met their final end. In this area, too, the Japanese had defeated the Russians in 1905. The waters, considering modern diving techniques, were ideally suited to exploration.

But the Friedman-Naguchi Expedition clearly had its work cut out for it. Its stated goal, as John Osgood had elaborated on their way across the street from the bar to the hospital, was to find the actual ruins of one of the Mongol vessels, not merely pottery shards, pieces of weaponry, and stone anchors. Because of this, and one reason why the Freidman-Naguchi Expedition had not broken off for winter, there was an elaborate platform constructed that was mobile, and was able to be anchored to the sea floor and fitted with heavy lifting equipment.

The season was definitely wrong for marine archeology, with sudden winter storms and heavy rains to be dealt with. It was almost as if the relics that had lain beneath the sea for so long had some new urgency attached to them. It was hard to believe that, even in view of the diamonds story John Osgood had given him.

He found information on the Freidman-Naguchi Expedition—on Lawrence Friedman and Hideo Naguchi, its architects and leaders.

Lawrence Friedman, like Naguchi a Ph.D. in archeology, was a graduate of the University of Chicago's Oriental Institute. Naguchi, the son of Japanese aristocrats, was a graduate of Oxford University and had studied extensively in Germany and Brazil. They had worked together over the years at marine archeological "digs" all over the world, but most of these had something to do with massive naval engagements from the World War II era, with a large number of these in the Pacific.

It seemed obvious—but he'd learned never to trust what seemed obvious—that if Ladislaw Gorchek was backing this expedition as a means of recovering a half-billion dollars in diamonds, neither Friedman nor Naguchi was aware of his true purpose.

Learning as much as he could, Mulvaney walked to the el station, using the time to think. Clearly, Gorchek wanted him as security chief on the expedition as a means of getting revenge. But was Gorchek stupid enough to place revenge as a priority higher than that half billion in diamonds?

That just didn't make sense, which reinforced Mulvaney's opinion that John Osgood had either lied or left out some necessary details. But why did John Osgood want him in on this expedition? The obvious answer was to aid in recovering the diamonds. Gorchek wanted him, too. But why not arrange things so that it would be impossible for him—Mulvaney—to take the job, and then Osgood would somehow insinuate himself or some CIA person into the job? The answer to that was something Mulvaney didn't like.

Gorchek really did want him on the expedition for the purpose of killing him, and Osgood considered him—Mulvaney—dumb enough and hungry enough to take on the assignment even though it smelled.

Osgood was right, there, because Mulvaney planned to do just that. Over a fast breakfast, with Andy already running late for work, he told her. "John's got a job sort of lined up for me."

"John Osgood?"

"Yeah."

"Don't take it; we don't need money that badly."

"It's in Japan. Some kind of sunken treasure thing, and there's a really big finder's fee, a kind of reward."

"Don't take the job."

"I'm going to take the job, for us."

"Ed, what happened to Lew could have happened to you, ya know?"

"I know, babes."

"But this is leaving the frying pan to go into the fire if it's one of Osgood's deals."

"Sounds pretty straightforward. A whole shitload of diamonds were lost after the war and this expedition's looking for them and they need a security man. Osgood wants me there to get my hands on the rocks after they're found. But you can't tell anybody about this, because it's all still top-secret stuff. He'd shit a brick if he knew I told you."

"He knows you'd tell me, which means he probably hasn't told you the truth. Need a ride? I'm late for work." She kissed him, picked up the keys to the used Chevy they'd picked up cheap, and left.

He let her go. Rather than take the Porsche out of the garage and get it all screwed up with salt stains, he called a taxi to take him to the library.

By the time Mulvaney reached Eleventh and State, Chicago police headquarters, Osgood's promise of killing departmental charges, reprimands, and the like had come true. How this had been accomplished Mulvaney did not want to ask. He suspected it was through the CIA's resident agent, a nasty guy named Dern. There was a polite note waiting for him, instead, that he was expected for lunch with Deputy Police Superintendent Lattimer and a Dr. Edith Blandish at the Italian Village. Lunch wasn't for two hours still, and he used the time to catch up on reports, check the hospital on Lew Fields's progress—which was good—and make some mental notes on what he would tell this Dr. Blandish, reminding himself all the while that he was supposed to be totally in the dark concerning the purpose of the luncheon meeting.

Lunch hour came and Mulvaney bummed a ride in a blue and white. Light snow was falling and a police car was a better bet to get where he wanted to be on time than a taxi. Crossing the Loop was never the easiest thing at the noon rush, and snow only compounded that.

He'd shaved in the morning, which he usually did anyway, but with special care. His field jacket was mud-stained and dirty and he'd worn his old peacoat, but the left sleeve had a large hole in it. He left it in his locker and braved the cold in his tweed sportcoat. He even wore a tie.

Deputy Police Superintendent Lattimer was polite to the point of nausea, telling Dr. Edith Blandish, "Sergeant Mulvaney is, indeed, one of Chicago's Finest, madam." Mulvaney was vaguely amused, wondering what Lattimer would have said had the deputy police superintendent known he—Ed Mulvaney—had, less than a year ago, offed a Chicago Police captain who'd been tied to the Japanese Yakusa. The captain, who played the Yakusa against the Chicago Crime Syndicate, raked in enormous illegal profits and was responsible for numerous deaths. But Mulvaney decided to pass on mentioning it.

Dr. Blandish was blandish. Her suit looked like something from the women's department at Brooks Brothers, and her hair, rather short and mousy brown with some streaks of gray, looked generally ignored. But she had a pleasant enough voice. "I'm very familiar with Sergeant

Mulvaney's background, and I must say I'm very impressed."

The menu was expensive, but Mulvaney didn't care because he wasn't paying for it; he had the veal parmesan. If Andy had been with him, he would never have ordered veal. She became incensed at the very mention of it because she considered the animals from which it came abused. He'd joked about baby veals when she'd first mentioned her feelings, only later realizing she was deadly earnest.

Over lunch there was small talk about the Friedman-Naguchi Expedition, about maritime archeology (which he'd studied up on just a little at the library), and Japan in general. He didn't tell the woman about the love hotels, about the Yakusa killers, about the ninja assassins, nor did he tell her anything concerning his own maritime experiences off the Japanese coast. He remembered swimming underwater and breathing through the scabbards of ninja Katanas in order to reach the island stronghold of a rival ninja clan, in order to rescue the relative of a Chicago Crime Syndicate figure—who had Soviet defense secrets locked in his head.

Instead, he told her how he'd always enjoyed the limited training he'd had in scuba techniques when he was with Special Forces, and continued on his own after Vietnam to polish those techniques.

"I'll come to the point, Sergeant Mulvaney," she said at last over a frosty metal cup of lime sherbet, which she ate in infinitesimally tiny spoonfuls. "We have no idea what actual monetary value there might be regarding the finds we anticipate—unearthing, if you will. Therefore, security is important. Aside from that aspect of it, reporters and the like are constantly after us for details to the point where work is interrupted. If we are able to raise something of significant size, we will need to focus all our attention on the work at hand, not on curiosity seekers. Certain materials which may have been preserved for centuries underwater will deteriorate with amazing rapidity when brought to the surface. We require someone to have a firm hand on overall security. Your lack of Japanese won't prove a handicap since all our personnel—with a variety of national backgrounds —speak English. We'd like you to take over."

"From whom?" He couldn't pass it up.

For the first time he noticed her eyes, a very pretty blue, the only bright thing about her appearance. "Thomas Westinghouse, a private investigator based in San Francisco, was our security chief and did admirably. He, uh, died." Her eyes looked down into her sherbet.

Mulvaney asked, "Old age?"

Deputy Superintendent Lattimer cleared his throat.

"No," Dr. Blandish said softly. "The nitrous oxide used for diving—I assume you're familiar with it?"

"To a degree, same components as laughing gas but in different amounts. Allows you to stay under longer at greater depths without increasing decompression time."

"Exactly. You're also aware of the fact that it is extremely volatile. There was a fresh shipment en route to us, one of the jobs of the security team; and someone made a spark. Mr. Westinghouse and two of the Japanese crew members on the vessel bringing it in were killed. Their bodies were lost, and the entire vessel was lost as well."

Mulvaney smiled and told her, "Well, it sounds very exciting, but I suppose my participation all depends on whether or not the department will release me temporarily from duty."

He didn't look at Lattimer, but listened as Lattimer said, "Participation in a project of this nature—which will advance the cause of science and the cause of international understanding—is to everyone's benefit. Consider yourself released for as long as it takes, Sergeant."

"Gee," Mulvaney said to Lattimer. And then he looked at Dr. Edith Blandish. "Just how much will this pay, ma'am?"

She cleared her throat, then looked directly at him. "We have no accurate way of estimating just how long we will be on site, Sergeant. For that reason we'll pay you on a retainer basis along with a structured system of bonuses. Eight hundred dollars per week, all expenses to and from the site, plus all expenses on site. A signing bonus of ten thousand dollars. A completion bonus will be awarded at the termination of your duties, assuming—as I'm sure will be the case—that you have carried them out to everyone's satisfaction. That amount will be a minimum of ten thousand dollars but could be substantially higher."

"Make it a thousand a week and pay the ten thousand bonus before I leave for Japan, and you've got a deal."

"Mulvaney!" Lattimer said.

But Mulvaney ignored him.

Edith Blandish closed her eyes, as if somehow looking at something on the insides of her lids, then opened them. She told him, "All right."

That was when Mulvaney extended his hand across the table.

He extended his hand now toward the small carry-on bag he'd fished out of the rest of his luggage. It was a black fabric bag, and he zipped open the main compartment after unlocking the zipper pulls. Inside it was his one actual weapon, although the human mind was always the greatest weapon regardless of how else one was armed or equipped. This had been difficult to get through customs even in spite of the arrangements that had been made for him by Dr. Blandish. It was technically listed on the customs manifest as a diving knife, but was his Cold Steel Tanto rigged out in a black fabric Southwind Sanctions Sheath he could lash to his leg—which added to the impression that it was a diving knife.

The Tanto design originated in Japan, but in a modified form; and the knife itself was made in Japan as well. He thought of the old expression about bringing coals to Newcastle, which indeed was the case here. But he would have felt considerably more comfortable were he bringing his Smith & Wesson revolvers to Springfield, Massachusetts, or his Beretta semiautomatic back to Accoceek, Maryland.

The death of the San Francisco P.I., Thomas Westinghouse, was a perfect cover for a homicide. Not only blow up the victim, but blow up the evidence as well. And whatever survived the explosion goes down at sea.

If Westinghouse had been murdered, Mulvaney doubted it was done merely to create a job opening for him to fill. Westinghouse might have discovered something about the diamonds (or whatever was really under the sea) or, perhaps, discovered the tie-in between Friedman, Naguchi, and Ladislaw Gorchek, or uncovered information on Gorchek's terrorist connections.

There was no way to tell, but if Mulvaney started getting close to something, he'd probably know it, especially if someone tried to kill him.

He set down his bag and looked out the window again. He could make out a large vessel with several small ones at anchor around it, and something that looked like a small version of an offshore oil drilling rig.

Mulvaney lit a cigarette. He'd checked the helicopter when he came aboard, and as far as he'd been able to tell, there was no nitrous oxide aboard. . . .

The skipper of the tender servicing the *Archimedes* had a sense of humor. The name painted on the bow of the fisherman was *Kanpai,* which meant "Cheers." John Osgood nodded his head toward her and murmured, "And cheers to you." He swept his binoculars along the dock to the right and left of the *Kanpai.*

There was nothing suspicious about any of the cargo going aboard the *Kanpai,* much of which he'd examined at close range in the predawn hours. Food, toilet articles, and equipment related to utilizing and maintaining the diving gear were included, just ordinary things.

Osgood put down the 8 X 50s, left the window, and

returned to the small desk at the far corner of the Western-style room. The only thing Japanese about the office he was using was the *tokonoma*. Within it hung the customary *kakejiku* or *kakemono*. The scroll was unremarkable, the sort of thing found in cheap gift shops all over the world. The flowers in the ordinary vase were plastic.

He looked at his watch. Mulvaney would be arriving aboard the *Archimedes* soon.

Osgood lit a cigarette, walked back to the window, and sat on the stool there, just watching the water.

The docks, primarily for small, privately owned fishing vessels, were small and rough. Disregarding objects of apparel which were distinctly Japanese—such as the short, kimono style *hantens*—the scene could have been any of a hundred places around the world.

But at any second the people on the dock—and he—might be obliterated in a blinding flash of light.

He smoked his cigarette and watched the fishermen in the *happi* coats.

The platform was about two hundred yards square with the helipad offset to the north, the crane offset to the south, and metal buildings to the east and west. As the helicopter dipped to starboard and started in, Mulvaney saw divers working off the northern side. Then the platform itself blocked them from view.

The pilot, an Americanized Japanese who hadn't given his name, announced over the intercom, "We're down, Mr. Mulvaney. Watch your head, please."

Mulvaney unbuckled, grabbed his three suitcases, and was at the fuselage door by the time the copilot, a quiet-seeming man who looked more Korean than Japanese, had the door opened. The copilot let out fold-down steps.

Mulvaney stepped out onto the pad and lowered his head and hunched his shoulders to avoid decapitation by the rotor blades. A strong, cold wind whipped across the platform. Three people—all dressed identically even

138

though two were male and one was female—walked onto the pad. Mulvaney recognized the female as Edith Blandish. The coveralls were actually an improvement over her attire during their lunch in Chicago five days ago.

The two men—one tall, broad-shouldered, fiftyish, and Caucasian, the other short, lean, about Mulvaney's own age, and Japanese—were Friedman and Naguchi.

"Sergeant Mulvaney! I hope that your trip was pleasant," Dr. Blandish enthused at the top of her lungs. Mulvaney smiled, looked back over his shoulder, and realized the helicopter was starting to lift off again. Like it or not, he was here to stay.

"Yes, Mulvaney, welcome!" The Japanese moved forward quickly, smiled, made an almost unnoticeable bow, and extended his right hand. The handshake was solid and dry.

Friedman offered his right hand, his left hand shielding the bowl of his pipe. "So you're our new policeman. I don't really like policemen, but as you're necessary to the success of our activities here, you're welcome."

"Gosh," Mulvaney said, smiling, shaking Friedman's hand. The handclasp was dry, but very brief and lacking in enthusiasm. Mulvaney barely considered the remark about cops. There were a lot of people who felt nervous around police and disliked being anywhere within a block of a cop. More often than not they were good citizens with nothing to hide. That was probably why Friedman made the remark in the first place.

Edith Blandish offered her hand. Mulvaney took it. She smiled at him, her eyes just as pretty as he remembered them, and the rest of her just as uninspiring. Her mousy hair was covered by a blue baseball cap pulled so low that it masked her forehead and made her ears stand out. "You just couldn't imagine how happy we all are to see you."

Somehow, he felt she meant it, but Mulvaney wasn't certain about the other two at all; and, of course, there was always the possibility that their happiness might mean his misery.

Chapter Twelve

Unofficial Strategy

Gonroku Umi's watery dark eyes looked very serious tonight.

There was good reason for that, of course.

"Oyabun, this will soon end, in one manner or another, as all things eventually do," Osgood whispered, lighting a cigarette as he sat down in the Western leather chair beside the old man he called, out of respect, master.

The old man touched the back of Osgood's hand briefly, and then the touch was gone. *"Kobun"*—Gonroku smiled indulgently—"nothing ends, but all things change. When this matter has completed the metamorphosis, either good or evil will have come from this, and this good or evil thing will continue on until it, too, has completed its metamorphosis. It is our goal, Osgood-san, to see to it that this change is for the better, not the worse. Nothing ends, but nothing remains the same."

Osgood watched as the others filtered into the room,

many of them veterans of World War II, as was Gonroku Umi. "Gonroku-san? How goes the history?"

"Each time, Osgood-san, that I think the book is completed, I realize that it is not. It is merely changing," he said and smiled. This was one of a half-dozen times or so John Osgood had seen the old man away from his home and wearing Western clothes. Both sacrifices were for a good reason tonight.

Everyone around the table began to stand. Osgood looked toward the conference room door, then stood as well. "Minoru Toshiyuki," Gonroku Umi advised, as he stood as well.

Most Japanese, if they knew this man had ever existed, would never have thought that he still did. Toshiyuki Minoru, John Osgood had learned some years ago from Gonroku Umi, was the man who, during World War II, had been in charge of Covert Operations for the Japanese Secret Service. It was to Toshiyuki Minoru, perhaps, that Gonroku Umi had presented information concerning the devastating new weapons the United States was preparing to use against Japan in the late summer of 1945. Whether or not Gonroku Umi had possessed such knowledge and transmitted it to his superiors prior to the bombings of Hiroshima and Nagasaki, John Osgood did not know. Gonroku Umi had never told him. But both men, at the close of the war, were under house arrest by the Fascist military leadership of Imperial Japan because they spoke the truth. The men who ran Japan's war machine refused to hear it.

Gonroku's book was a definitive history of World War II told through the eyes of a Japanese, but not an exposé.

As all bowed around the table, John Osgood caught a glimpse of Gonroku's eyes, and then looked quickly toward Toshiyuki Minoru. He saw the same look there. Toshiyuki said in British-accented English (Gonroku-san told Osgood earlier that Toshiyuki-san had learned his English in Hong Kong years before the war), "Sit down, gentlemen." The English was a courtesy to John Osgood, because everyone else at the table—thirteen men in all besides himself—were Japanese. All, Gonroku-san had assured Osgood, spoke perfect English. "We have not met like this for some considerable time. Osgood-san, how much do you know of us?"

Such directness was very un-Japanese. Gonroku-san nodded slightly as Osgood's eyes went to him, and Osgood looked directly then at his inquisitor. "Minoru-san, it is not the character of Gonroku Umi, my old and dear friend, to tell secrets, nor is it mine."

Minoru, very old, very conservative in his Saville Row suit, laughed. "You are very much like us, Osgood-san. I seem to think that Gonroku Umi would have told you of my humble attempt long years ago to serve my nation as I best saw fit. To a degree, I still persist in this attempt. I understand that you serve your nation as well. Good fortune and history find us allies today, whereas yesterday we would not have been. Tomorrow is another story. Our prime minister knows of the reason for this meeting, as does your president. All here know of this, because they are important men. I assume others from your nation are informed?"

"A very few, Minoru-san, because, as you know, the fewer the better."

"Indeed, however the situation is resolved. Tell us your theory."

John Osgood stubbed out his cigarette, then leaned back slightly in the suddenly uncomfortable Western chair. It was built to Japanese proportions, smaller than furniture of its type built for Americans. But that was not the cause of his discomfort. "Sir, I am of the opinion that Japan may soon be under nuclear attack."

There were no sighs, and no sudden rising from chairs. Not even a nod.

Osgood's palms sweated slightly. "As all here are aware, when President Truman ordered that Hiroshima be bombed, he was unaware of the awesome destructive power

142

of the atomic bomb. When the first bomb was dropped, Japanese authorities felt that what occurred was an anomaly, a firestorm—combined with other factors. All of us today know the results were merely the by-products of a very low yield fission bomb, crude by today's standards. Twenty kilotons, the equivalent of twenty thousand tons of TNT. These days the nuclear arsenals of the superpowers include fission devices in the twenty-megaton range. A megaton, of course, is one thousand times greater in destructive potential than a kiloton. When Japan did not surrender and the second bomb was dropped, anyone who thought what had happened in Hiroshima could never happen again was proved wrong. And Japan sued for peace.

"However," John Osgood continued, "the Japanese penchant at that time for fighting to the last man, for expending vast casualties if need be, was well known. Or, at least, that was the interpretation of Japanese military policy and tactics at that time. Because of that, a third bomb on a third aircraft was in readiness, ready to be delivered should Japan still fail to surrender. One must remember the times, of course. President Truman firmly believed that use of the bomb was saving lives, American lives, of course, but saving lives nonetheless. Intelligence suggested to him that the Japanese people, never successfully invaded throughout their national history, would fight off an invasion force every inch of the way."

"Do you feel compelled, Osgood-san," Minoru interrupted, "to justify what occurred to us or to yourself?"

John Osgood looked down at his hands, then across the table into Minoru's face. "Sir, it is impossible for me to consider what happened without considering the far-reaching consequences. I am a man of the postwar period, so I cannot judge the correctness of actions that to me are part of history, not personal experience."

"Continue, then, Osgood-san."

"Very well, sir," Osgood answered. "The third plane with

143

the third bomb was airborne. A recall code message was sent. But by that time the aircraft was caught in a storm and swept off course. It went down and was never heard from again. There was a search effort, although those personnel involved in the search were not told they were supposed to find the third atomic bomb. The search yielded nothing. It was thought, at the time, that the sea would never yield the third aircraft and its cargo. And considering the horror the first two bombs precipitated, it was best for all concerned to write off the aircraft and its crew as ordinary casualties in the closing days of the war. It was never mentioned to the press, or to anyone, that such a powerful instrument of destruction was lost.

"But there is substantial reason to believe that the location of the third aircraft has been discovered and that the bomb can, indeed, be recovered. If it is, it will be utilized by the right-wing fanatic Takeuchi Arisato as a means to destroy Japanese-American relations and bring Japan, one of the most heavily industrialized nations in history, into an adversarial relationship with the United States. This would be a prelude to reestablishing the Fascist Pragmatist rule of the prewar and wartime period."

Minoru Toshiyuki, if Osgood's words moved him in any way at all, did not reveal this in his face. He looked across the table as he lit his cigarette and spoke through a cloud of smoke. "Osgood-san, you have not chosen to reveal how little or how much you know of the men at this table. Gonroku Umi, as I am sure you know, served under me in our secret intelligence service during World War II. He was my most apt pupil, so adept that his abilities eventually surpassed my own humble skills in the tasks patriotic necessity called upon us to perform.

"All of the men at this table, today among Japan's most dedicated industrial and governmental leaders, served with me. I was and still am a Christian, and my favorite tale in Western literature was that of King Arthur and his knights."

Osgood's hands moved along the curving edge of the table.

Minoru smiled indulgently. "As one of us would join his ancestors, I would select one from those remaining to join us here. Only six of us are the original members of this company, but all of us serve Japan now as we did then, and shall endeavor to do so until only one of us sits alone at this table and takes the secrets of this company with him. We have no ritual, other than respect, no code other than truth, no duty other than justice. The emperor knew of our existence, as do very few others. We have become the persons to whom our nation turns when our nation can turn to no others. This is our honor.

"During the war," Minoru-san said in almost a whisper, "many Japanese felt that Japan had been betrayed by men who sought only to increase their power at whatever the cost. I should say that across the world, there were many Germans who felt similarly about Hitler and his Nazis. We did what we could, but fought for our nation's life, hoping that someday, with victory, we would be able to overturn those men who had misled our beloved emperor and the people he so dearly loved all his amazing life. When defeat came, our job was done for us, but at a terrible price. Yet we knew that even though many of those men were dead, the philosophy to which they adhered was not. It is no surprise that a man such as Takeuchi Arisato would be party to such a horrifying plan."

John Osgood took the moment's pause to speak. "The Friedman-Naguchi Expedition, of course, is the cover for the retrieval of the bomb. Friedman is a neo-Nazi, and Naguchi, the son of one of the men of whom you spoke, is his fellow traveler. The financing for the Friedman-Naguchi Expedition comes through a man probably well known to you, the renegade Communist arms smuggler Ladislaw Gorchek. There is reason to believe that Gorchek's funds emanate from certain persons who intend to reap huge

145

financial rewards from the collapse of United States–Japanese relations.

"A while ago, Minoru-san, Gonroku Umi instructed me that nothing ends, that there is only metamorphosis. It would seem that I have discovered the perfect illustration of Gonroku-san's wisdom, because the era of a half century ago has not ended, only changed." Osgood lit a cigarette in the flame of his Dunhill.

"A word to the right ear, Osgood-san, and the Friedman-Naguchi Expedition can cease to exist. Why not, then?"

"Sir, if we assault the expedition, and arrest or kill all there, what then? Evidently, they know where the bomb is. We do not. Others might possess this information and use it. While that bomb exists, there is only peril."

"Can that bomb, Osgood-san, after all these decades beneath the sea, be detonated?"

"This twenty-kiloton device utilizes a six-digit entry code. There is no way possible that this entry code could be known to Takeuchi, to Gorchek, or to anyone with the Friedman-Naguchi Expedition. Without that entry code the bomb cannot be armed, and its utilization would be exceedingly limited, if it could be detonated at all. The casing would be so corroded that opening the bomb to remove the fissionable material would be all but impossible without accidental detonation. These men with whom we deal are fanatics, but fanatics who wish to live. Anyone in their service stupid enough to open the bomb would not be bright enough to open it successfully. So the six-digit entry code is imperative.

"The single piece of data which made me realize that this threat was real was connecting the theft of a prototype Japanese supercomputer and the theft of the American 486 SX chip." Japanese intelligence was very good, and the American superchip would be known to these men. As he looked about the table, he saw no shocked looks, not even mild surprise. "With the 486 SX chip and your high-speed computer, the process of arriving at the correct six-digit entry code could be accomplished successfully in, it is estimated, forty-five minutes."

Now there were looks of surprise.

Gonroku Umi looked at Minoru Toshiyuki, then spoke. "Osgood-san?"

"Oyabun?"

The old man alone smiled. He continued. "Could you enlighten us as to the mechanics of detonation?"

"I am, of course, not a physicist, but I can humbly try, if you like." Osgood looked first at Gonroku, then at Minoru. Then Osgood began. "There are a variety of ways, once the weapon is armed, to precipitate detonation. The bomb was designed to detonate at two thousand feet above sea level. Its system was identical to that utilized during an above-ground test on August sixth, 1948. It is widely held that the basic methodology of the first-generation atomic bombs was more simple than it really was.

"Of course, critical mass was needed. In this case, 3×10^{24} atoms of uranium. To detonate, the physical geometry of the device must be disrupted. Merely pushing the pieces together will not create critical mass, because the pieces naturally repel each other. In laboratory experiments, when this was tried, what resulted was a neutron incident, not an explosion. Such a neutron incident, even with a device of such modest yield, would kill every living thing within a one-mile radius due to the cosine effect, were the incident to occur outside of a properly shielded laboratory.

"To precipitate the vastly more destructive explosion, gentlemen," Osgood went on, "what is necessary is to cause the free neutrons to collide with a sufficient number of atoms of uranium 235, with a chain reaction occurring. The immediate by-products are Alpha, Beta, Gamma, and Fp1 and Fp2 radioactive discharges. In five tenths of a second, there would be a nine-hundred-foot-diameter fireball, at a temperature of 7×10^3 centigrade, and a kinetic energy main destruction factor of eighty-three percent. I can provide the destructive details, but the result is obvious—third-degree burns on exposed skin at four thousand feet from the center of the detonation as a result of infrared emissions. There would be horrible destruction, suffice it to say."

One of the men sitting to Minoru's right was very old and frail-looking, but his voice was still strong. He said in deliberate but well-polished English, "Minoru-san, I respectfully submit that we should take these people now, get the information they possess, then—" He didn't finish.

Gonroku asked, "Then what, Kenichi-san? We do not want the bomb. We would give it to the Americans if we successfully recovered the bomb. But men such as these may not surrender what information they possess willingly. Do we pluck out their fingernails or their eyes? Drugs? What if, after sinking to the level of those whom we stand against, the secret remains unknown to us? Ask the United States to search for the bomb? When the news leaks out, what then? Search for it ourselves? Violate all that our nation stands for concerning nuclear weapons? What if, after that, it is never found? I will tell you, Kenichi-san.

"When the sun rises, rather than considering its beauty, rather than being humbly thankful for the continued privilege to view it, we will think, instead, that this day tens of thousands, perhaps hundreds of thousands of persons will suffer the same fate of those at Hiroshima and Nagasaki, all because of the error we allowed. When the sun sets, there will be no peace, because the same danger of the day will be with us during the night, and if we see another dawn, the threat will not be abated. It will devour our souls. If the only certain way is to allow these desperate men to recover the bomb for us, then that we must do." Gonroku Umi laced his fingers together before him.

"If I may," Osgood said after he was certain his friend had finished speaking, "I would like to point out certain facts."

"Proceed, Osgood-san," Minoru told him.

Osgood nodded. "As long as the bomb is not recovered, as we have discussed, the bomb is a threat. Once it is recovered, it is not. It will be taken away from Japan with all

148

possible safety and speed, then disarmed or detonated in an underground vault or in some remote place if it proves unsafe to store. First we would notify certain governments of this decision, in no way implicating the Japanese government. If we go in heavy-handedly, the possibility of detonation exists. As does the possibility of publicity, which could bring down the current Japanese government because of the understandably great concern here regarding nuclear weapons of any type."

Osgood lit another cigarette. "To attempt to prevent the Friedman-Naguchi Expedition from recovering the bomb would probably achieve what Takeuchi, Gorchek, and Gorchek's supporters hope to achieve via detonation—the alienation of our two governments, and of our two peoples.

"And," Osgood said, "we must eliminate the threat posed by the right-wing terrorist faction led by Takeuchi Arisato. If we only eliminate the threat of the bomb, what will Takeuchi try next?

"I have deliberately entered Japan under my own name," Osgood said, "and made my presence in Japan as obvious as possible. Takeuchi's woman was killed when last we crossed paths in Canada. I was not responsible for her death, but I hope that Takeuchi thinks that I was, because I hope to draw him out. Meanwhile, a person whose talents, abilities, and integrity I deeply respect has been insinuated among the personnel of the Friedman-Naguchi Expedition. He thinks he is alone there, but he is not. Gorchek will attempt to kill him. This may serve to draw out Gorchek himself, and would most certainly implicate Friedman and Naguchi in the conspiracy. Should this person survive—and my faith in his abilities is so strong that I consider he does, indeed, have a chance to survive—he would be on the spot when the bomb was recovered."

"This man is your friend, Osgood-san?"

"Yes, Minoru-san. But like you, and I suspect, like all of us, he would willingly risk his life to bring this matter to its proper resolution." At least, John Osgood reflected, he hoped Mulvaney would feel that way if he knew about the bomb.

Minoru-san commented simply, "Osgood-san, it is necessary to discuss this matter."

Osgood understood, rose, picked up his cigarettes and lighter, bowed to the assembled company, then turned and walked toward the double doors.

He exited the expensively paneled boardroom and entered the hallway. It was as if he went through some science fiction writer's dimensional doorway, leaving the West, returning to the East.

Although the conference room had the air of a corporate boardroom on the top floor of a Manhattan skyscraper, it was situated, instead, in a magnificent home on a large, private estate near the northwestern coast of Kyushu, not far from the city of Fukuoka. The estate belonged to the family of Minoru Toshiyuki, and had for centuries.

Today, as Gonroku Umi had related to Osgood, Minoru conducted most of his extensive business dealings from a penthouse apartment in a complex he owned in an exclusive section of Tokyo. The family estate was a retreat.

As he walked from the open foyer toward the greenscape beyond, Osgood was stunned by the dichotomy. When he looked to the left, there was a helicopter pad with two helicopters waiting. When he looked to the right, there was a garden so pristine and perfect that it seemed like a three-dimensional painting rather than a real garden.

But it was real, and Osgood walked in the garden now, twirling his cane slowly. A path wound through the garden and around it. Osgood followed the pale gray gravel, each piece seemingly matched to every other. Though there were pine trees of all sizes everywhere around him, not a single pine needle lay in the path nor on the meticulously kept grass, despite the winter season which was upon them. Topiary, or the precise sculpting of living plants into shapes, was evident in the hedgerow near the far border of the garden. High trees were walled behind the hedges. An assembly of rocks looked all the more rugged compared to the mounded shapes of some of the ornamental shrubs. More of the rocks were set at intervals within the grassy expanses, black, gray, and white against the green of the grass and shrubs, and the rusty autumn coloration of some of the other foliage.

There was perfect peace here, and John Osgood silently envied the man who could walk these grounds each morning at his leisure and compose himself for the coming day.

A soft, cool, floral-scented breeze touched his cheek. He looked down at the face of his Rolex. He had been wandering here for nearly an hour. The voice that came from some distance behind him was that of Gonroku Umi. "Osgood-san."

"Yes, *Oyabun?*"Osgood turned and looked at the man for whom he held deep respect.

"The matter has been decided."

John Osgood realized he was holding his breath. "Yes?"

"You will be allowed to pursue that course which you judge as best. It is hoped that we follow the path of wisdom."

"Thank you, my friend."

"You should know, John, that it is you whom we trust, not the policy or the men whom you represent."

John Osgood nodded that he understood.

Chapter Thirteen

Bad Actors

The salon of the *Archimedes* was large enough to hold a small dance and was far greater in size than the living room and dining room of his house on the near West Side of Chicago. It was four in the afternoon, which meant it was three in the morning back home. Andy would be asleep.

Ed Mulvaney could picture how she looked. She sometimes slept naked, sometimes wore a pretty, feminine, long white nightgown, but sometimes wore a huge T-shirt that came down to her knees and was big enough that another person could get inside with her. One time they'd tried that, nearly ripping the T-shirt to shreds, but having a lot of fun.

She was probably wearing one of those, all bundled up against the winter cold under a pile of quilts, with her Colt Detective Special .38 beside the bed. He'd left all of his guns with her, but she was never much for semiautomatics and was set in her ways when it came to revolvers.

He told himself she was safe, because the house had sturdy doors with good locks, and she was a good shot. After all, she'd spent three years as a cop in Detroit, and all those years in the MPs.

As he sipped from the mug of coffee on the dining table in front of him, he wondered if she was at home at all. Distrusting Andy Oakwood's fidelity would have been absurd. She loved him, he loved her; it was as simple as that. But several times she'd lost time, money, and brownie points with the P.I. agency she worked for by not taking on jobs that called for her to work at night.

He wanted to think she was safe at home in bed, but she could be out on some lonely stakeout for a divorce case. At least divorce cases usually kept the operative in a decent neighborhood.

Wherever she was, she was tough, competent, and had a good head on her shoulders, Mulvaney reminded himself as he lit a cigarette. She was fine.

What if she wasn't?

He almost stubbed out the cigarette. If something happened to her it would be no one's fault but his own. She loved him and he loved her, and she was a woman and he was a man, and that meant there was no reason for her to be working some damned dangerous job when she could have been nice and warm and safe somewhere. She was doing what she was doing because he didn't earn enough money. He had taken the only money they'd had and used it for something else.

Never once had Andy said a word about his using the money he'd wound up with (after getting Ellermann out of the hands of the Yakusa) to help Bill Grimshaw's family. Andy was that kind of a lady, so why did she have to be out risking her neck every night?

This job would pay. The ten thousand up front was already in the bank. Of the grand a week he'd be getting, he figured that he could easily ship eight hundred or more of that back home. If this whole deal didn't blow up on him too fast—meaning the bad guys didn't find these diamonds or

153

whatever Osgood was really worried about—twelve weeks or so of this would be enough for a start.

With Andy's background and his own, they could get licensed in Illinois. They'd start their own P.I. firm and specialize in security, maybe industrial espionage, maybe some divorce and domestic work, but only quality stuff that paid. Nothing sleazy or under the table. And he could still stay on the cops. Two real incomes. Who could they get as operatives to work for them? Lew Fields would do it as soon as he was back on his feet. Some of the other guys, too, the good guys who really worked at being cops. They could always use a good part-time job, and being a cop on the side was easier than being something else.

With the ten thousand earned here, and the ten already in the bank, they'd get the license, a small office, telephones, business cards, some classy stationery, and a Yellow Pages ad. Maybe even run a few thirty-second commercials on WGN television, or on one of the smaller independents.

This was a start again.

Now, if only these bad guys would take their time finding the diamonds or whatever.

And if Osgood had shot him the straight shit, there was a reward on the diamonds. That would be big bucks, enough to do the private agency bit in style, make a splash, have some neat offices and stuff like that.

"Sergeant Mulvaney?"

His cigarette was burned down in his fingers, and he looked up. In the doorway at the base of the companionway steps was Dr. Edith Blandish.

Mulvaney flicked the inch or so of ashes off into the ashtray beside him and started to stand, saying, "Doctor."

"Please, sit down and relax. If you suffer from jet lag like I usually do, it's a wonder you're not sleeping."

"I slept most of the afternoon." He stood up anyway.

She crossed the salon from the base of the steps. The *Archimedes,* albeit a working vessel, was like a mini–luxury liner.

The salon was richly paneled in dark wood. On the bulkhead hung several dozen brass barometers. Nautical gear was sprinkled about the walls, tables and the back of the bar. This was a rich man's pleasure vessel that happened to be on duty at a work site, like a luxury motor home out of camera range on a movie location.

Edith Blandish was just unattractive despite the gorgeous eyes and the nice-sounding voice. She was too flat-chested for Mulvaney's taste, too hipless, and the hair was just there. She wore loose-fitting slacks and a mannish-looking shirt, its pink color the only marginal concession to femininity. The sleeves were down and the cuffs buttoned, as was the neck. Her wrists and throat looked skinny.

She sat down opposite him, and Mulvaney took his seat. "I wanted to talk a little, Sergeant."

"Do me a favor and call me Ed, okay?"

She smiled. "That's my nickname, too."

"Ed?"

"Short for Edith," she told him. "Could I bum a cigarette?"

"Sure." Mulvaney slid the pack of Pall Malls across the table. She took one, studying its filterless design, then tapped the end with the logo printed on it against the tabletop.

"In the spy stories they light the part with the name printed on so the enemy agents won't be able to track them down, right?" Dr. Blandish said.

"I don't read too many spy stories," Mulvaney confessed.

"Neither do I, Ed."

"Ed for Edith, huh?"

"Right—Ed for Edward."

"All right. So"—Mulvaney smiled—"to what do I owe the pleasure of this visit, Ed? Not just worried about my suffering from jet lag, I assume, and I bet you didn't come in to bum a cigarette." He extended the Zippo for her, rolled the striking wheel under his thumb, and produced a flame.

She inhaled. He closed the lighter. She exhaled smoke through her nostrils, not just blowing it out in a thin stream through her lips like some women did.

"You know, Ed, there are twenty-two parts in a Zippo lighter, and one hundred and eight manufacturing steps to make it. I remember stuff like that. I'm a professional smart person."

"I'm a professional stooge, myself. Somebody says, 'Run into that building and let people shoot at you!' and I say, 'Gee, can I?' and I do it. You probably make more money as a smart person than I do as a stooge."

"Maybe we're all stooges sometimes."

"If we had one more," Mulvaney began—but she wasn't laughing. "What's the matter, Ed?"

"Well, I just wanted to have a little talk about your health and well-being."

Ed Mulvaney stubbed out his cigarette and sipped his coffee. "Worried about my doing a dramatic reenactment of Thomas Westinghouse's death scene? I don't get killed that easily. And if you're worried now, why weren't you worried back in Chicago?"

"I didn't say I was worried, Ed, just concerned. We're pushing a lot of things to the limit here, and sometimes that lends itself to a careless mistake."

Mulvaney felt like the guy in a Lassie or Rin Tin Tin movie. Edith Blandish was definitely trying to tell him something, but what? He started to ask her that, then looked around the salon again. Behind one of the many barometers there could have been a camera lens. A microphone could have been anywhere. Fiber optics. Parabolic electronic eavesdropping gear. There were lots of ways to find out what people were doing, and maybe Edith Blandish was too aware of that. So instead of asking her to spit out what she wanted to say, he told her, "When we talked in Chicago, you warned me that I'd have to be more careful than my predecessor, and I intend to be. I realize the damn job's important, so just get off my back."

He'd thrown the remark out as a test.

She was startled for a second, then flashed a quick smile. The corners of her mouth turned down when she said, "I was only trying—" And she smiled that quick smile again.

Mulvaney winked at her, then rubbed at his eyelid. "Look, Ed, I wanna be friends. I know you're worried about everything going just right. Well, you can count on me to do my part, okay?"

Why was Edith Blandish warning him about everything from getting killed to getting listened to? And the next logical question was why was Edith Blandish interested in doing either? She couldn't be trying to flirt with him. He was reasonably certain about that. And John Osgood had said nothing about a confederate already aboard the *Archimedes.*

As if she read his mind, and at the same time wished to confuse him still further, she molded ashes off the tip of her cigarette, looked up at him, and smiled again. Then she said, "Tomorrow morning, if you've looked at your duty roster printout, you know you're supposed to go ashore and meet the local police chief, a Mr. Tadatoshi. He's a nice man, really. I have some things to pick up. Give me a lift. I want you to be familiarized with everything here as quickly as possible because there's so much to do. I'm in charge of the day-to-day running of the expedition, so you could say you work for me. Nobody's said anything yet, but I just have this feeling that we're getting closer to what we're looking for. I mean, the diving master doesn't report to me, but I could just sense it. Woman's intuition. " She smiled. "And Doctors Friedman and Naguchi will brief you from their perspectives on what they want you to know tonight, so tomorrow you can get to work. I guess what I'm saying is that breaking in a new man at such a critical time makes it doubly hard on everybody, so you'll really have to be alert for everything, stay on your toes, and be on the ball."

"How about watching out for trite expressions?"

She looked at him and laughed. His coffee was cold.

* * *

Friedman stared out to sea, as if only paying part of his attention to what transpired. Naguchi talked as the five of them—Friedman, Naguchi, Edith Blandish, Mulvaney, and Milo Weatherall, the dive master—sat around the small table in the sun deck over a drink. Mulvaney pulled on a bottle of Michelob, having passed on the Suntory. The others—all but Weatherall, who sipped at mineral water and constantly flexed the biceps of his left arm—had mixed drinks.

It was past dark but still relatively early in the evening. Mulvaney's biological timeclock was now thoroughly confused. A cool breeze blew from the southeast, and Edith Blandish had her legs wrapped over in a plaid lap robe, like somebody in an old movie sitting in a deck chair on an ocean liner.

Naguchi said, "You see, Sergeant Mulvaney, your duties here are relatively few in number, but quite important. Safety is of the greatest importance. Dr. Friedman and Dr. Blandish, Mr. Weatherall and I—all of us—we want to accomplish what we set out to do, but not at the risk of placing anyone in any greater danger than this difficult task already demands. As security officer for the expedition, you report directly to Dr. Blandish, of course, but will, in a very real way, serve as liaison between all elements of the group."

"I've told Mr. Mulvaney some of the problems he'll have to face," Edith Blandish interjected.

"Yes," Naguchi said, his little chubby face truly yellow-looking in the light from the lanterns. "No one has ever set out to do what we intend to do—will do, Sergeant Mulvaney."

Naguchi was having a hard time with the L in Mulvaney's name, so Mulvaney said, "Just call me Ed."

Naguchi seemed to approve of that, said, "Ed, you see, we have reason to believe that in this immediate area we will be able to find a vessel that is largely intact. The island of Tsushima itself serves as a barrier against some of the stronger currents, and the bottom is just at the right depth, not so deep that we cannot reach nor is the water so comparatively shallow that surface disturbances over the years would have destroyed what we search for. Yet there is considerable, constant, and very rapid erosion of the seafloor here, meaning that our treasure is buried, requiring of us a great deal of sophistication in order that we might achieve our goal.

"What we hope to find will prove of such great significance that we cannot brook interference from anyone, curiosity seekers, the press, the local fishermen, anyone at all."

Friedman turned his eyes toward them and spoke. "You see, Mulvaney, like any other human endeavor, archeology can be a cutthroat business. We don't want all the years of work which have gone into this to result in someone else getting their hands on what we want. Your job is to assist us by every means at your disposal in creating an environment free of hassles and safe for everyone to work in. Okay?"

"Sure. Better for all of us, and makes my job that much easier," Mulvaney agreed. "And I was figuring maybe I could help with the diving part, too. I mean, I should see the excavation site, if that's what you call it, so I'll have a better idea of what I'm protecting."

Naguchi said to Weatherall, "Any objections, Milo?" But Weatherall's first name came out sounding like *My-row*.

Milo Weatherall—blond, very muscular, very tall, a perpetual scowl on his handsome face—looked over and said, "I don't like amateurs getting in the way, Doc." Weatherall's voice didn't go with his body. It was pitched just a little higher than it should have been, came out sounding laughable rather than commanding. And Weatherall had to know it. "No dice."

Mulvaney told himself that Weatherall was only being sensible and might not realize that the expedition's newest member had some dive experience. "I was in Special Forces and got a reasonably good amount of dive training. I kept up with it over the years. I'm no expert like you, of course,"

159

Mulvaney buttered up, "but if I just go down, look around, and stay out of everybody's way, I don't see where it'll hurt."

Friedman said, "Let him go, Milo. He's right. Won't hurt, and we might benefit from his going down."

Mulvaney looked at Friedman, wondering just exactly what Friedman was saying.

But then Naguchi spoke. "I agree that Ed should go down, Milo. It might indeed be useful to us all."

Milo Weatherall flexed his arms outward to full extension. They were long and powerful-looking. The muscles were not large but long—typical well-conditioned swimmer's arms. Weatherall said nothing, merely scowled some more.

Mulvaney decided to change the subject, asking, "How did you guys find this one spot of ocean where the conditions were just so right and everything? I mean, with all those ships that went down when Kubla Khan sent out his two fleets, I'd figure there were ships all over the place. Why just this spot?"

He watched faces, trying not to be too obvious, but saw nothing in any of them. Friedman began to answer the question. "Basically, without spending several hours updating you on years of our research, we discovered an old reference. Careful analysis clearly indicated that what was being talked about had to be what we were looking for. Fortunately for us, for all of us, the undersea topography and other conditions were just right, as is the timing."

"Timing?"

Friedman, still looking bored, said, "Even just a few years ago, raising the craft we hope to find would have been an exercise in futility. But now, well, the technology exists to deal with it properly."

Mulvaney cupped his hands around his lighter and started to light a cigarette. 'Ed' Blandish's eyes seemed to be signaling him, but he couldn't understand for what. He finished lighting his cigarette, started to speak.

"Put that shit out," Milo Weatherall snapped.

"Oh, I'm sorry. Allergy?"

"No."

"Is the smoke blowing your way, then?"

"No."

"What, uh—I mean, we're outdoors."

"Smoking is bad for your body. No one should be allowed to smoke," Weatherall declared. "Put it out, or I'll put it out for you."

Mulvaney looked at his cigarette, then looked again at Weatherall. "Let me get this straight, Milo. May I call you Milo?" Weatherall didn't answer. "My smoking is causing you no physical discomfort, and isn't blowing your way so you don't have to breathe it. And we're outside. Was your mother frightened by a cigarette machine when she was pregnant or somethin'? I mean, what's the problem?"

"Smoking bugs me."

"Assholes bug me," Mulvaney said, smiling. "So don't get bent outta shape about my cigarette. Display the same tolerance toward me that I display toward you."

Milo Weatherall started up out of his chair.

Ed Mulvaney didn't move and didn't say a word, but just looked at him.

Edith Blandish sucked in her breath so loudly it was almost a backward scream.

"Milo!"

Mulvaney looked away from Milo, who stopped like he was a kid playing statue and somebody had yelled "Freeze." He looked instead at Lawrence Friedman. The familiar bored look was gone. The look that replaced it was a look Ed Mulvaney had seen before, too. . . .

Mulvaney stood by the stern rail, having another beer. The night was old and cold by now, but his body was still telling him it was morning. If he stayed up long enough, it would be.

When he was a kid in high school, he joined the drama club for a semester to get on the good side of Irene Malijewski, who had the biggest tits in the sophomore class.

The club put on two plays a year, one just before Christmas, the other in the spring. The Christmas play always had to do with Christmas. The one in the spring was usually a mystery. In that play that one semester during which he had—unsuccessfully, it turned out—pursued Irene's charms, he was cast as a bumbling police detective, a role he still pursued. The only things he distinctly remembered about the play were Irene's boobs under a pink sweater and the fact that he'd gotten ribbed by all his buddies because he played a cop. Nobody liked cops and everybody in the play did a lousy acting job because they were all so obvious.

If he hadn't known better, he would have thought his high school reunion was being held aboard the *Archimedes* in the Straits of Tsushima. All that was missing were Irene's tits.

Chapter Fourteen

Jigsaw Puzzles

It was intrinsic to the job to have faith in betrayal, to trust in the absence of trustworthiness, to view camaraderie as the cloak of deceit.

Based on such truisms, John Osgood expected his assassins to call, and hoped that they would. He was counting on at least one of Minoru Toshiyuki's twelve knights being into a rather peculiar stream of the Samurai tradition—less good than evil, less true than pragmatic.

Each second that passed without finding some clue to the whereabouts of Takeuchi Arisato heightened the chances that Takeuchi might somehow succeed, and that the forces of truth and justice—or at least what passed for them these days—would fail miserably.

In the days before Japan's reckless imperialism culminated in the attack on Pearl Harbor, there existed a group within the greater fabric of Japanese society which, in many ways, was similar to Hitler's brown-shirted stalwarts. The S.A. were murdered in 1934 during the Night of the Long

163

Knives. Although no dictatorship like that of the Nazis ever held sway even during Japan's darkest hours, nor did Japan, for all its atrocities, ever approach the level of race-motivated murder seen under national socialism, the idea of racial and cultural purity was dearly held by certain elements within Japan's right wing.

A society of terrorists who utilized death as a means of promulgating a philosophy of racial purity and hatred of all things Western—including suffrage and equality under the law—flourished.

It was called Ketsumeidan, or the League of Blood.

The League of Blood was never large. Successful secret societies that deal in death never are. But it never died.

John Osgood surveyed the *kazu,* or side dishes, before him, questioning whether or not another piece of raw tuna would upset his stomach. He'd already eaten a substantial quantity of deep-fried pumpkin and lotus root, mushrooms and shrimp in a custardlike substance, and Kobe beef. The beef was on the fatty side but melt-in-the-mouth tender. Realizing these dishes were a prelude to bowls of rice and miso shiru soup, his hand reached to his cold sake. Soon the rice wine would be replaced with hot green tea.

The room in the small, public restaurant was very much like the room in which he'd sat when he first learned of the Ketsumeidan's continued existence. Gonroku Umi had recounted to him the story of the Ketsumeidan.

"I fear, John, that at some time in the future as the trade imbalance between our countries grows and anti-Japanese sentiment increases in the West, the time may be right again for the Ketsumeidan."

"Ketsumeidan?"

"The League of Blood."

"From the prewar era, Gonroku-san?"

"Yes. And no. The League of Blood submerged itself within the maelstrom, but never did it cease to exist. What

164

the Ketsumeidan initially came into existence to combat exists, of course, on a vastly greater scale today. That was the Westernization of Japanese society, and the racial impurity that would eventually result."

John Osgood sipped at the Gekkeikan sake, revered by many as Japan's finest, the drink of the samurai. John Osgood found it oddly contradictory that the favored alcoholic beverage of a people noted for politeness and neatness had the rather incongruous side effect of serving admirably as furniture polish. He forced himself not to contemplate what this cold sake might be doing to his insides. It would have tarnished his enjoyment of it. He asked Gonroku Umi, "Are you implying that this League of Blood still exists?"

"Yes."

There were always old men who could not surrender their youthful fantasies, however violent or bizarre. He suggested as much to Gonroku Umi.

"No, Osgood-san. Although some few of Ketsumeidan's original membership doubtlessly exist, I have reason to believe that the average age of the members in the League of Blood is somewhat less than your own age."

"If you have evidence of this, Gonroku-san—"

"I am fond of American jigsaw puzzles, as you know. Being old, Osgood-san, yet still possessed of faculties allows the luxury of combining the events of today with the experiences of a lifetime. It forms many strange pictures. Have you ever taken several jigsaw puzzles and poured all of the pieces into a common container, then drawn from this container at random?"

"No, Gonroku-san, I have not."

Gonroku Umi smiled then. "I have, but then I am sometimes very foolish. To understand the world around us, it is necessary to do much the same, to draw out pieces which appear interesting to you alone, while someone else might consider these pieces similar to all the rest. Then take these pieces and see which will fit with which, never knowing if a piece that is rejected might indeed fit later on. The human mind, I have always felt, works in much the same manner.

"The pieces of the puzzle of today which I have examined throughout many yesterdays, setting some aside at times to examine once again in some distant tomorrow, will sometimes fit together to form the most bizarre images. You have come to me to solicit my aid in your quest for the terrorist Takeuchi, and I tell you that as I arrange these pieces from many puzzles one of the pictures which begins to take shape is the resurgence of Ketsumeidan."

John Osgood lit a cigarette.

That conversation with Gonroku Umi concerning the League of Blood had been in June. It was now December.

In the intervening months, John Osgood had come to believe in the continued existence of Ketsumeidan, and that Gonroku Umi was, indeed, correct in his reasoned assumption.

And today, when he met with Gonroku-san prior to the meeting at the estate of Minoru Toshiyuki, he asked one simple question: "Gonroku-san, I mean no offense, but is it possible that one man among these with whom we shall speak is Ketsumeidan?"

"I am one man, and I am not; I cannot speak for the others, Osgood-san. But men who profess to wisdom cannot dismiss even the most remote of possibilities."

John Osgood, although at times not certain of his wisdom, dismissed no possibilities. . . .

In the distance beyond the blue mists, beyond the fast-moving breakers that assaulted the black rocks here by the water's edge, there was a Chinese-style pagoda. It was black like the rocks, but rose against a blue deeper than that of the mists. That blue was night.

John Osgood walked here.

Such things as sleep, the crash of waves, or the musical

166

laughter of a small child were more appreciated when death might be waiting. While Elizabeth, John Junior, and Natalie had lived, he had failed to appreciate that fact. But from their deaths he had learned a great deal more about life than he had ever suspected.

So he walked here, at once enjoying the night, yet hoping that somewhere attackers waited.

In his hand was the cane. Beneath his overcoat was the gun. Around him was life. In the final analysis the end of life was inescapable anyway.

Chapter Fifteen

On the Death of
Thomas Westinghouse

He was up, showered, breakfasted, and ready to go by
quarter after six.

The standard routine, Ed Mulvaney discovered, was to
board a decent-sized launch from the base of the passenger
steps along the starboard side of the *Archimedes,* and then
go out to the platform. There were slips built into the
platform which made it a floating dock. From the three slips
expedition divers could board a larger launch out to one of
the work boats clustered around the *Archimedes.* He and
Edith Blandish boarded a vessel the size of a fully rigged-out
sport fisherman and made the journey between the seaside
village of Karagawa and Tsushima Island.

Karagawa had its own landing area for the vastly larger
Sikorski cargo helicopters, Edith told him, which could not
touch down safely on the platform. In rough sea or turbulent
conditions they could not safely hover and crane down their
cargo, either. In addition to this pad, there was a strip which
allowed the landing of fixed-wing aircraft. The strip dated

from the early days of World War II and was used by the Imperial Japanese Air Force as a base from which to attack coastal targets in Shanghai, mainland China.

Despite the impressive-looking modern fishermen, Karagawa was gray and poor. Mulvaney and Edith Blandish walked to the house of the policeman rather than wait for the village's single hired car. They didn't want to use one of the expedition's island-based pickup trucks. The morning was cool, and it felt good to Mulvaney to walk on dry land rather than through the aisle of an aircraft or on the deck of a boat.

"So nobody should be able to hear us now, Ed," Ed Mulvaney began. "What did you really want to tell me?"

"Do you realize why you were hired, Ed?" Edith Blandish said at last, answering his question with a question of her own.

"Because I'm so talented?"

"They don't need a security man like you. Milo handles all the real security."

"Why did they hire Thomas Westinghouse, then? Or, for that matter, why did they kill Thomas Westinghouse?" She stopped walking, looked straight at him, then looked away. Mulvaney lit a cigarette. "If this Westinghouse guy was hauling the nitrous oxide on a regular basis, he had to know the basic safety precautions unless he was an imbecile. If he was that big a dummy, he would have been killed his first time out, right?"

She didn't answer him, but began walking again.

"You were the one who wanted to talk, Edith. So talk."

"That's the house of the policeman, the clean yellow one at the head of the next block. It's the *chuzaiso koban* for the district."

"Gee, that's nice. What's he going to tell me?"

"Probably nothing, maybe something. This is just a courtesy call. It's expected."

They crossed the street, which was gray and dingy like the

houses, and barely wide enough for two Japanese cars to have navigated it safely in two-way traffic.

The yellow house positively gleamed. The front wheel of a brightly painted blue bicycle was set within a concrete well near the ground level entrance. "He'd cut his response time if he put the rear wheel in that little gutter," Mulvaney observed as they neared the house. "Then he wouldn't have to pull the bike out before mounting."

"Well, why don't you mention it to him, Ed?"

"Maybe I should, Ed," Mulvaney told her.

They turned in at the narrow walkway between the two equal sections of front yard. Edith Blandish said something about this being one of over nine thousand resident police boxes just like this—although not necessarily yellow—that were a part of Japan's National Police Agency. That every cop here was a Fed of sorts, Mulvaney already knew.

There was a plain door with some Japanese writing on it, which Mulvaney assumed indicated this was a police station. Edith Blandish knocked on it.

Mulvaney snapped his cigarette out into the street, saying to her, "Maybe he's not up yet. It's just a little after seven."

"I thought policemen never slept," she said matter-of-factly.

"Oh, yeah, we sleep every chance we get, but that's so we'll be properly rested when we fight the forces of evil."

"Oh."

The door opened. A skinny man dressed in a dark blue uniform reminiscent of a highway patrolman rather than a city cop stood there. He bowed, smiled, and said something totally incomprehensible to Mulvaney.

Edith Blandish responded. At least, this time, Mulvaney caught that it was Japanese. And then the man turned to Mulvaney. It was as if he chose his words very carefully, and he spoke them almost painfully slowly, but correctly. "Sergeant Mulvaney." He bowed. Mulvaney made a quickie bow back. "I am honored to meet the famous American policeman. Not long after the tragic death of Westinghouse-san, I was informed by Dr. Blandish that you would be arriving. Come in."

Mulvaney started to step aside to let Edith Blandish pass through ahead of him, but she nudged him forward. A memory clicked in of something he'd picked up on his last visit to Japan, that Japanese men did not hold doors, help with coats, or give seats to women. Mulvaney waited anyway, until the awkwardness of the delay forced Edith Blandish to pass through the doorway ahead of him.

Inside, there was a small desk, several neat stacks of papers, a plain vase with a single chrysanthemum, several chairs small enough to be used in a kindergarten, and a framed photograph of the late Emperor Hirohito. In one corner of the room, there was a modern-looking two-way radio set on a small wooden table with ornately carved legs. In the other corner there was a hotplate and a metal teapot and some pretty china teacups. Everything was small, clean, and devoid of anything similar to any police station Mulvaney had ever seen. Edith Blandish sat down in one of the chairs opposite Mr. Tadatoshi. Mulvaney sat in the other.

Tadatoshi folded his hands on his desk, smiled, and bowed his head slightly. "I appreciate very much the courtesy of this stopping by, Mulvaney-san."

Mulvaney smiled, bowed his head slightly, and said, "I appreciate your taking time from your schedule to see us, sir."

That evidently pleased the man, and he stood up, asking if they would like tea. Edith looked to Mulvaney, and Mulvaney supposed he was expected to say yes. He said so, and Edith Blandish offered to pour. She stood, went to the hotplate, and began to fix the tea. Tadatoshi said, "You would inquire concerning the death of Westinghouse-san?"

"Yes. Just what caused the spark that ignited the gas?"

"That is unclear, Mulvaney-san. But as one officer of law

171

enforcement to the other, I marvel at how rapidly the explosion and fire consumed the entire vessel so quickly."

Mulvaney shook his head at the redundancy, then asked, "Are you implying it might not have been an ordinary spark, sir?"

"Impry?"

"Imply. To say something without saying it, I mean."

"Perhaps, perhaps not. There is no evidenciary material."

Mulvaney felt a little more at home than he had when he'd entered. Here was a cop who smelled a rat but couldn't do anything about it. That was a song Mulvaney had played lots of times, and it was always a lonely tune. "Just a hunch?" Mulvaney thought better of the word as he said it.

But, evidently, Tadatoshi had seen a lot of American movies. "A hunch, but only that."

"What kind of man was Westinghouse-san, Tadatoshi-san?"

Tadatoshi seemed to consider his answer, or perhaps was just searching for the right English. "He was secretive, but Westinghouse-san was good."

"Secretive, Tadatoshi-san?"

Again, the policeman sat at his little desk with his hands folded, seeming to consider his words and collect his thoughts. "You have an expression, Mulvaney-san. Two sides to money?"

"Two sides of a coin, yes."

"One side of Westinghouse-san was funny man who talked a lot when he stopped here and drank tea. The other side I never saw."

"You never saw the other side? Then how do you know there was one?"

The policeman smiled as Edith Blandish brought the teacups and the pot of tea from the hotplate. "You see the front of my desk, but you know there is a backside."

Oddly enough, Ed Mulvaney understood what Tadatoshi-san meant.

*　*　*

"Who was he?"

"Who?"

"Westinghouse. And who are you?"

"What?"

"You heard me, Edith," Mulvaney told her. The boat wasn't loaded yet, and there was nothing Mulvaney had to do with it except check that the number of items on the invoice matched the number of items on the boat. So they walked along the beach just north of the harbor docks. "You want to tell me something and then you don't. Who said you shouldn't?"

"If I could tell you that, I could tell you everything. You ever hear of a man named Ladislaw Gorchek? Well, he's heard of you."

"Gorchek? Gorchek. Hmm," Mulvaney said, shaking his head.

"I've only seen him once, when he flew in to the platform late at night and Dr. Friedman and Dr. Naguchi were there to meet him. But they didn't know I was there, because I wasn't supposed to be. But I was catching up on still photographing some pottery shards and things brought up earlier in the day. We get a photographic record of everything just in case a sample should be damaged while it's being flown out. Well, I was catching up. I figured I'd just curl up under a blanket on the couch in the office. I was finished, and I tried going to sleep, but around two in the morning the helicopter noises woke me up."

"There's a couple of things wrong with that, Edith," Ed Mulvaney told her. "First of all, if you were sleeping on the couch in plain view and this Gorchek or whatever his name is is so much into secrecy he comes in by chopper at two A.M., Friedman and Naguchi would have checked the place, made sure everyone was accounted for. And if you were hiding, how would you get close enough to recognize this Gorchek guy? Was he wearing a name tag? And how come you know he's heard of me?"

She exhaled, steam on her breath, put her hands on her

hips, and just stood there a few inches from the line of surf. "Give me a cigarette."

"Great. You mooch cigarettes and Milo hates them. And who is Milo, anyway? Why don't they need me because they've got him? You've got a lot of cutesy things to say, Edith, but you don't back any of it up." He lit a cigarette for her and one for himself, too.

"I don't want to see you get killed like Tom Westinghouse did."

"Who was Westinghouse, really? What was this other side of the coin thing Tadatoshi talked about?"

She exhaled smoke this time, looked down toward the sand, then looked up into his eyes. "I was out there with Tom, all right? Tom and I were—" She looked away, looked back at him, her blue eyes somehow different now. "Tom knew who Gorchek was. After Tom, uhh—" She looked down at the sand again. Mulvaney noticed the hand that held the cigarette was shaking, so he put his arms around her. She looked up into his face, but not at his eyes. "Tom was my lover. He was so beautiful. You know what it's like to be me? You couldn't. Always the smart girl, and smart girls don't get men like Tom Westinghouse, but he really cared, really loved me, dammit! And if you laugh at me, I'll gouge your eyes out. It was after Tom was killed that I overheard Friedman and Naguchi talking, and they mentioned Gorchek wanting you dead, too."

"Too," Mulvaney repeated.

She bit her lower lip, tears starting from her eyes. "Too."

Mulvaney drew her close against him, touched his lips to her forehead, and wanted to tell her he was sorry.

174

Chapter Sixteen

Okane

Through the window of the small rented office, John Osgood saw the *Okane* moving in along the dockside.

He set down his binoculars, picked up his coat and cane, and left the office at once, taking the stairs down to the ground floor.

Okane would be thought a curious name for a ship of any kind, but not if one knew the owner, Steve Oglethorpe. Most men named a vessel after a girl or a hometown, but always after something well loved. Steve Oglethorpe was no exception there, because what Oglethorpe loved was *okane*, or money.

Oglethorpe, like Ed Mulvaney and thousands of other men, had his life irrevocably altered by Vietnam. Unlike Mulvaney, who had been an officer in Special Forces, Oglethorpe was a Navy SEAL, never high-ranking, but very good at his work. After the war Oglethorpe tried his hand at various jobs but as he told Osgood once over a drink, "I was tired of bein' a nigger, John. Inside me, I wasn't a nigger, I was a black man. Overseas, maybe they didn't like me, but they knew better than to treat me like shit. Back home I was one more guy who'd probably been a fuckin' baby killer an' a hophead. And I was the wrong color to boot. Shit, blame me for leavin'?"

Oglethorpe found three other friends who felt similarly, one of them white and one of them of Japanese extraction. The four of them, all SEAL-trained, went off to the Orient and did the stuff boyhood fantasies (and real-life nightmares) are made of—roaming the Pacific, salvaging, brawling, or working as mercenaries, and always for money.

Presumably, it was the Japanese member of the four who provided the name for the ship, although he had died in Jahor Baharu, near Singapore, two years ago. The other black man, like Ed Mulvaney's friend Bill Grimshaw, died of cancer associated with the use of Agent Orange. Only Oglethorpe and the white man, Norbut Kowalski, survived. And they still did what they'd always done.

Part of their repertoire was contract work for the CIA.

Osgood stopped dockside, shouting up to one of the deck apes, "Hello! Can you tell Steve or Norb that John is here?"

The man looked at Osgood strangely. Osgood was ready to try something other than English on the man, but the man—white, mid-thirties, long-haired—shouted back, "Right y'are, mate." An Australian, the accent hinting at Tasmania more than the mainland, Osgood thought.

Osgood lit a cigarette, remembering to lean on his cane while he waited, but in the next moment Steve Oglethorpe and Norb Kowalski appeared on deck. Norb was as fair of hair and eye as Steve was dark. Norb's skin was so tanned, however, that he looked almost like a light-skinned black. "John!" Osgood nodded toward Oglethorpe, Norb gesturing with the stem of his pipe. "We're coming down." Oglethorpe grabbed a line off a beam and swung across the six feet or so of open water to the dock, flexing the pectoral muscles under his shirt. "So, how ya doin', man?"

"Fine, now." Osgood shifted his cane to his left hand and took Steve Oglethorpe's right hand.

Norb Kowalski joined them on the dock, shaking Osgood's hand as well. "Dry land! I can't believe it!"

"Let's walk then, shall we?" Osgood suggested. As Oglethorpe fell in on his right and Kowalski on his left, Osgood asked, "What about it? Is it there?"

Oglethorpe took a pack of Marlboros from the pocket of his T-shirt, lit one with a Zippo lighter, and said, "I think so."

"You think so?" The wind was blowing harder, and they were running out of dock. Osgood steered them right, out onto the sidewalk over the seawall. "Couldn't you find it?"

"The electronic imaging equipment your people provided showed up a whole mess of solid objects, but we couldn't tell for sure if one of 'em was a plane."

"Damn." Osgood spat under his breath.

"It isn't as bad as Steve here's lettin' ya think," Norb Kowalski said. "We got a coupl'a good possibles right in the area those mothers from that expedition are lookin'. Steve an' me would swim out, go through their underwater perimeter security stuff and check out where they was workin' durin the day, see. And the last two nights they've been concentratin' their work in this one spot. We got it on the map. That spot matches up with one of the blips we got. Betchya that's your damn airplane."

Osgood looked at Oglethorpe as Oglethorpe snarled, "But we ain't sure. We were paid to be sure. I figure, Norb and me get in there again, maybe tonight, maybe a coupl'a nights if we gotta, and we push a probe in there with some plastique and—"

"For God's sake, no!" Osgood said without thinking.

Both men stopped walking and looked at him. They were almost to the end of the seawall, and Osgood gestured toward the street beyond and they kept walking. He could tell them the truth, but he wasn't supposed to do that. But

177

there were no viable alternatives. "I lied when I told you it was a fortune in diamonds you were looking for. And that's why you can't use any explosives, because explosives might bring on a disaster."

"What you talkin' about, John?"

Osgood looked at Oglethorpe, who'd stopped walking again. "I want your word that what I'm going to tell you and Norb right now goes no further than ourselves, ever. And before you commit, here are the options. If you betray this trust, despite our friendship over the years, I'll hunt you down and kill you both because I'd have no choice. If, for some reason, I were unable to, the Company would do it for me. This is that important." Oglethorpe's jaw clenched, his shoulders stiffened and for a moment Osgood thought they might come to blows right here on the street. Osgood kept talking. "If you opt to know this secret, you'll share knowledge that a select few men in Washington and Tokyo possess. I'd promise to double what we're paying you, but if I do that, then someone might decide to preempt any possibility that someday one of you might talk and have you killed anyway. Do you understand?"

Osgood looked at Oglethorpe and Kowalski in turn, Oglethorpe saying, "What the hell's so fuckin' important we gotta get into all this spy shit, John?"

"Do we have a deal, Steve?"

"We have a deal."

Osgood nodded and lit another cigarette. He shifted his cane under his arm. He pocketed his lighter and regrasped his cane. "All right, gentlemen. To make a long story short, there was a third atomic bomb that was to be dropped on Japan at the close of the war, only the Japanese leaders surrendered before it had to be used. The plane was called back, but never returned, and was written off as an ordinary casualty. It went down, we believe, right where the Friedman-Naguchi Expedition is looking. It is our belief—my belief—that the intent of the expedition is to salvage the bomb, which is still usable, and detonate it in one of the seacoast Japanese cities frequented by U.S. Naval vessels, laying the blame for the ensuing nuclear devastation on the United States. All this is a prelude to a coup against the Japanese government led by forces who are the spiritual descendants of the right-wing militarists who led Japan in World War Two. That, gentlemen, is why you cannot use explosives, because you might detonate the bomb."

"Holy shit," Norb Kowalski said almost as a sigh.

"After all these years the sucker'd still go up?"

"Possibly."

"But it can't be in one piece—"

Osgood didn't let him finish this time. "Do you think, gentlemen, that we are total fools? If the bomb were damaged, there'd be a radiation leak, right? So, instead of sending you to look for it with electronic imaging equipment, we would have sent you in with radiation detection equipment instead, wouldn't we? Those bombs were built," Osgood told them. "Ever see the kind of automobiles that were built following World War Two? Ever see a tank? Some—thank God, very few—bombs from that era still exist as bombs because to try to open them and remove the explosive elements might set them off; they're safer as they are. No. We're talking reality here, gentlemen. Clear?" He looked at Oglethorpe, then Kowalski.

"So, so much for an explosive probe, boss," Oglethorpe grinned.

He ate aboard the *Okane*, relishing the simple American fare. One of the deck apes doubled in the galley and had made thick, juicy hamburgers, French-fried potatoes, and chocolate pudding. And he served them all real American beer.

The plan was now to wait and observe while—hopefully—two things occurred. First, that Mulvaney, about whom he told Oglethorpe and Kowalski nothing at all, would stay alive long enough to witness the plane's discovery, then get word of that out through the established conduit. Second, that Takeuchi Arisato and his League of Blood followers would tip their hand, allowing Osgood the means of locating Takeuchi and killing him.

The one fault from the very beginning was that once the Friedman-Naguchi Expedition had located the bomb, the bomb might be spirited away and lost unless there was quick action. Interdicting any involvement by Takeuchi by killing the man first was the best insurance against that happening.

He said his good-nights, decided to forgo swinging over to the dock Errol Flynn style, and used the board gangplank. Then he started back toward his hired car which was parked near the rented office. The hotel—in the businessman style, and a member in good standing of the Japan Hotel Association—was twenty minutes away, near large horse pastures which, in the days of the shogunates, had been the breeding grounds for the horses of the samurai class. Today the horses were merely there as a beautiful diversion for the tourist trade.

As he walked, he was especially vigilant. Since Takeuchi's people had not tried for him last evening, the odds were greater they would try for him tonight. And, unavoidably exposing Steve and Norb, he had left himself intentionally wide open during the day.

Osgood worried little about some disaster befalling the men of the *Okane*. The ship would be gone with the evening tide. Takeuchi's men would have to strike with incredible precision and force because Oglethorpe, Kowalski and the four man crew of the *Okane* were professional and ridiculously well armed.

He worried more for himself at the moment. The Walther P-38K was out of its Sam Andrews shoulder holster and in his right hand behind the pocket of his coat. The coat was specially tailored to have a real pocket with a slit cut behind it through which a gun could be pushed, thus allowing free operation of a semiautomatic pistol which a normal pocket would preclude.

He reached his hired car without incident, checking the

back seat for unwanted visitors as he unlocked, then made a quick check of the vehicle—engine compartment, the pavement where a cut brake line would leak—and entered. He made it a general rule to rent either a Mercedes, a Jaguar, a Volvo or a BMW, the great European roadcars which combined speed and handling ability with mechanical reliability and creature comforts. The car he drove was a Mercedes, set up for standard drive from the left-hand side. He turned into the left-hand lane of the roadway—the Japanese drove like the British rather than Americans—and started out of the harbor district.

When he looked into the rearview mirror and saw two sets of lights that stayed with him when he turned onto the highway toward the hotel, he felt oddly happy.

Chapter Seventeen

The Shaping of Tomorrows

Mulvaney sat alone on the platform-like deck where, the previous evening, they'd discussed his job over drinks. After leaving Tadatoshi's *kōban*—Edith Blandish taught him that word and the word for police, *keisatsu*—and learning that Edith Blandish and Tom Westinghouse had been lovers, so many things had fallen in place for him.

Westinghouse had been Osgood's man aboard the expedition.

Edith didn't exactly know who Westinghouse had been working for, but knew he had been working for somebody. When the explosion and fire killed Westinghouse and the Japanese crew members on the delivery boat, she knew that Westinghouse's spying on Friedman and Naguchi was important.

Initially Mulvaney had wondered why, if Edith Blandish knew that Ladislaw Gorchek (whom she associated with Tom Westinghouse's death) wanted him to replace Westinghouse for the express purpose of murdering him, why had she been so enthusiastic about hiring him? But after a moment's further thought, that became obvious. Friedman, Naguchi, and Gorchek had killed her lover, but she didn't have any proof. They intended to kill Mulvaney once he replaced Westinghouse, but he was a cop, had a background in Special Forces, and was the perfect guy to either get the goods on the bad guys or kill them.

John Osgood was using him as bait and so was Edith Blandish—bait for the same catch.

Throughout the rest of the day Mulvaney familiarized himself with the other vessels in the expedition's little armada, checked fire extinguishers, checked storage of such hazardous substances as cleaning fluids and gasoline, reviewed emergency procedures in the event of fire or accident, and avoided Milo Weatherall. After examining the stowage of the diving equipment, Mulvaney was thoroughly convinced of two things: Milo, despite a poisonous personality, really knew his stuff; and the likelihood of the explosion and fire that claimed Westinghouse's life being an accident was even more remote than before.

There were certain sections of the *Archimedes* that were off-limits to everyone except Friedman and Naguchi themselves. Studies, they were called. As Edith Blandish explained it to him, both men were charmingly disorganized, and if someone moved the wrong piece of paper on a chart table or desk, finding it again might take forever.

Ed Mulvaney wondered what else might be in these studies. Possibly another radio, for use in contacting Gorchek, and probably an arms locker. Milo, a good number of his diving crew, and most of the deck apes gave every indication of being heavy-hitting professionals at more things than nautical-related duties.

He finished his beer, then set off in search of another one. He wanted a good night's sleep, with his diving knife beside his pillow, of course. By seven in the morning he'd be at a site briefing, then by late morning, as part of his safety inspection and familiarization, he'd be diving on the prime recovery zone with Friedman, Naguchi and Milo.

At the hotel John Osgood parked his car by himself rather than letting an attendant do it, wanting to keep his keys and wanting to know exactly where his car would be as well. He backed into the slot, too, in case he needed to make a quick exit.

The two sets of headlights, almost daring him to do something, had stayed behind him until he turned onto the hotel grounds.

The hotel room was very Western, like luxury-class accommodations at a Hilton, with a large bedroom, a sitting room, a large and comfortable bath, and a balcony. Being a business hotel, the businessman's amenities were in evidence everywhere—the desk in his room was actually large enough to work on, fax machines were in the lobby, Xeroxing services, secretarial services, and interpreting and translating services were available, as were full health club facilities, a jogging trail, horseback riding, and even a small man-made mountain, for persons who chose to get their exercise climbing.

Osgood checked the room for obvious things like explosive charges in the toilet, poison-tipped needles inside his pillow, and bugs. He found none of these, but had been at his profession long enough to worry about what he might not have found at all.

As Osgood sat at the desk and poured himself a drink, he called the concierge and made arrangements for a horse in the morning. If Takeuchi and the League of Blood did not try for him tonight, he wanted to give them a chance tomorrow morning that would be irresistible.

Chapter Eighteen

The Ketsumeidan Come

Catering to overseas businessmen as they did, the hotel stables offered a choice of western or English-style saddles. He chose western because it was the style to which he was most accustomed, although he preferred English for comfort. Horseback riding had never been his favorite outdoor pursuit, and such movie and television legends as Trigger, Champion, and the Lone Ranger's Silver notwithstanding, he'd always considered horses rather lacking in intelligence as well.

He checked the saddle and the adjustment of the cinch himself, then mounted. The horse, or *uma* as it was called in Japan, was enjoying a heightened popularity these days for sport riding and for racing. Historically, these animals— based in prehistory out of Chinese bloodlines—were restricted to the use of the samurai class. It had been a criminal act for anyone not socially acceptable to ride one. Japanese topography hadn't lent itself to the use of the horse as a farm animal, either.

He mounted carefully, the cane already lashed to his saddle, then gently heeled the animal away from the stable and onto the bridle path. The mare, a deep russet brown, and, typically of Asian horses, not terribly large, seemed gentle enough. They started into the forested area some distance to the rear of the hotel. The morning was beautiful and Osgood felt good, alert to the possibility of Takeuchi's people striking.

After arranging his morning ride and finishing his drink, he'd showered briefly, sat on his balcony with an afghan draped over his legs against the evening cold, smoked a cigarette, and lingered over a second drink.

It was often profitable to construct worst-case scenarios and plan in advance how one might turn them around. That was how he occupied his mind while sitting in the dark on his balcony. There were no lights silhouetting him, and there were no places within two hundred yards where a sniper could conveniently situate himself, so he was in relative safety; but his pistol was beside him nonetheless.

The ultimate worst-case scenario concerning Gorchek, Takeuchi, and the missing A-bomb was that Takeuchi would not show himself, Gorchek would successfully eliminate Mulvaney just prior to the bomb's recovery, and the bomb would be readied for detonation at some undisclosed site in the near future.

There were a variety of ways to detonate the weapon, but there were only two practical means. Since the bomb had never been armed, you could short-circuit the altitude switch, which would read zero or a little below, depending on how far below sea level it actually was. Or you could reset the altitude switch—which worked on relative air pressure —to some handy number, then convince the switch that number had been reached, perhaps through use of a decompression chamber such as the unit aboard the *Archimedes*.

Short-circuiting the altitude switch would result in imme-diate detonation. Fanatics were available by the bushel basketful almost anywhere in the world today, but not fanatics skilled enough to be able to penetrate the case, execute primary arming, then short-circuit the altitude switch. Once the altitude switch was short-circuited successfully, the bomb would immediately explode, vaporizing anything in the immediate vicinity. Such a technician would have to be a fanatic of world-class order.

The best method involved decompression, to fool the altitude switch. Essentially, it gave the device the convenience of a time bomb, allowing the persons who wished to detonate it to be far away when the device actually went off.

In either case, there was still the six-digit entry code which was linked to an elapsed time device. The entry code could not be discerned one digit at a time. One had to know the entire six-digit entry code, as there was a timer that reset if the code was incorrect.

This could be done without a computer, but might take years. With an ordinary computer the time frame would still be great. But by using the 486 SX chip in conjunction with the stolen Japanese supercomputer, forty-five minutes or less would get through the nine hundred nintey-nine thousand, nine hundred ninety-nine permutations of the six-digit number and the primary arming sequence would be achieved. All that would remain would be to fool the altitude switch and detonate whenever one wished.

There was always the possibility of a plane being used to drop the bomb, but if, after nearly five decades inside a B-29 at the bottom of the ocean, something went wrong with the altitude switch, the bomb would just fall like a grand piano in a Laurel and Hardy movie, never going off at all. With the decompression method, if the bomb didn't go off, the site where it was planted could be returned to and adjustments made. And detonated at ground level, the scenario that there was a nuclear accident concerning some U.S. Naval vessel would be more believable, at least in the media. That was what seemed to count more than anything these days.

If Takeuchi didn't show, if Mulvaney died prematurely, if the bomb wound up in enemy hands, what would his options be? Evacuate one hundred twenty-one million people from the four principal islands and the smaller islands offshore? Just sit tight and wait?

Neither of those options was viable.

As the bridle path curved off counterclockwise toward the north, the animal he rode reared her head, edged sideways along the path, and seemed to balk at going on.

John Osgood patted her neck. Perhaps horses were brighter than he'd always supposed. He urged her ahead, the reins in his left hand, his right hand by his belt, ready to slide up beneath the goatskin bomber jacket he wore to the pistol in his shoulder holster.

The animal moved slowly around the bend. Osgood thought he heard something in the trees. And then he knew what he heard. His right hand flashed toward his pistol while his left hand hauled back so hard on the animal's reins that she reared under him. A motorcycle dodged past the horse, steel flashing in the helmeted driver's right hand, just missing the horse's abdomen. Osgood could not reach his pistol; the placid trail horse was now a creature terrified by noise and a primitive sense of danger, bucking insanely under him. The first of the riders wheeled his machine to charge again, and two more roared out of the treeline toward him.

Osgood did the only thing he could do, tearing his cane from the thongs by the saddle horn and using it like a quirt on the mare's right flank as he dug in his heels. She vaulted ahead, almost colliding with the second biker. Steel whistled by Osgood's left shoulder as a foot-long sword—or *tsuto*—passed inches from him.

Osgood looked back and saw a fourth motorcycle joining the other three in pursuit. In a cowboy film the hero would have drawn his gun, twisted round in the saddle, and laid down withering fire against his opponents, shooting from his trusty steed. But John Osgood realized that if he fired as much as a single shot, the already terrified animal would become so totally uncontrollable she'd probably throw him.

His left hand grabbed the reins and the animal's short black mane. Osgood lowered himself in the saddle, rapping the cane along the horse's flanks again for more speed.

The motorcycles, of course, were gaining.

As the path turned south and clockwise, two more motorcycles came from out of the treeline to Osgood's left. Helmeted men were aboard, with knives the length of short swords mounted beside the farings of their machines. Osgood wheeled the animal right, off the path, and into the trees. These were scrub pine, evenly rowed, but wide enough apart so that when he kept his head low and hands in, only his trouser legs and the upper portion of the sleeves of his leather jacket were beaten by the boughs.

The ground began to rise. Suddenly he was out of the trees and climbing toward a ridgeline. Osgood looked back—the motorcycles were close behind him, weaving through the trees, but coming fast. To Osgood's left the ridgeline became progressively narrower and the ground rose still more sharply. To his right the ridge leveled out into a ravine, the ground on either side rising sharply. "Damn," he said. Osgood wrenched the animal's head to the right and gave her the cane again. She bolted forward, Osgood clinging to her.

Sweat already stained her neck and flanks in white crusty lines, and froth from her mouth sprayed Osgood in the slipstream around her. He kept urging her on, into the defile, the ground simultaneously rising upward and spreading outward on either side of him. In the distance was a crater lake.

The motorcycles were louder now, and without looking back, he knew they were closer. At any second they'd be flanking him, their riders hacking at him and the animal he rode. He should have gone to the left, trusting the narrowness of the ridgeline to keep them behind him rather than allow them to get on his flanks.

Twenty-twenty hindsight.

Beneath him the russet-brown trail horse was starting to

founder. Her stride was now uneven, her body seeming to lurch slightly forward as if she were throwing herself ahead rather than running. In a few minutes she'd be done for and he'd be afoot, if she didn't collapse under him and get him a broken leg.

"Come on, girl!" It was the sound of the voice, not the language, which mattered to children, to animals, and, he thought, sometimes to women. He stopped using the cane, knowing the animal was going as fast as she could already.

The ground began to rise as he neared the rim of the crater. The animal was stumbling, going on, and stumbling again—still running, but almost staggering, too.

He reached the height of the rim and started to rein her in so he could dismount, but she started collapsing under him. Osgood pushed away from the saddle and threw himself onto the ground, hitting it hard, coming up to his knees in a roll as the horse fell.

He grabbed his cane from the ground and ran, along the rim of the crater toward the water's edge. The sounds of the motorcycles behind him buzzed in his ears.

He didn't look back and didn't try to draw his gun. Instead, he ran into the water, wading in up to his waist, sucked in a deep breath, then dived in. His legs were brushed by the front wheel of a motorcycle as he breast-stroked into the cold depths. His gun might still function underwater, at least for a single shot, but accuracy, range, and terminal ballistics would be radically altered. If he surfaced, as long as the pistol was completely out of the water, it would function as normal. Modern ammunition was essentially waterproof—for a short period of time, at least.

The important thing was the motorcycles would be useless here.

John Osgood judged that he was about fifteen feet down and at least twice that distance from the rim of the crater. The water surrounding him was ice cold but crystal clear.

On the surface he could free the sword of the Crawford cane from its shaft, ready for use, in under fifteen seconds. It took a little longer underwater, and once he was through, he still had to unscrew the end cap with the rubber tip over it, all the while gliding slowly downward.

At last the cap was removed, and John Osgood started for the surface. He was temporarily disoriented as to which direction he'd come from. He broke the surface for an instant and reoriented himself. Three of the motorcycles moved along the crater's rim, patroling, to catch him when he came out. One of the motorcycles was parked near his entry point to the lake, two others were partially submerged, and three of his pursuers stood in water up to their waists, stripping their leathers.

John Osgood shook the tube free of most of the water, then tucked downward, the handle end of the cane to his lips and the opposite end protruding just above the waterline. An important question was answered for him when he surfaced for those few seconds. If they had seen him, as he knew one of them must have, and no one had opened fire, that meant his enemies were without guns or, for some reason, chose not to use them.

He swam toward the center of the lake, the sword in his right hand, the shaft he now used as a breathing tube in his left.

He thought of the assault on the castle of Tsukiyama Koji and of the affair in Rio off the Island of Love.

Events were repeating themselves, or his solutions to them were.

The goatskin bomber jacket was becoming progressively heavier. The only items in his pockets were the black driving gloves he rarely used for driving but often used for other matters, and the Leatherman Tool. He took the Leatherman Tool and the gloves, stuffed the tool into his right front trouser pocket, and packed the gloves in over it, securing the tool and his money clip.

Osgood shrugged out of the jacket and pushed it upward, letting it float away. He wanted further proof that his enemies had no intention of using firearms. There were no shots, and the jacket started to sink. He treaded water just beneath the surface, trying to plan his next move.

Suddenly that move was planned for him—response. As he looked right, he saw two of his pursuers closing on him, their knives—short sword-sized knives like the ones he'd seen earlier—out ahead of them, one man coming toward him from either side.

Osgood edged back through the water, using his breathing tube until the last possible minute when he would have to use it as a weapon. The only place to fight these men would be beneath the surface.

One of the two went to the surface, took in air, and started downward again as the second man went up for air. Now, as he should have seconds earlier, John Osgood struck. He inhaled as deeply as he could, pulled down the breathing tube, and launched himself through the water toward the man going toward the surface. Osgood ran the man through with his rapier, blood clouding the water instantly. As Osgood swam away, the second man closed on him very quickly. When the second man thrust with his knife, Osgood parried with the shaft of his cane, then lunged forward with his blade, opening up a wound across the man's left rib cage and under the left biceps. Nothing instantly fatal. At this stage John Osgood couldn't have cared less if the man died of old age with his grandchildren at his knee; he just wanted the man out of commission.

The swimmer fell back, surfacing for an instant. Osgood took the opportunity to break the surface as well. He tucked down just as the second man came for him.

Again Osgood parried the thrust of his assailant's knife with the shaft of his cane. He sliced the blade of the rapier through the water, just missing the man's throat.

The killer's knife and Osgood's cane shaft were no longer

locked, and the edge of the enemy weapon swiped within inches of Osgood's left arm. Osgood stabbed the sword forward, punching the spike-shaped tip into and through the left side of the man's neck. A cloud of blood larger than anything before nearly engulfed John Osgood as he wrenched the blade of his sword free and swam for the surface.

He inhaled the cold air, his throat and lungs aching. His left hand shook the cane shaft clear of water. The third man he'd seen by the rim of the crater wasn't there anymore. The other three were still patroling near the water's edge on their motorcycles. Again John Osgood brought the shaft to his lips and tucked beneath the surface.

He looked around him, saw the body of one of the two men he'd killed floating up toward the surface, but there was no sign of the man from the crater rim. Keeping the end of the shaft just barely above the surface, he swam thirty-one inches below the surface. The length of the shaft was precisely thirty-three inches.

Where was the third man?

Osgood kept moving. His plan was a simple one. The men sent to kill him would assume he would make for the side of the rim where the unattended motorcycle was, attempt to steal it, and use it for his escape from the crater.

That was his plan, except for one slight modification.

Osgood reckoned that by now he was nearing the opposite rim, as the lake bottom was shoaling upward steadily. Behind him, he saw the third man coming down from the surface and looking side to side. Osgood broke right and swam parallel to the rim now, not toward it, realizing that if he tried to race toward the rim, the third man would merely surface, shout to the others still on shore, and his plan would be blown.

John Osgood turned in the water, keeping the shaft protruding just above the surface so he could breathe. It was hard to see perfectly, because to use the cane shaft as a breathing tube it was necessary to crane the neck back or turn the head to the side. He chose the latter, but this severely cut down on peripheral vision and made a radical alteration in his field of view. It required a one-hundred-eighty-degree turn of his body.

He kept the third man in sight. Osgood's eyes were riveted on the weapon the man held. This was the ultimate Samurai weapon, a three-and-a-half-foot-long *Katana* sword.

The man surfaced, taking his last breath before the fight commenced. Osgood still utilized the tube. Mulvaney's skill with a blade was the one thing John Osgood envied of his friend. Osgood possessed no such skill. With an ordinary knife he was better than average. With his sword cane against a shorter blade, he was evenly matched or better. But against a full-length sword, Osgood was at a distinct disadvantage, assuming the man knew how to use it. The only hope John Osgood had was that the water so telegraphed physical intent and so slowed movement that he might have some chance to hold his own and win.

The man was coming full at him now. John Osgood took his last deep breath through the shaft of the cane, then brought it downward to parry any thrust made by his opponent. His own blade was clutched tightly in his right fist.

To use a sword, Osgood was convinced, there was some genetically based talent. Mulvaney had it. He didn't. And he hoped his assailant didn't have it, either.

But the third man evidently did. Despite the water retarding his speed of motion, John Osgood was barely able to parry the sword thrust with the shaft of the cane. And he was unable to strike with his own weapon.

The third man's sword moved again, missing Osgood's throat by inches.

Osgood made his decision.

He edged back through the water, closer to the shoaling bottom, nearer to the rim.

The problem with guns and water was that the gun needed to be entirely submerged or entirely free. If it were partially in and partially out, pressures could cause even the best gun to rupture a barrel and possibly explode.

John Osgood let the sword and the cane shaft fall from his hands toward the bottom just below him. To get his gun in time, with its holster sodden, would take both hands.

As the third man started for him, an evil look on the water-distorted face, Osgood's left hand clutched at the top of the holster. His right thumb broke the snap, and his right hand pulled. The gun didn't budge for a split second and Osgood almost panicked. But he'd realized years ago that panic only helped his opponent.

He kept pulling on the butt of the P-38K. He cleared leather and pulled the trigger when the man was about five feet away. The first shot would have to count, since the gun might jam after that.

The pistol bucked oddly in Osgood's right hand, and Osgood was shoved back, his right wrist aching.

The man trying to kill him with a sword just floated there for a second, and then the fingers of the man's right hand opened. The sword floated away and downward, and the man stared blankly at Osgood. Air bubbles spread from the man's open mouth almost as quickly as the blood spread from the fatal wound in the man's chest.

John Osgood realized he was out of air. He pushed himself upward through the water, his head breaking the surface, his mouth gulping air for his greedy lungs. There was no way to tell if the shot he'd fired was perceived on the land. As he looked at his gun, he saw that it wasn't jammed. The action was closed, and the hammer was cocked for the next shot.

He silently thanked West German craftsmanship, then worked the decocking lever to lower the hammer, breaststroking downward after his cane and his blade. Osgood recaptured them both, then stuffed the pistol into

195

his right hip pocket and broke the surface again. He cleared the tube and went down after a quick glance shoreward. Nothing had changed. He thought he'd caught a glimpse of a body floating on the surface, but wasn't sure.

Osgood swam toward the rim, adjusting the angle on the cane shaft so very little of it would protrude above the surface. This also made the positioning of his head and neck more comfortable.

Although it was like looking through the bottom of a Coke bottle, he could see the rim—just clearly enough so that the mass of a man and a machine passing was discernible.

He treaded water near the surface, the cane shaft extended almost horizontally now. He shifted the sword to his left hand as well and drew the pistol from his hip pocket. There was one other problem with guns and water. When one came out of the water with a gun, the barrel had to be cleared of the water inside to keep the barrel from rupturing.

He thought of the best, most logical way to do that.

Osgood worked the heel of the butt magazine release for the Walther, freed the magazine, and put the magazine between his belt and his abdomen for a second. Then, clamping his teeth tightly on the shaft of the cane/snorkel, and keeping the sword under his armpit, Osgood had both hands free to rack the pistol's slide rearward, ejecting the chambered round. Osgood held the slide back and worked up the slide stop.

He retrieved the magazine from his waistband, put the magazine up the butt of the 9mm, but left the action locked.

He regripped the sword and the cane in his left hand and stared upward through the water, waiting for his target to come.

And he saw it—a red motorcycle with red farring just like the others—coming toward him around the rim.

Osgood stroked forward as powerfully as he could, letting go of his cane and sword as he rose out of the water, punching the pistol upward, the water in the barrel spilling rearward over the barrel's feed ramp, his right thumb working down the slide stop, his left hand cupping around his right hand. The action closed, but hesitantly.

It was too late now for anything else. The motorcycle-mounted killer saw him and started to turn his machine.

John Osgood pulled the P–38K's trigger and hoped.

The pistol bucked once in his hands, and the man grasped at his chest, falling from his machine. The machine spun out onto its side, with the rear wheel still turning. Osgood simultaneously decocked and bent into the water, grabbed his sword and cane, then started running toward the overturned motorcycle.

He slipped where sand and rock met, fell to his right knee, cursed, and ran on, his knee hurting. He looked to his right. One of the two remaining killers was coming toward him full tilt. Osgood wheeled toward the man, hoping the Walther would keep right on working, and fired it, then again and again. He hit the man with the second and third shots.

There were only three shots remaining in the Walther. It carried an eight-round magazine plus one in the chamber, making nine. Osgood had fired one underwater, one breaking surface, three more now, and ejected one round from the action before he surfaced.

And he wanted one man alive.

The sixth man would have to be the one.

Osgood, limping from his banged knee, climbed out of the water onto the crater rim. He saw the sixth man now turning his machine, starting away from the rim.

There was no time to change magazines, and a gun was not the answer here, anyway. John Osgood limped toward the overturned Kawasaki Ninja.

He cast down the shaft from the Crawford sword cane, but lay the sword itself across the handlebars as he righted the machine.

As he jump-started it, he sucked in his breath against the pain in his knee.

Twisting the red motorcycle under him, Osgood revved

the engine, then let out the clutch. The machine moved so suddenly beneath him that Osgood nearly fell. He hadn't ridden a motorcycle in more years than he wanted to remember, and this was hardly the ideal terrain for a refresher course. He held on, throttling up once he was off the rim and onto a more forgiving surface, in pursuit of a killer he had to take alive.

The last of the six men was retracing the original course of the pursuit, heading up the ravine and toward the ridgeline. Osgood matched the man's speed, not gaining, but not losing. Near the crest of the ridge where they had come out of the pines, the sixth man cut a fast left, the bike nearly skidding out from under him. Osgood increased his speed now, realizing that if he did not intercept the man in the trees, he'd never get him at all.

Like the swordplay, John Osgood knew his own limitations all too well. This man was a better biker than Osgood had ever been or ever would be.

But there was something to be said for reckless abandon. Osgood tried that as he reached the turnoff from the ridgeline, his right knee screaming with pain as he torqued the bike into the turn with the sheer force of his legs, whacking himself in the testicles against the saddle, and cursing aloud as the pain radiated outward. He doubled forward in a wave of nausea, but he kept control of the Ninja. He got his speed up again, throttling into top gear.

The cold air around him dried his sodden clothing against his bare skin and made him shiver. The pain in his testicles subsided, but not the pain in his knee. He leaned his body low over the handlebars, realizing that he was gaining on the man he chased.

They were in among the trees now, dodging their machines around the tree trunks, zigzagging right and left at full speed. A spray of dust and gravel was thrown against Osgood's face as he narrowed the gap. He squinted his eyes, clutched the handlebars, and clutched his sword as well.

He came up on the left of the enemy biker. The man's right hand held a long-bladed knife, possibly a Cold Steel Magnum Tanto. If it was, it was a good knife, stout, strong and sharp, and vastly heavier than his own blade. Osgood pressed nearer, not three feet behind the man he pursued. His right leg slammed against a tree's trunk.

Osgood nearly lost control of the machine, but kept going.

They were nearly to the bridle path where the other man, a superior rider, would escape.

Osgood tested the machine to see if there was an ounce more speed in it. And he found the three feet between the two machines now two, then one. Suddenly, as he bounced the Ninja over a hillock and swerved around a pine trunk, they were side by side. The would-be killer hacked cross body with his blade. Osgood let the bike drift left and away, then cut the fork hard right. Osgood's right hand, holding the sword, hacked outward.

Osgood's blade sliced through leather and across the back of the other man's right wrist. The long tanto-shaped blade fell from the man's grasp, bouncing along the ground beside them.

They hit the bridle path, their machines still side by side. Osgood cast his sword down into the path and reached out and grabbed for a handful of the man's leather jacket. He threw himself from the saddle of his own machine against his would-be killer.

Osgood's body slammed against the man. Osgood's frame vibrated with the impact as he twisted right, throwing his body weight hard, his hands locked to the man's neck and shoulders.

The motorcycle jumped something, and Osgood, still holding the man, was airborne. He hit the ground, and the Japanese rolled over him, slamming down.

Osgood lay on his back, breathless, head aching, with his knee on fire.

The Japanese was up and threw his helmet toward

199

Osgood's head. Osgood's left arm blocked it, and the face of his Rolex took the impact and shattered. Osgood sucked air, launched himself forward, and caught the man's right ankle, pulling him down.

The Japanese was large, but wiry and strong. He twisted free, kicked toward Osgood's face, and missed, but struck Osgood's right shoulder. Osgood was drawing the Walther from his right hip pocket and the 9mm flew from Osgood's right hand onto the bridle path.

The Japanese was moving again. Osgood scrambled to his feet, throwing himself toward the man, and caught him by the shoulders, bulldogging him to the dirt. They rolled over and over. When Osgood was on the bottom, the Japanese's right fist crashed down toward Osgood's throat. Osgood dodged his head right, and the Japanese's fist smashed the ground. Osgood's right hand moved, and the Crawford Special Dart snapped from its sheath on the magazine carrier under his right arm. As the Japanese—the knuckles of his glove torn away, his right wrist dripping blood— started another hammer drop blow, Osgood rammed the spike-shaped custom knife into the man's left kidney. Osgood's left knee smashed upward simultaneously.

The man shrieked in pain and rolled back onto the ground. His back arched, his hands grasped at his testicles, and his lips drew back over his teeth in a rictus of agony.

Osgood was up, his left foot snapping out, catching the man at the side of the head, and slamming him to the ground.

Osgood bent his left knee and dropped his full weight onto the Japanese's chest. There was a rush of foul-smelling air as Osgood brought the blood-smeared blade against the man's throat.

Osgood didn't waste time on Japanese. If this man didn't understand, it was his problem. Osgood took a deep breath, felt better, and said, "You have two kidneys. This is a mathematics quiz. How many throats?"

For a split second the man said nothing, then answered, "One!"

"Good. Takeuchi Arisato's League of Blood sent you to kill me, friend. Tell me where he is. Otherwise, that will be the last word you'll ever say."

The Japanese hesitated all of four seconds, then nodded his head once and grunted, *"Hai,* Osgood-san!"

Chapter Nineteen

Down to the Sea in Tiny Yellow Submarines

She was pointing to a map. "This is where the north equatorial current swings upward, toward us," Edith Blandish told him as he leaned over the chart table. The map was of the Northern Pacific, specifically Japan, the Philippines, the China coast, and the Korean peninsula. "See?"

He told her he saw and her eyes went back to the chart table.

"You see, Ed. All the oceans of the world are broken up into temperature and salinity belts. The greatest surface salinities in the Pacific occur in the southeast, where they can get as high as thirty-seven parts per thousand. In the extreme north they can be less than thirty-two parts per thousand. Rainfall and surface temperatures lead to evaporation, and all of this affects the ocean.

"The majority of the north equatorial current veers northward to make up the Kuroshiro Current. Off to the east it forms the Kuroshiro Extension. But a branch of that comes from the Straits of Tsushima. Now, Ed, the Tsushima-kiakyo is part of a deep basin, but the sill depths, where we're at, can be less than seven hundred feet. Right in the heart of the basin you've got depths in excess of six thousand feet, which of course makes any kind of recovery work impossible for divers. You can use remote probes, unmanned submersibles, and things like that. But we're very lucky."

Mulvaney looked at her while he lit a cigarette, smiled, and said, "All right, I'll bite. Why are we so lucky?"

She smiled. Her smile was a nice one—very warm.

"The reason we're so lucky, Ed, is that the shelf here off the island is very similar to the shelf structure off the four main islands. Aside from the usual collection of troughs and basins, we're looking at depths ranging from four hundred thirty feet to thirteen hundred feet."

"Yeah, Edith, but how does that make us so lucky? You're looking at maybe a hundred thirty feet or so for any kind of practical repeatable dive without going through tons of hassle. But thirteen hundred feet?"

"You're right, Ed, and you're wrong. When you really know what you're doing and you're damned careful, about three hundred feet with twenty decompression stops, and with an exotic gas mixture is about the practical limit. And then you're talking about an hour and a half's worth of bottom time at the most. But what we're using to get down to the site where we think the wreckage is are NEWTSUITs. But we don't have that many NEWTSUITs to use, and we need divers midwater to help pull up items that we recover and to operate some of the electronic equipment that we're utilizing to pinpoint the wreckage site. What we've got on average is three people in the NEWTSUITs working at the eight-hundred-foot depths and the rest of the diving team down around a hundred twenty feet or so on Nitrox."

Mulvaney started to say, "And that's the stuff that—"

Edith Blandish's voice was low when she looked at him and said, "That's the stuff that exploded and killed Tom."

"I've never used Nitrox," he told her, "but when I was in Special Forces, we did some stuff with oxygen-enriched air to fudge on Equivalent Air Depth."

"It's basically the same thing, Ed, but it's a lot more precise. As an experienced diver you know that the two biggest problems when you dive on straight air are narcosis, and if you're going to any good depth much below thirty feet or staying down at that depth for any protracted period of time, the decompression. Now, if you stick with the U.S. No Decompression tables and follow them religiously, which you're supposed to do, theoretically you won't get into any trouble. But No Decompression tables don't take into account—and can't take into account—flow rate. That's dependent upon the amount of physical activity you're performing and the amount of carbon dioxide you're producing.

"What the Nitrox does," Edith Blandish continued, looking at him, "is allow you a vastly greater bottom time. When Milo was giving his briefing this morning, he was talking about total dive times exclusive of surface intervals in excess of an hour and a half, which is only possible with a sixty-eight/thirty-two nitrogen-oxygen mixture. All it does is give you the same bottom time at a greater depth than you have on air at shallow depths. So we'll be spending a good hour down there the first time before we ever have to surface, still have plenty of reserve in case something comes up that would keep us down longer. We'll be able to make repeat dives of shorter duration with that same safety margin, and we won't require any additional surfacing beyond what we did initially.

"Now," Edith said, "the guys in the NEWTSUITs could stay down at a greater depth for as long as forty-eight hours without any kind of decompression worries or any kind of special gas mixtures."

Mulvaney mentioned, "They'd be awful hungry after a while, not to mention having to take a quick whizz."

Edith Blandish laughed, and if he hadn't known her better, he would have thought she was blushing. "I'm not saying anybody would stay down for forty-eight hours, but they could! In the NEWTSUITs they can work in a normal one-atmosphere habitat without any custom decompression tables or anything like that. The man inside the suit—now these things weigh about eight hundred pounds and are all aluminum—can move around on the bottom, walk comfortably, and have almost a full degree of motion. The joints, Ed, are fluid-filled for low friction, yet give you mobility at those enormous depths. When we go up on deck, you'll be able to see for yourself. If you get the chance while you're here," she said, the enthusiasm in her voice something she wouldn't have been able to disguise even if she tried, "you've gotta try one."

He'd seen the suits during his safety inspection. They looked like little yellow submarines. . . .

Although it was the middle of winter, the wind that blew across the deck of the platform was almost warm. The sky was bright, but there were dark clouds to the south and west. Here rain would fall, but as the clouds reached the coast of the main islands, there would be snow.

Mulvaney ran his hands back through his hair, but the wind was blowing the wrong way and his hair kept blowing into his eyes and face.

Along the far side of the platform from where he and Edith Blandish stood, both of them wearing black dry suits, there were three teams of three men each, each team helping a fourth man into one of the yellow, self-contained NEWTSUITs. The suits separated into upper and lower halves. One of the men had only partially suited up and had the lower half on. The other two were fully suited, breathing through their systems. Edith was pulling on her dry suit's hood. She said to Mulvaney over the wind, "See those propellers behind the arms on the right and left side?" He nodded that he did. "They only rotate in one direction, but the pitch is variable, so in mid-water you can use them to take you forward or backward. Whatever. Once you get the hang of it—so they tell me—it's like flying through the water. Neat."

"Yeah, neat. What do you do when you're on the bottom?"

"Just walk. Sort of. The sole of the right boot has a system of pressure-sensitive pads built into it. When you want to go forward, you just push down with your toes. Backward, you push down with your heel. Sideways, just angle your right foot in the direction you want and you go. To keep you going, when you're in mid-water, each suit has two sets of thrusters. Just like a mini-sub that encapsulates only you."

"Do they build 'em for two?"

She looked at him and laughed as she stuffed fringes of her hair under the hood like a bathing cap.

"Doc! Mulvaney!"

Mulvaney looked behind them. It was Milo, waving them over toward one of the launches that would carry them out to the *Kiji,* the work boat off which Mulvaney, Edith Blandish, and three actual diving team personnel would be working. Mulvaney caught up his gear, except for tanks, which would be provided on the *Kiji.* He knew a little bit more about Nitrox than he'd let on, having done some research on his own with some help.

Years ago he'd made the acquaintance of Jim Foley, a diving expert who'd worked in the Midwest and just recently moved to Colorado. Foley, a lean, muscular guy with a good sense of humor, had been at diving since 1955, for the Navy mainly, and had almost as many certifications in diving as he had gray hairs. After talking with Edith Blandish in Chicago, he'd called Jim and mapped out where the Friedman-Naguchi Expedition was working. He called Jim again when he'd changed planes in Honolulu. Jim had already put together a package of material for him, and Mulvaney took notes over the phone. Nitrox had to be what they were using, Foley had told him, and then gave him some information concerning the NEWTSUITs (which Foley had theorized the expedition would be using). Foley did emphasize one thing about Nitrox. Any traces of oil or rust, or any other foreign compound, in a tank where Nitrox was to be used would result in one thing—an explosion.

The normal air people breathed was seventy-eight percent nitrogen, twenty-one percent oxygen, and one percent inert gases. Below one hundred thirty feet the Nitrox mixture was no longer safe. It would be like breathing toxic gas because of the effect the pressure had on the oxygen.

One could add nitrogen in two ways: one could mix nitrogen and oxygen together, or trickle oxygen into a stream of compressed air. The first process was expensive and necessitated resupply all the time. The second process could be dangerous. Just the friction of the molecules contacting one another, then coming into contact with something as simple as a silicone lubricant, could make a spark and blow the mixture.

Once Mulvaney had learned the details surrounding Tom Westinghouse's death, he'd known for certain what the Japanese policeman he'd met suspected but couldn't prove. The only way Westinghouse and the Japanese crew personnel could have had an explosion, unless they were trying to cause one, would have been if they were filling tanks aboard the vessel which blew up. They hadn't been doing that, because the tanks were already filled.

Someone had done something as simple as setting a very small explosive charge on one of the tanks, perhaps disguised as a pressure-check valve, or shot into one of the tanks. The sun deck of the *Archimedes* would have been a perfect spot for that, commanding a good overview of the target area but obscure enough so that the casual observer wouldn't have noticed anything. The sound of the cartridge firing would have been immediately masked to all but the most well-trained ears by the louder sound of the explosion aboard the tender vessel.

If he made it up from this dive alive, Ed Mulvaney intended to check the off-limits areas aboard the *Archimedes,* find the arms locker, and look for a sniper rifle. The rifle shot would have been a clean operation. If Tom Westinghouse was a pro sent in by John Osgood, something abnormal on one of the tanks would have attracted his attention and enabled him to avoid the blast.

It had to be a rifle shot.

Milo stood on the edge of the platform, waiting for them. Despite Milo's height, his heavy musculature made him appear stocky. A stocky build was the perfect build for a sniper. . . .

The equipment was all the best, from Delphi digital readout dive computers to Mares MR 12 V vortex-assisted regulators—the same kind NASA used in the astronaut training program. They were diving on single tanks, something Mulvaney had done but had always inherently distrusted. On dual tanks, if there was a problem, the diver had the option of switching off one tank and running on the other. With a solo setup, when one tank went, it was all over unless you were close to the surface or had a buddy you could share air with.

Mulvaney sat on a utility chest cover, pulling on his black fins. He hated fins because they made his feet sweat, so he always pulled them on just before going over the side. He checked his snorkel and his regulator one more time.

The leader of the dive team on the *Kiji,* a Japanese named Taihei, stood aft and called to them. "You guys ready?"

Mulvaney looked at Ed and she nodded. He called back to the American-sounding man, "Ready as we'll ever be, man."

"Right." Taihei signaled them over toward the open railing on the stern gunwale.

One thing Mulvaney hated more than putting on his flippers was walking in them on the deck of a boat. It was like walking in cement, or something that smelled worse, looked worse, and washed off less easily.

He helped Edith into her tank, checked her regulator for her, and checked her BC vest. He imagined, if you were female, diving had to make you feel good, because women had more natural body fat and floated more easily. Either that, or it made you feel bad if you had too much fat to begin with.

Taihei looked down at Mulvaney's right leg and the Cold Steel Tanto sheathed there and laughed. "That's a diving knife, man?"

Mulvaney told him honestly, "I dive in rough neighborhoods."

Chapter Twenty

Water

Mulvaney came out of the roll and breathed, Edith splashing in beside him. Through the wireless communication system built into his regulator, he asked her, "Where'd they park this thing?"

"Should be that way." She gestured to the north with her right hand, her left hand holding a spear gun.

Mulvaney checked the computer, reading the Allowable Nitrogen line, the Remaining No Decompression Time, Depth, Time into the dive, Tank Pressure, Water Temperature, and maximum time on his tanks. The No Decompression numbers and the tank time numbers were not supposed to coincide. Everything read out as it should be.

Edith was already swimming toward the central open space within the circle made by the tender vessels and the platform itself. The *Archimedes'* hull was visible as a blurred white shape off in the distance.

Ahead, he could see the yellow deep-dive suits spiraling downward ahead of a wake of foam. Below them, but well up in mid-water, were the two- or three-person open-top mini-subs Edith had told him about. He recognized them from some James Bond movie. Called Reef Rangers, from Submersible Systems Technology, they were operational to a depth of 120 feet with a range of about eighteen miles depending on speed and payload. Maximum speed was three and one-half knots. The advantage of the mini-subs for the Friedman-Naguchi Expedition was obvious—the less exertion, the less carbon dioxide the diver exhaled, and the longer the Nitrox supply would last. With only one diver aboard, the submarines could be used for light hauling. If the dig site had been nearer the surface, tubing hooked to the prop (after it was shrouded) could channel the backwash and be used as an economical means of cleaning the area.

The same part of him that took pride in owning an antique Porsche held a fascination with gadgets. But since he'd never operated one of the Reef Rangers and Edith ran one frequently as actual supervisor of the dig, she would pilot and he would be the passenger. If Gorchek wanted him dead, there was no better place for making that happen than underwater.

There was something nagging at the back of his mind, too—something about Edith. One of the divers directed them toward one of the subs, and as they buckled in, Mulvaney asked her, "What exactly is your function here? I mean, I know you're the liaison for everything, but in terms of the project, I mean."

He heard her laughter through the earpiece under his hood. "I'm the field supervisor, Ed!"

"What's a field supervisor do?"

"Years ago, when the Treasures of Tutankhamen were on display in Chicago, did you go?"

"As a matter of fact, I did. I'm not as totally, irredeemably acultural as I lead people to believe, Ed," Mulvaney told her. The machine was coming to life under her hands now, the prop wash spilling out behind them. "I had a friend whose aunt or something was a museum member, and I used the membership card and got in without all the waiting in lines. I gotta confess, it was really something."

"Oh, I agree. But if you remember, Lord Carnarvon was the actual archeologist, while Howard Carter was the field man who actually made the find. I'm sort of like Carter to Friedman and Naguchi. They're too busy to be down here, seeing that the work goes the right way; so here I am!"

And now it hit him, what had been nagging at him since they'd first started talking about the NEWTSUIT and the depths at which the actual work was taking place. "You said you never wore a NEWTSUIT."

"They keep promising me," she told him.

He wondered how much range there was on the two-way radios they used. So he told her, "Take us for a ride, over that way," and he pointed toward the farthest edge of the circle, where the platform was. There was something he had to talk to her about, and fast.

Water could ruin a gun, of course, but wasn't like acid. There were some terrible problems that required instant solving once he'd apprehended the sixth and last of the men sent to kill him. He found a convenient pine tree and had the man climb the tree at gunpoint, then shinny down it with legs crossed beneath him. The pain this caused was excruciating, and in a short period of time if the man were not helped out of this position, the muscles would automatically contract, his body would snap rearward, and his back would break. It was an old trick from World War II that one of his instructors had taught him when he was just getting started in the spy business. It was still effective.

John Osgood had no intention of letting the man die, of course, so time was of the essence. He could not walk into his hotel wearing sodden clothing and a wet shoulder holster, with his hair askew and shoes squeaking with water. And his knee hurt very badly. At least now the limp he affected to cover for his carrying the cane was genuine.

Instead of coming back toward the hotel's entrance, he made his way toward his own small suite, climbing up into his room along the network of balconies with some difficulty, hoping he would not surprise the chambermaid.

There was no time to run through the shower, so he just changed into clean, dry clothing. While he did that, he called the private number of Minoru Toshiyuki. A servant answered, and after a couple of minutes the old man himself was on the line. "Minoru-san?"

"There is something of urgency, Osgood-san?"

"Yes, Minoru-san. Six came visiting me; one stayed behind to converse with us at greater length, but he and I will need some transportation in order for all of us to get together."

"I understand. Where shall we meet, Osgood-san?"

"If you are familiar with my hotel, I would suggest the road beyond the bridle paths, or the field beyond should you decide on arriving more rapidly."

"Your transportation will, indeed, arrive rapidly, Osgood-san. In the field beyond the bridle paths." He hung up.

John Osgood finished buttoning his shirt, quickly disassembled the Walther P-38K, and used the hair dryer to dry some of the moisture. Then he lubed the weapon overgenerously with Break-Free CLP. As soon as time and circumstances permitted, he would have to strip the gun. There was nothing for the shoulder holster now, but he did run oil over the Special Dart and the rapier blade of his sword cane. The rest was aircraft aluminum and essentially insusceptible to rust.

The cursory attention to his weapons took three minutes, and then he was gone. He limped leaving the hotel, as a large bruise surrounded his right knee. Considerable stiffness was setting in.

With any luck, he'd be able to extricate the Ketsumeidan assassin from the potentially fatal hug with the pine tree before the man's back snapped like a twig.

* * *

The Reef Ranger was well out of radio contact area with the other personal submarines, the NEWTSUITs, and the surface vessels. Ed Mulvaney already had a story ready in case anyone asked why they'd gone that far afield. "I was curious how fast this sucker'd go, and Edith wouldn't let it full out where there were divers around who might get hurt." That sounded dumb enough and at least marginally plausible.

He asked Edith the important question. "If you've never been inside a NEWTSUIT and there aren't any mini-subs with the expedition that are capable of traveling as deep as the NEWTSUITs, have you ever seen the actual site of the dig?"

She laughed. "Of course I have, Ed. Video. We've got video feed going up to the *Archimedes,* and we keep a tape of everything."

Mulvaney considered that, then said, "Remember all the talk there was in the late sixties and early seventies from some people about the United States fixing the moon landings?"

"Yes. Why? You don't think our country—"

"No. I believe the moonshots were real, but consider what I'm implying, Ed," Mulvaney told Edith Blandish. "Three NEWTSUITs are down there. How many have you ever seen on video, live, I mean, at once?"

There was a long pause as she piloted the Reef Ranger through a school of fish. Almost mechanically she told him, "Those are bluefin tuna. There used to be a lot more of them around here in years gone by, and herring and sardines, too."

"I like herring."

She turned her head and looked at him over her left shoulder. "Only one suit, Ed, but in the taped stuff I've seen—"

"All three, or maybe two, but sometimes all three, right?"

"Yes." Her voice came back to him over the link almost as a whisper.

214

Mulvaney, without thinking, checked the Delphi computer. All conditions were normal, and because of the Reef Ranger, his tank supply was down even less than he would have thought. "They're not looking for some boat Kubla Khan lost, Edith. They're looking for a World War II vintage B-29 bomber. According to the people who sent me here, there's maybe a half-billion in diamonds aboard her, but there might be something else. I think I'm Tom Westinghouse's replacement in more ways than one."

She looked at him again, and the mini-sub seemed to stutter as she said, "Then—"

"Then, what you're seeing has been set up for you to see, Edith. You said yourself that the guys can stay down as long as forty-eight hours in a NEWTSUIT, so there's nothing preventing them from staging a little play for your benefit each time they're down, leaving one guy on camera working away—in the suits you couldn't tell who was who—while the real work goes on off camera."

"But diamonds? In an old plane? How would they have gotten there, and how would Dr. Friedman or Dr. Naguchi know anything about diamonds?"

So Mulvaney told her the story, leaving out Osgood's name, any reference to the CIA, or the government. As he told her the story, half-formed thoughts were beginning to take shape on another level of consciousness, and were beginning to bother him.

About what was true and what wasn't.

About Gorchek.

About the 486 SX chip.

About a B-29 eight hundred feet down in the water.

Chapter Twenty-one

Inquisitors

He'd read western novels as a boy and seen his share of theatrical and television westerns as well. An overwhelming impression drawn collectively from these was that the American Indians were a stoic people. His experiences as an adult had taught him much the same about the Japanese.

And stoics seemed remarkably unaffected by pressure.

John Osgood respected stoicism, more as a way of life than a stated philosophy, but this afternoon Osgood's perception of stoicism had turned into what Ed Mulvaney would have called "a royal pain in the ass."

According to Minoru, one of the three finest gunsmiths in all of Japan was now detail stripping and cleaning Osgood's gun and the two spare magazines that had been drowned with it. The weapon had been flown to the expert by helicopter, to be returned within the hour. Meanwhile, his shoulder holster was being carefully dried and treated to retard the effect of the water, and to restore the leather. His hopes for his gun were, justifiably, he felt, quite high. His hopes for the holster were not. The Andrews holster was among the finest gun leather to be had, he felt, and perhaps Sam Andrews himself could restore it, but that was its only chance. The most likely process was getting Andrews to make him another once he returned stateside.

His cane and the Crawford Special Dart were on the small table in front of him in the cellar of Minoru's home. What the cellar—a bare room with nothing but a Western-style table and several chairs—was routinely used for Osgood did not know. Today, it was an interrogation chamber.

Compounding the natural tendency toward stoicism, which Osgood viewed as a Japanese racial trait, there was also the matter of this man, who would divulge only that his given name was Akio. As member of the Ketsumeidan, or League of Blood, a follower of Takeuchi Arisato, and ready to kill because Takeuchi said so, the odds on this man divulging anything useful in the short term without sophisticated drug therapy were minimal.

And time might be running out, both for capturing the bomb and preventing Ed Mulvaney's being killed over it.

Minoru Toshiyuki and three Japanese men in their late twenties or early thirties, the latter in conservatively tailored business suits, shared the basement chamber with Osgood.

Only Osgood, Minoru-san, and Akio, the sixth and possibly most hapless of the assassins, sat. The three young men, not a tie at half-mast, not a jacket removed, not a short, black hair out of place, stood silently—one on either side of the table, one beside the solitary doorway.

Minoru-san spoke to Akio, who seemed perfectly bilingual (not all that common in Japan), in English rather than Japanese. Perhaps he sensed somehow that Osgood didn't trust the situation and Minoru-san's committee one hundred percent.

"You are aware that you have committed very grave crimes."

"Yes."

"You are aware that I have the authority to have you summarily executed."

"Yes."

"Where is Takeuchi Arisato?"

"I will not tell you."

"You know that I can have tortures used against you."

"Yes."

"You are aware that eventually you will tell me what I wish to know."

This was sounding terribly like a World War II B-movie, Osgood thought. All that was needed was for Minoru-san to be wearing a khaki uniform, smoking a cigarette with an ivory holder, and holding a Nambu pistol casually in his hand.

And suddenly John Osgood realized that that was exactly what it had to be.

He decided to pay close attention to the next reel to make sure.

Minoru asked Akio, "Do you wish to die for the Ketsumeidan?"

"That is my honor."

"Then why did you not stay and continue in the attempt made by your brothers to kill Osgood-san?"

"I was a coward. I am unworthy."

"Will you tell us what you know concerning Takeuchi?"

"I will not."

This next reel was more revealing than the first. Plot exposition was subtle. Minoru-san reminded Akio of the latter's responsibilities to Ketsumeidan, and Akio apologized for his earlier weakness and promised that he would stand fast.

The classic actor's question haunted Osgood now: "What's my motivation?" Not his motivation, but Minoru-san's. Minoru-san clearly was willing to see this man, Akio, die, and clearly wished to draw out what transpired here. Why?

Not for a single second did Osgood consider that Minoru-san might be a *member* of the Ketsumeidan; Minoru would only be its leader, and perhaps had been its leader since before the war. Perhaps he was not a victim of the Imperial Japanese military leadership, as Gonroku Umi had been, but a party with it. When Gonroku Umi reported to his superiors, theoretically, that he had information concerning the atomic bomb, Gonroku Umi and his information were suppressed. So, too, supposedly, was Minoru Toshiyuki. What if, instead, Minoru had covered his actions regardless of which side won?

Minoru's intentionally removing himself as head of Covert Operations could be made, to his superiors, to look as if he were preparing, in the proper fashion of the zealot, to go underground to fight the Allies to the death when the invasion came. But to the Allies it would look as if, seeing the inevitability of Japanese defeat, Minoru chose to disassociate himself from war and study the ways of rebuilding Japan during peacetime. The knowledge Gonroku Umi brought him could have been the immediate catalyst, and likely the only reason Gonroku survived was because Minoru saw him as too challenging to kill. Despite Gonroku Umi's current age, John Osgood would never intentionally incur the man's wrath.

Maybe Minoru was hedging his bets again, working with his American friends to defeat the evil enemy Takeuchi, all the while Takeuchi's leader in the Ketsumeidan.

Osgood had no choice but to sit here, play through the charade, and hope that Minoru did not realize he—Osgood—knew. The three young men in business suits were all carrying firearms under their coats, skillfully hidden, but not skillfully enough. On the other hand, Osgood's gun was out of his control for now.

Osgood realized that if he did not betray his suspicions, and admittedly, they were nothing more than that, he would walk out of here alive.

But then what?

There was a lull in the inquisition, so John Osgood

decided that he should attempt to fill it. "Listen, Akio, with men like Minoru-san against you, you cannot hope to win. If you tell the truth now you'll know that you've done the right thing for your country and for all of mankind. We need to find Takeuchi, need to know his plans."

The Japanese said nothing. After a moment, Minoru-san said, "There are drugs that are being brought to us even as we speak, Osgood-san. Once they are administered, our problems will be solved."

John Osgood doubted very seriously that his own problems would be solved, but doubtless one of Minoru-san's problems would be out of the picture—namely, Akio.

Chapter Twenty-two

Surface Time

He'd fooled around with surveillance equipment enough during stakeouts to know his way around video. If Edith Blandish was right, that a continuous video record of the expedition's activities was being recorded, he could see for himself about the B-29 and, perhaps, what was really there.

There was always the chance, of course, that Osgood had told him the truth, that there really were diamonds aboard the old plane. Ed Mulvaney trusted Osgood's integrity in all matters except one: telling him the truth regarding a matter of national security. What Osgood had told him in the bar across the street from the hospital back in Chicago was almost certainly a lie.

Assuming the part about the B-29 was true, what was inside it?

His plan involved looking for two things: videotape evidence of what was in the actual dig site; and the arms locker. He'd already made a decision. Once he had the arms locker open, he would liberate something to help keep him—and Edith—alive. The time for subtlety was passed. Another thing he'd learned as a cop was how to use a lock pick set.

There was no lock pick set available, but he had credit cards, a couple of borrowed bobby pins from Edith, and some scrounged pieces of heavier wire which, when doubled, were essentially rigid. He'd wanted Edith to stay behind and keep watch for him, but she'd been frightened and insisted on coming along. The lock on the off-limits below-decks stern of the *Archimedes* was disappointingly simple.

As soon as he had the door open, Ed Mulvaney realized why it was so easy to defeat the lock.

"Come in, Sergeant Mulvaney, Dr. Blandish," Dr. Friedman said cheerfully.

At least one mystery was solved. There was, indeed, an arms locker aboard the *Archimedes*. Friedman and Naguchi each held pistols, and Milo, who objected to smokers, had a mini-Uzi submachine gun. Mulvaney closed the door behind him, leaning against the jamb with both hands on the knob. "I guess with Milo around it sort of rules out a last cigarette before you burn me, right?"

Friedman actually laughed. "Don't be upset with yourself, Sergeant. If you hadn't come here, we would have eliminated you and Dr. Blandish on your next dive a half hour from now. And since you won't be dying any sooner, you've really lost nothing."

Milo's perfect white teeth were clenched, and the muscles in his jaw twitched. "Let's see your hands, asshole!"

"Milo! That's why you want me to give up smoking! Well, sorry to disappoint you, but I'm saving my hands for that certain someone and you aren't the one." Mulvaney smiled. Milo did just what Mulvaney hoped and charged across the cabin toward them, Mulvaney bracing himself against the doorway. His right foot snapped up and outward, catching Milo right at the tip of the jaw. Teeth and blood sprayed from Milo's mouth.

222

Mulvaney wrenched open the door, throwing Edith through, and started after her.

Taihei, the friendly diver, was standing there with two other men. Like Milo, they held mini-Uzi submachine guns.

Mulvaney had Edith behind him again and walked backward through the doorway. The muzzle of one of the guns pressed against his left kidney. He heard Naguchi's voice. "Would you not care to know what we're doing before we kill you?"

Mulvaney looked over his shoulder at Naguchi, smiled, and asked, "Is this like in the spy movies? You run your ego trip on me before I die a cruel death, but that gives me the chance to escape and blow up the whole boat?"

"Only the first part," Friedman said.

"Damn," Mulvaney groaned. "How about I blow up part of the boat? Maybe just my own cabin?"

Friedman spoke again. Mulvaney honestly would have rather heard Naguchi, because Friedman's voice was like death incarnate. "You can die now and we'll have to carry you both to your final resting places, or you can die in about a half hour and go there under your own power. A moment ago I would have been easier to deal with, but now that there's blood all over the carpet, it really doesn't matter, Sergeant. If you wish to delude yourself, there's still that old expression, 'While there's life there's hope.'"

"I saw Bob Hope once, ya know. Even as old as he is, he's sharp as a tack, rippin' out that monologue and rollin' 'em in the aisles. Hell of an entertainer."

"I'll buy tickets to see him first chance I get, rest assured," Friedman said without a trace of humor in his voice. "What's it going to be?"

"Show me your plan for world domination. I can dig it," Mulvaney told him.

Chapter Twenty-three

Fatalities

Osgood watched as they administered the drugs to Akio, watched as Akio willingly let himself be sacrificed for the greater good of the League of Blood, and watched as Minoru-san's men murdered Akio. To say or do anything to stop it would have been to invite himself to be the next victim. If he did not walk out of here alive, not only would Mulvaney surely die, but there might be no way to prevent the Ketsumeidan's detonation of the twenty-kiloton atomic bomb snatched from the bomb bay of the B-29 *Satin Lady*.

So he politely watched the murder, knowing that the likely instrument of death would be embolism.

While Akio was falling under the influence of the drug from which he would never return, another of Minoru-san's three-piece-suited aides entered the room with an exquisitely made wood-inlaid box. He showed this to Minoru-san, received an approving nod, then presented it to Osgood. Osgood examined the exterior of the box admiringly, also looking for evidence that it was somehow lethal.

Finding no such evidence, and having admired the box sufficiently, he opened it. There was no spring-loaded needle containing poison. There was no gas billowing up toward his face. The box was lined in silk, and set in the box were his Walther pistol and the two spare magazines. As he was expected to do, Osgood set the box on the table, then carefully inspected his weapon to the point of stripping the slide/barrel assembly from the frame, removing the barrel from the slide, and checking the firing pin. All seemed in order, and before he would rely on the pistol again, he would test it. "Thank you, Minoru-san. The skills of your gunsmith are great."

"You honor me, Osgood-san." Minoru smiled, nodding. While Osgood examined the pistol the young man left the room and returned with another box, this one of plain cardboard—the sort of box in which an expensive present from Marshall-Fields or Saks might be packaged. Again the box went to Minoru-san for an approving nod, then was given to Osgood with a deferential bow.

As Osgood opened the box lid, he watched Akio dying.

Inside the box was his Andrews shoulder holster—dried, supple where it should be, not overly oiled, and as good-looking as it had ever been. Osgood was amazed. "I must ask, Minoru-san, how was this accomplished?"

"Try your gun in it, Osgood-san." Osgood did, and the fit was as precise as ever. The knife sheath accommodated the Crawford Special Dart just as well as before. "It is a special process that was used first in the great days of the samurai. I am pleased that you find the humble efforts of my gunsmith to your satisfaction."

"Commend the man for me, please," Osgood said with perfect sincerity. From the pocket of his coat, which hung on the chair back, Osgood took out the green plastic hinged-lid box containing fifty rounds of Federal 9BP, then began slowly loading the magazines.

Akio's eyelids were fluttering. The doctor who had administered the drug stood beside him, monitoring his vital signs on equipment as sophisticated as any Osgood had seen in hospitals around the world.

Osgood was chamber-loading the Walther, replacing the eighth round in the magazine as he heard the electronic whine. It was a single pitch, irritating but not loud. He looked over at the monitor screen. The lines that before had shown pulse, respiration, and other signs were now flat.

The doctor bowed to Minoru-san and announced, "It is to be regretted that the patient has reacted badly to the drug and has expired."

Osgood held his pistol as casually as he could.

Minoru-san said, "Try to revive him, Doctor."

The doctor bowed, began to administer a shot, and ordered that the four young men in three-piece suits assist him with the heart machine.

Somehow John Osgood had a premonition that their efforts would be to no avail.

Edith sat pressed close beside him on the small sofa. Mulvaney reflected that this was what man had come to. Only minutes remained before Friedman, Naguchi, Milo, and the others would carry out their plans for execution. What was he doing but watching television, not a sunset (it was the wrong time of day), not the smile of a pretty girl (or even Edith's), and not the rolling of the sea.

The video was surprisingly clear on both screens. The one to his left showed a man in a yellow NEWTSUIT sifting through bottom sediment. This was the sort of exciting stuff Edith had seen all along. The one on the right showed two men in NEWTSUITs working alongside a partially buried but surprisingly intact World War II bomber.

"The B-29 Super Fortress," Naguchi said venomously. "Were you able to see the underside, you would detect that her only defense was a tail turret. She was stripped to fly over Japan and rain death on the Japanese people. The primary target was Hiroshima, the secondary target the arsenal at Kokura, the third target Nagasaki. The weather was bad. Kokura was not destroyed. People, animals, rivers, canals, houses, all were vaporized."

Ed Mulvaney realized he was biting his lower lip.

Friedman spoke, but there was no trace of Naguchi's emotion in his voice. "See, aren't you glad you stayed alive for the show, Sergeant? Now, a quick test. How many cities did my colleague mention?"

Mulvaney looked up from the sofa, first at the muzzle of Friedman's pistol, then at Friedman's eyes. The muzzle of the gun looked friendlier. "Three."

"Right! Now, it would stand to reason that three bombs were ready to be dropped, wouldn't it?"

"Yes."

"Well, three bombs were ready. One was dropped on Hiroshima, and another on Nagasaki. On the evening of August fourteenth, 1945, one hundred sixty B-29 Super Fortresses left Kumagaya and Isezaki. On that same evening, the plane you see on the monitor, the plane out there just below us, was bringing the third atomic bomb. Its mission was to drop that bomb from an altitude of twenty-eight thousand feet, the ceiling altitude thirty thousand. The aircraft was to travel at precisely two hundred miles per hour. That was the same technique used over Hiroshima and Nagasaki.

"The blockade of oil and other raw materials was crippling Japan. Yet there were still more than two million troops ready to fight, and thousands of Kamikaze aircraft ready to fly. The Japanese had not surrendered, even after two cities had been totally destroyed with the new super bombs. That was the mindset when the aircraft left on its mission. Then news of the Japanese surrender was broadcast to the aircraft. The mission was to be aborted," Friedman went on. "Some say that it was the same Divine Wind which had destroyed the two invasion forces of Kublai Khan, but who knows? There was—fact—a sudden, violent, localized storm of such enormous intensity that the B-29 was forced down over the open sea and lost."

"Why didn't our government search for it?" Edith interrupted him to ask.

Friedman smiled.

Naguchi said, "There were many searches, but the aircraft and its cargo of death eluded the victors. When the world learned what horror the United States was capable of unleashing simply because its enemies were of a different race—"

"Fuck off, Naguchi," Mulvaney said through his teeth. "Truman inherited the damn bomb from FDR, and nobody knew what the hell it'd do. We thought the Japs'd fight to the last friggin' man."

Mulvaney shut up. Naguchi's pistol was two inches from his forehead. Edith screamed.

Friedman said, "To answer Dr. Blandish's question more completely, the United States searched diligently. But in the end the search was fruitless. Lucky for us. No mention of the third bomb was made because by then the war was over and no one wanted to dwell on the destruction the other two bombs had precipitated. Why make the United States look bad? The bomb was lost. It was constructed in such a manner that it could not be detonated without being armed, and it was never armed. Portions of the ocean here are more than a mile deep. The sea does not give up such mysteries easily."

"How did you find it?" Mulvaney asked, still looking at the pistol Naguchi held.

"What does logic tell you, Mulvaney?" Friedman asked, smiling.

"An accident?"

"We prefer to call it serendipity. A happy accident."

"What do you plan to do with it?" Edith asked. "Extort money from your own countries?"

Naguchi laughed, took his pistol away, doubled over, and laughed some more.

Two thoughts crossed Ed Mulvaney's mind: Friedman and Naguchi were going to use the bomb, not for extortion, but really use it; and if he lived long enough to see John Osgood, he'd really beat the shit out of him.

On the right video monitor, he saw the starboard wing, one engine ripped away, the propeller twisted into some sort of Rorshach test shape, the inboard starboard engine seemingly intact.

This was tape, not live feed. The fuselage was nearly uncovered. Powerful water jets washed away the silt.

Mulvaney figured he couldn't get in worse trouble by asking some obvious questions; and anyway, Naguchi still had a smile on his plump face. Mulvaney tried the first one. "How do you know the bomb will still work?"

"Elementary research, really. The casing for the bomb will be corroded, but we can penetrate the casing with perfect impunity. There's a six-digit combination that works on a timer. The digits have to be hit within the established time frame or the combination won't allow primary arming. That was a big problem. We solved that by stealing the prototype of Japan's latest supercomputer, faster than anything in the United States. But we still needed to be able to speed up the process. You see, to accomplish our intended task using an ordinary mainframe computer would have taken upwards of two years, and the cost and security arrangements for that length of time are prohibitive. Then Mr. Gorchek, whom you've met and will be meeting again very shortly"—Mulvaney didn't like that at all—"kindly provided us with the 486 SX chip, which was not lost, by the way, when you attempted to kill Mr. Gorchek. Mr. Gorchek was assisted in obtaining this chip and the knowledge of how to use it, as well as in maintaining his curious status as an illegal alien resident off the southeastern coast of the United States, by the very man who hired you to retrieve it."

"Tom Peterson?"

Friedman smiled. "The 486 SX was government-funded research and is the property of the United States government. Peterson, justifiably, I think, was miffed that his

229

organization had built the ultimate mousetrap, so to speak, but wouldn't be able to profit from it beyond the already exorbitant overcharges billed to the U.S. Defense Department. When the chip was 'stolen,' he was told to find a means of getting it back or the government would come in officially to recover it.

"Peterson couldn't let that happen, of course," Friedman continued, "because then his complicity in the theft might have been discovered. He persuaded the Defense Department that he could get the job done. So he did two things. He told the D.O.D. people that he knew Ladislaw Gorchek, the international arms smuggler, through a mutual friend. Gorchek, who had the KGB after him, could be bribed to try to intercept the 486 SX chip with temporary political asylum in the United States. In fact, whoever had the chip might go to Gorchek with it while Gorchek was right off American shores. How convenient. The other thing he did was equally ingenious. Peterson hired your late friend, Mr. Grimshaw, to find the chip. Grimshaw was getting uncomfortably close to the truth, namely that Gorchek already had it but was waiting for the data that would allow use of the chip with the stolen Japanese supercomputer. If Grimshaw hadn't gotten so suddenly ill, Grimshaw would have met with an accident." Mulvaney balled his fists into his thighs. If he jumped Friedman, he'd get both himself and Edith Blandish murdered on the spot.

"But," Friedman went on, "fortunately, Grimshaw was out of the picture. The necessary data that Gorchek would need to utilize the 486 SX chip in conjunction with the computer was coming, but the D.O.D. people were after Peterson because his investigator, Grimshaw, was dead. So he hired you, and he told you that Gorchek had the chip, in the event Grimshaw's data on the case came to light at a later date, thus covering his actions. If you had waited for your friends to join you in the commando raid on the island, Sergeant Mulvaney, Mr. Gorchek and his information would have gotten away and you never would have met Gorchek."

Mulvaney looked down at his hands. They shook. "What about the girl Gorchek killed?" When he closed his eyes, Mulvaney could still see Gorchek ripping her throat out.

"Presumably, she was in the employ of Grimshaw. She would have been killed anyway, but our Mr. Gorchek does tend to indulge himself with his sense of the theatrical."

"With this chip and this supercomputer—"

"How long will it take to accomplish primary arming?" Friedman smiled indulgently. "Mulvaney, even if you escaped, which is, obviously, what you're hoping to do, nothing I've told you would stop us. By way of confirming that, I'll tell you how long, because that should prove to you how hopeless it would be. With the 486 SX chip and the Japanese supercomputer, our best estimates indicate forty-five minutes, perhaps a little faster."

Mulvaney asked one more question, but he thought he already knew. "How soon before you're bringing the bomb up?"

Friedman looked at his watch. That was a bad sign.

Chapter Twenty-four

Options

If there had been more time, he could have gotten together a small army of the most highly trained commandos in the world—the Ninjas of Tsukahira Ryoichi, with whom he and Mulvaney had worked a year ago.

There was no time.

The Friedman-Naguchi Expedition could have been days or weeks from uncovering the bomb, getting it to the surface, and getting it ready for detonation. But, instinctively, John Osgood knew they weren't, and he felt that everything was going to happen very quickly. Otherwise, Minoru-san would not have let him walk out of the house alive just for the sake of keeping up the charade. Minoru felt something might still conceivably go wrong. In that case Minoru wanted it clearly demonstrable that he had bent over backward to aid his established government and his government's ally, the United States.

That meant the bomb wasn't up yet, or wasn't in place.

But it would be raised soon. If days or even weeks still

remained for the bomb's retrieval, killing Osgood would have been the only insurance that Minoru-san's connections to Takeuchi and the Ketsumeidan would not be discovered.

Once the bomb was detonated, whatever happened would be too late. Who would believe an American agent that one of the pillars of Japanese industry, confidant to the imperial family and the leaders of the Diet, had intentionally caused the deaths of hundreds of thousands of Japanese citizens?

John Osgood stepped into the waiting helicopter which would return him to his hotel, having received assurances from Minoru-san that everything would be done to trace the now-dead sixth assassin, Akio, and somehow find the elusive Takeuchi Arisato before it was too late.

As Osgood buckled up, he thought that the smart thing to do would be to file a full report to his superiors, let them run with the ball, and get himself safely out of Japan. Minoru-san could even have things in motion that would somehow implicate him—Osgood—as being involved with the bomb. There was no way to tell.

But officialdom moved too slowly. Giving up now, when everything looked hopeless, wouldn't get the job done, nor would it do anything for the man he'd thrust right into the middle of the entire mess, Ed Mulvaney.

The helicopter was airborne, and Minoru-san waved at him from the ground below. John Osgood waved back. Then he decided to do the one thing that made sense under the circumstances. He closed his eyes and tried to fall asleep, confident that Minoru-san had no lethal surprises in store for him. Right now, with victory all but assured, the risk would outweigh the benefits.

They were marched onto the deck of the *Archimedes* in plain sight of everyone. Friedman's and Naguchi's guns were away, but Taihei and his men were visibly armed. Milo had to be restrained from going berserk. So everybody in the crew was a bad guy.

Although he cultivated the "wild man" image because it

aided him in his police work, what was required now was cold logic if he and Edith Blandish were to have a prayer of getting out of this alive. And a prayer was probably all they did have.

Why hadn't the bad guys let Milo go wacko berserk? After all, Milo's pretty teeth were all over the floor—and Milo was still bleeding. The only reason, discounting kindness, was that Friedman and Naguchi were concerned that the bodies of their intended victims shouldn't look brutalized. Maybe Gorchek wanted the fun of starting on bodies that were virgin territory.

Mulvaney tried to ignore that possibility for the moment.

There wouldn't be a second Nitrox explosion. The Japanese cop would figure that one out and get the law out here uncomfortably fast for the bad guys. And since the bodies would be blown to bits and the bits charred to ashes, condition before the explosion wouldn't really matter.

A diving accident?

They went down the passenger steps and onto one of the launches, with Milo, Taihei, and one of Taihei's gang accompanying them. A second launch pulled up. Friedman and Naguchi got aboard along with more of the armed divers, and this second launch followed the first.

Coming up over the horizon from the direction of Kyushu, Mulvaney saw two helicopters. One of them was a Bell Long Ranger, the kind used by police departments and as traffic helicopters by television and radio stations. They were also popular for executive transport. The second was considerably larger. Mulvaney hadn't seen one in person since Vietnam. It was an old Sikorski Sky Crane.

And then his eyes moved from the sky to the water.

The crane on the platform was in operation.

They were hauling up the bomb. . . .

Ladislaw Gorchek stood some distance away from them, scowling and grimacing, naturally. Friedman and Naguchi were with him.

Edith Blandish held Ed Mulvaney's left hand. Milo held a mini-Uzi. The look in Milo's eyes was something Mulvaney had only seen once before, in the eyes of a serial rapist and killer, the instant before he and Lew Fields shot him to death.

The bomb rested inside a cocoon of sorts near the center of the platform, well away from the helicopter in which Gorchek had arrived. The Sikorski Sky Crane hovered well above the platform. The bomb casing was originally black, and this was visible in bands near the front and rear. The rest of the casing was a mottled green and brown and encrusted with the bodies of dead sea creatures. Here was the perfect idea for a 1950s horror movie. The sea creatures that had attached themselves to the bomb received trickles of radiation and mutated. And just as the Sikorski would start craning the bomb upward to a safe berth beneath its fuselage, some giant sea horse would rear its head out of the water near the platform and destroy the helicopter. The good guy and the beautiful babe—Edith would have to do—would then be saved from the evil villains. And then, as the man and woman found a life raft conveniently floating by, the camera would pull back and cut to Mt. Fuji, maybe, and the words *The End* would flash on the screen, then scraggly-looking letters beneath them would read, *Or is it just the beginning???*

No sea monsters were on the horizon, however.

The bomb looked about ten feet long and was shaped like a fat version of those cap bombs you could buy as a kid. It seemed to be a little bit greater in diameter at its widest part than his watch commander's wife.

"I'm afraid," Edith whispered to him, as if it were some big secret.

He squeezed her hand more tightly, not telling her that he was afraid, too. . . .

John Osgood stood under the hot water, his hair washed twice, his body scrubbed, but no desire in his heart to leave the warmth. He was cold inside, tired, disgusted, and at a loss. And his right knee throbbed. He'd have to get it looked at, although he doubted anything was permanently damaged. There was a large dark bruise surrounding it.

His gun was wrapped in a towel and within reach of the shower, just in case Takeuchi's people (working without authorization from Minoru-san) came after him again. He'd tested the gun, making certain that it worked. He'd fitted the suppressor (which he rarely used) to the muzzle, then fired the Walther through the mattress. Two shots convinced him that there had been no tampering. He wouldn't worry about the bullet holes in the mattress.

He stood there in the shower, most of his weight on his left leg, closed his eyes, and put his head under the water.

There had to be some way to act rather than just—

He opened his eyes under the water.

Osgood smiled. . . .

Two folding chairs were brought onto the platform.

Wearing a navy blue swimsuit which did nothing for her, Edith Blandish was brought out of the small building near where the chairs were situated. She hugged her arms around her, half against the cold and half in modesty. Taihei and one other of his men had accompanied her while she changed.

As she neared him, he could see that her arms and thighs were goosefleshed, and he put his arm around her.

Mulvaney was still attired as he had been, swimming trunks and a sweatshirt, and his legs were cold, too. If the wind kept increasing, he supposed there was always a chance that the Sikorski Sky Crane wouldn't be able to safely haul off the bomb.

"What are they going to do to us, Ed?"

"I don't know, Ed," Mulvaney told her. Then he tried to add something reassuring, but realized it didn't sound that good after he said it. "We're not dead yet, Edith."

He heard Gorchek's voice behind them, and Mulvaney

didn't turn around. "Sergeant Mulvaney, you have no idea how happy I am that you didn't die during that storm."

Why was Gorchek happy? Mulvaney had a sick feeling in the pit of his stomach that he was about to find out.

Gorchek came to stand in front of them. His nasty eyes were lit with a smile that looked like a sneer. Milo stood behind him, the muzzle of the mini-Uzi aimed at Mulvaney's chest.

Friedman and Naguchi could be seen near the cocoonlike affair which was being closed around the bomb.

Gorchek spoke. "Once I was certain I could get you out here, Mulvaney, I realized I was being foolish to waste you on something as counterproductive as revenge. Until I came to that realization, I envisioned getting Milo to soften you up a little—which he'd still love to do—then having you slowly skinned alive. Have you ever considered what salt will do to an open wound? Think how it would feel to have large slabs of skin removed and then be packed in salt."

"You're insane!" Edith shrieked at him.

Mulvaney held her tighter, telling her, "He already knows that, kid."

Gorchek laughed, evidently quite happy with himself. "No, I decided to sacrifice my own pleasure for the good of the project. You see, the realization I had was exquisite. We're planting a bomb aboard a U.S. ship so it will appear to be a nuclear accident. But just in case something goes wrong, we still want to do as much damage to your country as possible, Mulvaney. That's when the realization came to me."

"Were you watching one of those religious shows on cable?"

Gorchek just kept smiling. Mulvaney shut up.

Gorchek said, "You will both be my evidence of U.S. involvement in this little affair. The Japanese government will be able to trace your identity easily and connect you to the CIA. As for Dr. Blandish, well, we knew she was keeping company with Westinghouse. Westinghouse was another

CIA plant. That will be discovered, too. Your bodies near the wreckage of the B-29 from which this bomb was recovered will just add that extra element of credibility."

Gorchek said nothing, and suddenly Mulvaney realized Gorchek was waiting for one of those "You'll never get away with this" speeches. Of course, Gorchek wanted to point out how he had already gotten away with it. And Mulvaney knew that Gorchek really had.

"Don't you want to know how you'll both die?"

Mulvaney looked at Edith and asked her. "How about it?"

She leaned her head against his chest, but she didn't cry.

Mulvaney looked at Gorchek, shrugged his shoulders, said, "Sure, I've got the time."

"Very little, Mulvaney." Gorchek folded his hands over his abdomen like a statue of Buddha, looking disgustingly pleased with himself. "You are, of course, familiar with the NEWTSUITs?"

"You bet."

"What we'll be doing is marvelously simple. Both you and Dr. Blandish will be administered rather powerful muscle relaxants. Before that I'll give you each the option of self-administering enemas or having Milo do it for you."

"That's about all Milo's good for, anyway."

Gorchek went on, as if Mulvaney had said nothing at all. "A short time after you've been administered the muscle relaxants, you will both become unable to move unaided. You should be able to blink your eyelids."

"I like blinking," Mulvaney said, his mind racing to find a way out where he knew there wasn't one.

"You will each be placed inside one of the NEWTSUITs, helpless to activate any of its systems, helpless to move. Your radios will be on so you will be able to listen to each other as you die. The tether lines for each suit will be entangled in the wreckage eight hundred feet below us by Taihei, who will be wearing the third suit. Then Taihei will leave you down there, alone, return to the surface, and extricate himself from the third suit. The third suit will be disabled." Gorchek was enjoying this.

"I'll admit to some disappointment," Gorchek told them, "because I'd hoped to watch you suffer, Mulvaney. However, I'll know that you and Dr. Blandish might well survive for as long as a day. The suits will not be recharged, so a full forty-eight hours won't be possible. Even so, those twelve, thirteen, possibly fourteen hours should be exquisite agony for you both. Watching each other, hearing each other, perhaps your suits touching each other, but unable to move to aid yourselves. When and if your bodies are found, they'll be well preserved enough to identify easily. Think of it as predeath mummification. The Japanese, after the bomb is detonated, may search, may realize that this expedition was somehow involved in the bomb's deployment. Your bodies will serve to implicate the United States even more."

Edith, her voice trembling, asked him, "Why would the United States want to do something so disgusting to a friendly nation?"

Gorchek laughed a little, reached into his pocket, and drew out a wad of American money, fifties and hundreds. "This is why. Money, Doctor, good old money."

Mulvaney gestured with a nod of the head toward Friedman and Naguchi. "What about them?"

"You are clever enough, Mulvaney, but you guess incorrectly. Evidence will be left behind that you and your evil CIA associates attacked the expedition. Some of the personnel here will be left behind, dead. It will be assumed that Friedman and Naguchi and the others were murdered and their bodies pitched into the sea."

"Gonna kill Milo? Go ahead, kill him," Mulvaney urged.

Gorchek laughed. Milo actually growled.

The other man who'd gotten out of the Bell Long Ranger with Ladislaw Gorchek started walking over to join them. He was Japanese, but very tall for a Japanese—almost Mulvaney's own height. As he came still nearer, Mulvaney noticed that the man smoked a pipe.

Chapter Twenty-five

No Way Out

When he opened his eyes, Ed Mulvaney felt drunk. The pain that he suddenly remembered should be in his head wasn't very noticeable at all.

He remembered the rest.

When Milo turned to talk to the tall Japanese pipe smoker, Mulvaney made a try for Milo's gun, knocking Gorchek down to the platform deck and breaking Milo's nose this time—the right way, so that Milo died.

Mulvaney remembered having his left hand on the mini-Uzi submachine gun, the pleasant smell of pipe tobacco, and the pain starting in his head.

He tried to turn his head around, but his head didn't turn too well. He tried to touch at his head, but his arms wouldn't move.

He remembered it all now.

On the edge of unconsciousness some of them dragged him into one of the blue, telephone-booth-shaped chemical toilets and pulled his swimming trunks off. Edith was screaming outside. They shoved something up his butt, and what seemed like a few seconds later, he was dropping everything he had into the toilet.

He remembered what happened next very vividly. Maybe it was what his body was doing, or maybe the effect of whatever had hit him wore off, but he reached out and grabbed one of the Japanese guards and slammed the man's head into the side of the toilet. Then something hit him again.

When the Japanese guy with the pipe hit him, it was across the neck. He'd gotten hit in the head when he was half in, half out of the porta-potty. Probably a gunbutt.

He didn't remember the needle. He hoped it was clean. He laughed at that.

His laughter sounded hollow to him.

He realized his eyes were closed again and he opened them.

He felt like he was inside a small television set, or a goldfish bowl. He could see out through glass in front of him. He could breathe okay. And he was moving.

Fish came up and looked into his face, then sped away. He saw a yellow submarine near him, and he saw Edith's face inside it. He wondered what Edith would have looked like with the right hair, the right figure, the right clothes. Probably she would have looked okay.

The sensation of movement stopped, and he could see something that looked like a lot of twisted metal. There was another of the yellow things, moving around him, between him and the third suit. That's what the things were, the NEWTSUITs.

Then one of the helmets was pressed flat up against his, and he could see the face inside. Taihei. Taihei's voice filled the inside of the helmet. "Eight hundred feet down." And then Taihei's face was gone.

Another voice. "Ed?"

That was Edith now. "Yeah?" Where was she? Inside the

little yellow-colored submarine. The one that stayed behind with his. He remembered.

"I can't move at all. I—I'm drunk?"

He started to shake his head, but his head wouldn't shake. "No, Edith. They gave us—"

He remembered what Gorchek had said, about the muscle relaxant, the twelve hours or so of air, and he realized he was dying and that this time there really was no way out. . . .

"When I was in school, none of the boys liked me."

"They had bad taste."

"I wasn't pretty, Ed." And she began to cry again.

He'd been listening to her crying on and off. The thing was, he'd been the kind of teenage boy who'd gone after Irene with the big tits and never looked twice at—what was her name?—the girl who'd wound up valedictorian. This muscle relaxant stuff, Mulvaney realized, was like alcohol, a psycho deinhibitor. He wanted to cry, cry for Edith being lonely all her life, cry for Bill Grimshaw's family, cry for Andy, who loved him and would never see him again, cry for himself, because he didn't want to die and he was going to die. At the edge of his mind he realized that there was no reason to hold back tears, but he had to, because all his life he had held back tears. Except for a few times when they really came and he couldn't stop them at all.

Edith started talking about the bomb. "The bomb could kill hundreds of thousands of people, Ed."

"My friend, John Osgood. I never told you about him. He's a son of a bitch, but he's a good man. Osgood and Lew Fields, they're the best friends I have. And Andy." He didn't tell Edith that Andy was a she, not a he. Why rub it in? "Osgood's still on the job. He'll maybe find those guys, find out where they're putting the bomb."

"Maybe they'll find our bodies in time."

Mulvaney didn't understand that one. He was starting to nod off again, maybe from the drug, maybe from lack of oxygen. He had a hell of a headache. But this was important. He blinked his eyes a lot. "What's it matter if they find our—find us first?"

"They changed your shirt, Ed."

They changed his shirt. He blinked his eyes a lot. What did changing his shirt have to do with it? But she'd been talking like that ever since they'd started talking, sometimes sounding perfectly sober, sometimes sounding perfectly daffy. "This is an okay shirt, Edith. Don't worry."

"No, the pocket."

He thought about that. He'd been wearing a sweatshirt, but not the kind with a hood and a muff pocket in the front, just a regular old sweatshirt. "What about the pocket?"

"They needed you wearing a shirt with a pocket, Ed, so they could put the map in your pocket. It shows where they're going to blow up the bomb."

Ed Mulvaney closed his eyes. Gorchek really did get the last laugh. By the time the muscle relaxant wore off enough so that they could try to move around and find some sort of way to get back to the surface, the air supply in the suit would be gone and they'd die. And all the while the information that could have prevented the bomb from being detonated, that would implicate the United States as the perpetrator when their bodies were found, was right in—"

My fuckin' pocket!" Ed Mulvaney snarled. And when he did that, the pain from when he'd gotten slugged in the portable toilet came back sharper. He was able to turn his head a degree or two to the right.

"Edith!" He shouted her name with a vengeance. "Edith! Get mad! Think about all those pimple-faced little motherfuckers who never looked at you once. Think about all the cheerleaders with the big tits that every guy wanted to grab, but you knew wore falsies! Think about it! Get so damn mad you've never been that mad before! There was

243

this guy I busted once when I was rookie, ya know? I'm gonna get real damn mad tellin' ya this one. He pulled maybe a hundred B&Es and I nailed his ass and the judge let the asshole walk, right? Turns out the judge was his fence. When I tried bustin' the judge, I got suspended. Me! They fuckin' suspended me for doin' my job! Come on, Edith, get mad! Think about those falsies! Come on!"

"Ed? What's—"

It was working, not miraculously, but it was working. "Come on, Edith!"

"I just wanna go to sleep!"

He could wiggle the little finger on his left hand, but it hurt like hell to move it. If Edith fell asleep, if she didn't get so angry that she wanted to kill somebody—"That what you'd do every time somebody wanted to give ya a roll, Edith? Fall asleep, huh?"

"Ed!" She was bawling now, loudly.

"Betchya when you wore falsies, you were still flat-chested, huh?"

"Damn you!" There was silence except for her sniffling. It lasted a long time. Mulvaney was blinking his eyes to the point of making them tear and moving his little finger and concentrating on the pain in his head where he'd gotten cold-cocked, trying to make the pain feel worse. And she said to him, "Adrenaline?"

"Damn right! Think about everything that pissed you off in the last fifty years, Edith!"

"I'm thirty-eight, dammit!"

"Thatta girl!" He started running his bust record through his head, trying to recall every time somebody he'd nailed good and tight had walked because of a crooked lawyer or a liberal do-gooder imbecile judge. He started to think about how ticked he was with John Osgood, about beating the crap out of Ozzie if he ever saw him again.

But Ed Mulvaney gave up on that. If he ever got out of here, could get the map Edith told him he had in his pocket into Osgood's hands, and Osgood could somehow help them stop Gorchek and the others, instead of kicking him he'd be tempted to kiss him.

So he thought about Ladislaw Gorchek and Friedman and Naguchi and that schmuck Peterson who'd sent him after the 486 SX chip.

Chapter Twenty-six

Another Monster to
Lay Waste to Tokyo

He expected to fall over, but did not. Never in his life had Mulvaney experienced such pain. It started in various places—his rectum, his knees, his elbows, and his neck—and all came to focus behind his eyes. But he could move both his legs, and he could move his left arm within the suit, but not enough to draw it back from the NEWTSUIT's arms to get it inside and adjust the oxygen flow.

Once the adrenaline surge had come on full tilt, he'd started asking Edith about the suit, knowing that she knew its intricacies even though she had never worn one before. She asked him, right in the middle of telling him how to adjust oxygen flow, if he'd really meant what he said about her. He told her, "Edith, there's a woman I'm in love with. She lives with me, and one of these days we'll be getting married. But when you and I are out of these suits—" There was still no chance for survival, but at least he could keep her and himself working at trying to survive until the air in their suits ran out. "When we're out of these, I'm gonna kiss you so hard, your lips are gonna be stuck to the back of my neck, so help me."

And she laughed, a nice girl sort-of laugh.

It was odd looking at her through the suit. Through the transparent faceplate of the rounded helmet portion, he saw too much of her forehead and her hair. It was as if she were standing on her toes inside of it just to look out.

"The air you're breathing is processed through dual rebreathers, and once you can get an arm inside, you can adjust the mixture, although you should be on seventy-nine/twenty-one nitrogen-oxygen anyway."

"A little more oxygen will goose things up, right, Edith?"

"Yes, I guess."

He still couldn't get his arm to move inside, but now Edith seemed able to move her legs a little, too. Mulvaney moved like a little old lady on January ice along the shelf beside the B-29, and tried to figure out what to do next. Their tether cords were hopelessly tangled in the wreckage. If he could get his hands moving enough to figure out how to manipulate the tools attached to the ends of the suit arms, he could either untangle the tethers or cut them against the wreckage itself, which was very jagged in spots.

Maybe there was hope, real hope, that they could use the mid-water maneuvering system to get themselves up.

As he contemplated this, Edith told him, "Ed, I think my suit's running out of air. I'm getting a really bad headache—"

"Hell, Edith, you're just trying to back out of that kiss."

She laughed, but it didn't sound natural. "No, you see, the level of carbon dioxide is too high. We've been under for over eleven hours. I can move my left arm enough to read my watch. And the oxygen adjustment isn't doing anything."

If he could have sat down and cried, he would have, but

247

sitting down was impossible and crying was counterproductive. Instead, he told her, "If you can move your left arm enough to tell time, start moving your ass instead, and see what you can do about getting us out of these tether lines."

"I don't feel good."

"Edith!" And, he realized, the anger they'd generated to build up adrenaline and increase their blood circulation had also increased oxygen use and doomed them.

He tried moving his legs more, but maneuvering the suit was hard because his feet were asleep. He couldn't control the toes and heels well enough to make the suit march forward or backward when he wanted to. He fell onto his side, but the tether line kept him from going all the way down. The fall was so slow and so gentle he didn't notice it until it was too late.

Now Edith was crying very hard. "We're going to die!"

Big revelation, Mulvaney thought, his mind racing to find some way to—"Edith. How do these suits stay down?"

"What?"

"We've been so friggin' concerned with how to get back up, we forgot why they stay down."

"You're right, Ed. My God! There are levers inside the suit, and if we can get ourselves free of the tethers, we can release the ballast and trim weights, and we'll go up to the surface and we can get ourselves out. But—"

"The damn tethers!" They had to be attached with some kind of release mechanism right at the top of the helmet section. He began moving his feet within the feet of his suit.

Edith was moving toward him now. "What are you doing?" he said.

"I'm going to try to use the pincer on my right arm to release your tether from the helmet of your suit. I'm going to have to swing my arm against it, because I really can't use my hand that well, Ed," she told him, her voice as breathless as Marilyn Monroe's.

"We can get outta here now, Edith. We can do it!"

248

"Oh, Ed."

"Come on, Edith!"

He was still at a diagonal to the shelf on which the B-29 lay. Edith was slightly over him. He could hear her metal hand clanging against the aluminum of his helmet and felt the vibration in his head. He was working madly at wiggling his toes, getting enough circulation into his feet so he could reliably maneuver the suit.

"I think—think I've got . . . I have it. . . . Oh, Ed . . . I'm so tired."

Edith stumbled against him, and the bubbles of their helmets touched. He didn't know what he had at the end of his left arm, but *thwacked* with that against the tether connection at the top of her helmet. There was a safety lever, with a hook passing through a flange that ran like an exposed spinal column from the crown of the helmet downward. The appendage at the end of his left arm was like a pair of pliers. He got these on the hook and started working the release.

He was moving his right arm inside his suit, getting feeling back very fast in both arms. "Edith. I've almost got you unhooked, Edith. Edith!?"

"Ed?"

"Don't you pass out on me! We'd be idiots to pass out now. Think about those ballast and trim controls. That's what I want you to do." A fish swam up to Mulvaney's face, made a kissing motion with its mouth, then swam away. Mulvaney was too tired for a wisecrack. The release lever opened and the tether slipped from the crown of Edith's helmet. "Edith! Edith?!"

There was no answer. If Mulvaney could somehow flip the right switches inside his own suit, would there be enough force to pull Edith's up, too? And how would he hold on to her?

"Ed?"

"Edith. Thank God. Where are those switches?"

"You can get to them with either hand. I don't think—"

Mulvaney could see her face, the bubbles of their helmets touching again. Her lids were nearly closed. "Edith! Edith, dammit!"

Her lids fluttered and opened fully. "Ed?"

"Hit your switches now. You can do it."

"But your arms. You can't—"

"I've got full control of my arms now," he lied. "Meet you topside. Go on."

She nodded her face and edged her suit back from his. He thought he saw her blowing him a kiss. And then the suit started rising, slowly at first, then more rapidly. Soon it was gone from his sight.

Ed Mulvaney, his air going, tried dragging his left arm into his suit.

A lot of switches, Mulvaney thought. He'd probably flip the ones that separated the halves of the suit and drown while his body got crushed by the pressure.

His eyes were closing.

There were no breathing sounds from Edith, and he realized just how comforting those had been throughout the hours.

His left arm was inside the suit.

He flipped as many switches as he could, his lids becoming heavier and heavier.

And he was moving.

He opened his eyes.

He was rising through the water now, with fish staring at him, and entire schools breaking up around him.

There was a loud rushing sound all around him. It was dark, but not as dark as it had been. He was getting sick to his stomach with all the rising and falling and spinning around. He thought he saw a glimpse of yellow. And he realized he was gone. He had to be dead, because that giant sea monster he'd been thinking about was rising up out of the water and coming straight at him.

As he closed his eyes, Mulvaney told himself those plucky Japanese people had so much experience dealing with monsters. It seemed they were always able to bounce back after some giant tyrannosaurus or some turtle the size of a football stadium demolished Tokyo. What the hell difference would another one make?

Chapter Twenty-seven

How to Fight Monsters

Edith was wrapped in a gray blanket. She was kneeling beside him and was stroking his forehead with cool fingertips. John Osgood was sitting on his haunches a few feet away. Mulvaney—cold and queasy—looked to his right and saw whitecaps on the open sea. Maybe it hadn't been a monster coming to get him after all. Maybe Tokyo would be safe.

When Osgood started talking, two Americans, one black and the other dark from the sun but blond-haired, crouched down on either side of him. "This map doesn't indicate when, but it certainly indicates where. Another case of Minoru covering his actions just in case something goes wrong. If everything is carried off as planned, the bomb will explode aboard a ship in Yokohama Harbor, halfway up the west side of Tokyo Bay, where there are plenty of U.S. ships that might be carrying nuclear weapons."

"Might?" Edith asked.

"U.S. policy is never to affirm or deny that nuclear

weapons are aboard." Mulvaney enjoyed listening to the sea more than listening to Osgood. But Osgood started talking again, anyway. "On the water precise placement of ground zero might just be difficult enough that the authorities will attribute it to a careless nuclear accident on the part of the United States. But if the bomb is somehow discovered, it will be linked to the *Archimedes*, there'll be the bodies and other evidence of a slaughter, and then divers would find Mulvaney and Dr. Blandish. Just to make sure they'd know how deep to look, the third NEWTSUIT was partially destroyed and left at the scene. And they would have found this map, in Mulvaney's blasted pocket. They'd blame the Central Intelligence Agency for it and have the evidence to back it up. Damn!"

The black man, when he spoke, sounded like he was from Chicago. "Can't you get your buddy Gonroku Umi to pull this Minoru asshole's plug with the authorities?"

"That would probably take too long, and Umi has to know that Minoru would openly cooperate, but would delay things just enough to give Takeuchi and the Ketsumeidan terrorists the opportunity to detonate the device without delaying too long to make himself look suspect. And if he isn't able to hold things off, then the Japanese come in, find incriminating evidence pointing to the Company, and Minoru-san's backup plan is in full swing. I can't accuse Minoru-san without starting a diplomatic incident all its own. Even with Mulvaney and Dr. Blandish to swear to the events aboard the *Archimedes* and on the platform, we'd still be unable to prove our case. After all, Gorchek was given asylum within the United States by the Department of Defense, and the 486 SX chip is a D.O.D. project. Minoru is so well respected here, a national hero, we'd never be able to convince the authorities he was responsible, no matter what we said or did.

"The point is," Osgood continued, "Yokohama is the third largest city in Japan, with millions of people, and industry—everything from automobiles and ships to food.

If they put Dr. Blandish and Mulvaney into the water at around one o'clock in the afternoon, as Dr. Blandish indicated, they've had twelve hours to get their plan into operation. That's ample time, with their stolen supercomputer and the 486 SX chip, for them to have accomplished primary arming, flown the bomb to its destination, and perhaps transferred it to the ship from which it will be detonated."

It was the blond-haired guy talking now. "You got any idea, John, how many damn ships there are in Yokohama Harbor? How we gonna find the thing?"

Mulvaney was losing it, starting to fall asleep, but he heard Osgood say, "If I'm right, I know which kind of ship to look for. We have to steal a helicopter and pray we can get there in time, because we'll have to refuel two or three times along the way. If I'm wrong, we'll probably be dead, and so will hundreds of thousands of others. For best effect, they'll wait until the morning rush hour, which means we have between seven and eight hours until detonation—seven or eight hours to cover about six hundred miles. If they detonate in the morning rush, more people will be out on the streets, more people will be killed outright, and the radiation and burn factors will be multiplied. And if we tried to evacuate Yokohama, we'd have to evacuate Tokyo and every city in between. Aside from the thousands who might be killed during the evacuations, there'd never be enough time to effectively clear the cities anyway. And they could always move the bomb to a secondary target, perhaps Tokyo itself. The damned monsters!"

Mulvaney just let his eyes close.

Mulvaney looked pale and shaky, but when he awakened Osgood gave him a thumbnail sketch of the plan. Mulvaney had insisted on coming along. Under the circumstances, Osgood could not refuse.

The helicopter was coming up over the city of Yokohama toward the rising sun. Busy streets filled with cars and

254

bicycles below them. Children made their way to school. Life started for a new day as commuters rushed to fill the city and perhaps rushed to their deaths.

John Osgood would assume the responsibility for his actions, if he lived that long. If he failed, his worries would be over. If he succeeded, he'd be made the whipping boy for not alerting the proper authorities and not suggesting that Yokohama and Tokyo and all the other cities on the western side of Tokyo Bay be evacuated. He was doomed even if he succeeded.

Edith Blandish was aboard the *Okane*—Oglethorpe and Kowalski's boat—en route to South Korea. In the event everything went wrong, it would not be good to be an American in Japan. At least someone would be alive to tell the story.

The last thing Osgood had said to Edith at the small airfield before they entered the Bell Jet Ranger helicopter that Steve Oglethorpe and Norb Kowalski had stolen for them was, "If things go wrong, Dr. Blandish, you must not only tell representatives of our government in South Korea, but you must somehow get word of everything that has transpired to Gonroku Umi. If Minoru is successful, some way must be found to bring him to book for the enormous loss of life."

"I understand, Mr. Osgood." She allowed him to shake her hand.

And then Ed Mulvaney did something John Osgood thought rather odd. After all that Mulvaney and Dr. Blandish had been through, Osgood could have understood a friendly good-bye kiss. Mulvaney was, after all, engaged to be married to Andy Oakwood, and Mulvaney didn't seem the type to cheat on a woman.

But Mulvaney walked up to Dr. Blandish, looked at her for a moment, then took her into his arms and kissed her with such obvious fervor that Osgood looked away embarrassed. When he looked back, Mulvaney was getting up into the helicopter. Dr. Blandish was returned to Osgood's hired

255

Mercedes, with one of Oglethorpe and Kowalski's men driving her.

At maximum speed of just over one hundred thirty miles per hour, and allowing no reserve, with the single refueling stop, the flight had consumed almost exactly six hours. Better than an hour was consumed in getting the *Okane* to port and stealing the aircraft to begin with.

It was now almost eight-thirty, and the bomb might be detonated at any second.

Osgood put his Walther away after one last check, then picked up his binoculars. They were nearing the harbor, and there seemed to be thousands of ships there.

Needles in haystacks would have been easier to deal with, he told himself.

"I'm getting some flack from some airport ground control guy that I'm off my flight plan or something," Oglethorpe announced. "Which is pretty cool, since I don't have a flight plan. I'll let you know if they decide to send up something after us."

Osgood murmured, "You do that, Steve." He'd slept a few hours so he'd be at maximum alertness for the coming task. But his eyes burned and were tired.

Mulvaney's voice came through his headset. "John?"

"Yes, Ed."

"I fluctuated from wanting to kick the shit out of ya for getting me into this to praying for a while that you'd come and rescue us, which in a way you did. However this turns out, you did what you could, man. That's what I wanted to say."

"I'm sorry I involved you in this, but when I made the connection between Gorchek and the chip and the computer, and learned where Takeuchi was—he's the one I told you about."

"I remember."

"Well, I remembered something I shouldn't have ever known in the first place. A very good friend of mine who died several years ago was involved with U.S. Intelligence before World War Two, during the war, and for a short time after that. He told me the story of the third aircraft, about how it really did seem Japan was protected by a 'Divine Wind' because it was a sudden storm that brought down the plane. So I remembered that I knew the basics of how the World War Two atomic bombs worked, and I realized that if somehow the bomb had been located, with the chip and the computer they could activate it without ever having the access code. Anyway, I'm sorry."

"Don't be, John," Mulvaney told him. "Just for your information, though, if you'd told me the truth, I would have come along for the ride anyway."

Osgood lit a cigarette, safety precautions be damned. "I know that, Ed." All his life he'd had a very difficult time dealing with the concept of friendship as anything but an abstraction, and after the death of Elizabeth and the children, that problem had become more acute.

He'd spoken of the man who'd first told him the story of the third atomic bomb as a friend, but the man was merely a drinking buddy—a regular acquaintance. Throughout his life, only Gonroku Umi and Ed Mulvaney were real friends to him. "Thank you," Osgood said a little hoarsely.

"For what?"

Osgood put down his binoculars and looked at Ed Mulvaney for a moment. Mulvaney was checking his weapons again, the Tanto which had been strapped to Mulvaney's leg when they'd pulled him out of the NEWTSUIT and the two handguns Mulvaney borrowed from the arms locker of the *Okane*. Mulvaney had been doing that—checking his weapons—throughout the flight, almost compulsively. "I want to thank you for being my friend, Ed. Not for being here, not for holding back your complaints. Just for being my friend. I thank you for that."

Chapter Twenty-eight

Brothers in Blood

Osgood sounded like a priest reciting a litany. His voice was low, even, never rising, never falling, and serious—very serious.

"I am gambling that they will utilize the simplest and—for them—the safest method to detonate this very old and very dirty bomb. That method is, rather than short-circuiting the altitude switch—as the altitude switch is the secondary arming procedure—to fool it, instead. The only way I can think of to do that is by utilizing a full-size medical decompression unit. The smaller types found on so many ships which are used to service scuba divers would be too small to accommodate the bomb. But by removing the fins and some other portions of the original casing, they could fit the bomb inside one of these full-size medical units.

"Then to make the bomb detonate, they set the unit to slowly decompress until the atmosphere inside the unit matches the setting on the altitude switch. Once that occurs, the nuclear weapon will detonate.

"A twenty-kiloton weapon will produce one million centigrade degrees of heat. Chain reaction by-products will break down primarily into alpha, beta, and gamma radiation. The kinetic energy main destruction factor should be in the neighborhood of eighty-three percent. Casualties should be divided roughly into sixty percent from the blast itself, twenty-five percent thermal-related, and, the most insidious of all, fifteen percent from the radiation.

"The duration of the blast will be short, only ten to the minus seven seconds. But the pressure developed from the bomb will be enormous, roughly ten to the fourth power atmospheres, or ten thousand times normal atmospheric pressure. A three-pounds-per-square-inch overpressure would cause deafness in any exposed persons within a radius of three miles.

"In five-tenths of a second there will be a fireball approximately nine hundred feet in diameter, and temperatures will have risen to seven times ten to the third power degrees centigrade.

"The shock front will be traveling at the speed of sound, and will pass within one second.

"There will be an underpressure, or negative phase, in the wake of this shock front which will last for two to three seconds, essentially creating a vacuum.

"The fireball will rise at a speed of two hundred miles per hour to an altitude of fifteen hundred feet. In ten seconds it will have reached eleven thousand feet from ground zero.

"Third-degree burns will be experienced to exposed skin from infrared radiation alone as far away as four thousand feet.

"The figures are based on an air blast, of course. If the detonation were to take place in Yokohama Harbor, millions of gallons of water vapor would be sent skyward along with irradiated dust particles, forming vast clouds of water vapor, which would eventually fall to earth as rain. It would carry down the radioactive debris, possibly taking it as far away as the west coast of North America."

As Mulvaney watched him, Osgood stared through his binoculars, presumably looking for some sort of hospital ship that would have this large medical decompression chamber.

No one else aboard the helicopter spoke.

Mulvaney looked at the fuel gauge. He'd gone for a lot of helicopter rides in Vietnam. This helicopter would be landing—the hard way or the soft way—in under five minutes, but landing nonetheless.

"Gentlemen," Osgood murmured. "We are in luck."

Ed Mulvaney wanted to ask him just which kind of luck this was, good or bad.

Mulvaney realized he was becoming obsessive about his weapons. John Osgood could compile lengthy dissertations loaded with gloomy statistics, Oglethorpe could fly the aircraft, and Kowalski could look out from the copilot's seat. All Mulvaney had to do was smoke, check his weapons, or go nuts. And smoking right now hurt him.

The guns he'd been given from the *Okane*'s arms locker were good ones. The revolver was a Smith & Wesson Model 25-5 in .45 Colt—the cowboy cartridge. The semiautomatic was a SIG-Sauer P-226 9mm, in many ways similar to the Beretta 92F he'd left stateside with Andy. Osgood, in addition to his antique Walther P-38K, had an Uzi semiautomatic carbine with metal folding stock and a good supply of twenty-round magazines. He'd chosen the Uzi over the M16s in the arms locker, saying the gun would be more maneuverable for him and not excessively penetrative.

Both Oglethorpe and Kowalski, in addition to handguns, carried M16s.

Osgood began talking again. "As best I can tell, there are two ships in Yokohama Harbor that meet our requirements, gentlemen. Would you concur, Norb?"

"Two hospital ships with helipads on deck. One with a chopper, one without."

"Then our decision is clear, gentlemen. You will hover over the deck of the hospital ship with a helicopter aboard and Mulvaney and I will drop off. You'll then proceed, Steve, to the second ship, where you will land. We'll stay in radio contact as long as we can. You have the radio, Ed?"

"Yup."

"Excellent. Steve, if you and Norb locate the bomb, advise us at once, and we'll somehow get over to you. In the meantime, do what you can to prevent detonation. Watch out for booby traps on the medical decompression unit, however."

"I messed with that shit a lot in Nam, John. Don't sweat it. But if we can't stop the bomb, what can we do besides puttin' our heads between our knees and kissin' our asses good-bye?"

"There would be one chance, a very risky one, yet under the circumstances worth trying. If you determine that detonation is imminent, smash one of the view ports in the decompression chamber so the machine is inoperable. It is conceivable that, if the bomb were near enough to detonation, you might shock the altitude switch and actually cause the detonation yourselves. Then there'd be no other options left. If we find the bomb, we'll need help, because that helicopter would only be on board for one reason: Takeuchi and his League of Blood followers would still be guarding the bomb, counting on leaving by helicopter at the very last minute in order to get a safe distance away before they themselves are killed. Or they might be that fanatical that they would stay and blow up with it."

"What about personnel on these ships, John?" Norb Kowalski asked.

"If they are friendlies, advise them to evacuate. That won't save their lives, but it will get them out of your way. If they are unfriendly or friendlies who refuse to cooperate and inhibit your abilities to search for the bomb, do whatever is necessary. If that results in fatalities and we survive this thing, I'll assume all the responsibility I can. If we don't survive, I'll try to intercede with Saint Peter. Now, let's go."

Ed Mulvaney's stomach lurched as the helicopter slipped to starboard and started down. The only holster that had been aboard the *Okane* was a Southwind Sanctions Lifesaver universal belt holster. It was an open-bottomed fabric unit that was constructed to allow almost any size handgun to be worn in it. Mulvaney had the SIG semiautomatic there now, beside his right kidney, under his borrowed shirt. The Pachmayr-gripped N-Frame Smith & Wesson revolver was in his right hand, his trigger finger well away from the guard for safety's sake.

The helicopter was making a nosedive toward the deck of the hospital ship, and Mulvaney forced himself not to look at the fuel gauge just in case it showed empty.

Osgood stripped away his jacket and tossed it to the cabin floor, revealing a shoulder holster holding Osgood's pet pistol. The Uzi semiautomatic carbine was in Osgood's left hand. Osgood's right hand was on the handle of the cockpit door.

The helicopter leveled out, and now Mulvaney could see the afterdeck clearly. There were men near the helipad. The grounded machine's main rotors turned lazily, as if the helicopter had just arrived or was about to take off.

Shots were fired, a bullet spiderwebbing the Bell's chin bubble.

Osgood declared, "Well, that rather settles which ship we're looking for. Steve, join us after you ditch the helicopter. But we won't wait for you. Norb, come with us."

"Right, John!" Norb Kowalski shouted, his headset thrown down now, the M16 in his left fist.

"I'm going out over the forecastle. I can get about six feet over the deck for about twenty seconds tops, if the vapor in the fuel tank holds out!" Steve Oglethorpe shouted.

A rifleman fired from the radar mast amidships, the glass on the starboard side of the Bell helicopter shattering. Osgood hit the release latch, and the door beside him fell away, slicing through the air like a Frisbee. It hit the radar mast and made a shower of sparks. No more shots were fired by the sniper.

"Ready! I'm comin' down!" Oglethorpe shouted.

The chopper slipped right again, just forward of the flying bridge.

"Go! Go! Go!" Oglethorpe ordered.

Osgood jumped, then Norb Kowalski. Mulvaney pushed between the seats, held his revolver tight in his fist, and jumped. The Bell slipped left and up as Mulvaney hit the deck in a roll. Gunfire ricocheted off the deckplates on either side of him. He punched the big, blued revolver toward the gunfire's origin and fired as he hauled himself to his feet.

Osgood was crouched beside a smokestack, his Uzi to his shoulder. "Come on, Ed!"

Mulvaney ran and skidded down beside him. Osgood made rapid-fire three-round semiautomatic bursts toward the flying bridge. Gunfire came back at them.

There was a companionway ladder leading to the flying bridge, and Mulvaney saw Norb Kowalski taking it upward, his M16 in his right fist. As Kowalski reached the top of the ladder, Mulvaney snapped to Osgood, "You take the right side!"

Mulvaney threw himself flat. He had five shots remaining in the revolver. Both fists were on the gun as he emptied it toward the flying bridge. The sharper, lighter crack of Osgood's carbine made his ears ring. Bullets from the flying bridge pinged off the stack.

There was a burst of assault rifle fire and then Norb's voice, shouting, "Got the mother!"

Mulvaney had the empty revolver in his left hand, the SIG in his right. Osgood shouted, "Let's go, Ed!" And both of them ran toward an open companionway door at the base of the flying bridge.

Norb Kowalski joined them near the entrance.

"Down there, Kowalski, back us up!" Osgood changed magazines as Mulvaney loaded six fresh rounds into the revolver, giving him a loaded gun in each hand.

"Gotchyas covered!" Kowalski shouted.

And Osgood was gone, down the steps. Mulvaney was right behind him. . . .

Osgood heard gunfire from overhead, wondering if the Ketsumeidan were firing at shadows or if Steve Oglethorpe had gotten aboard somehow.

There was no time to worry about it.

The hospital ship—a converted passenger liner—was too large to search every cabin at every deck level. So he gambled. "We're getting aft, as fast as we can, Ed."

"You know where it is?"

"No, but anything involving decompression is an emergency procedure, so logic dictates the emergency room area would be as close to the accommodation ladder as possible. That should put it aft on one of the upper levels on the portside, probably near an elevator. Let's go." He broke into a run, careless of how he crossed intersecting corridors. The moving rotor blades of the helicopter were in his thoughts—that Takeuchi's Ketsumeidan terrorists were ready to leave, that the bomb was ready to blow. . . .

Gunfire tore into the bulkhead between Mulvaney and Osgood. Mulvaney shouted, "John! Look out!" and fired both guns toward the suddenly opening doorway. He fired through the door itself, and a man tumbled out from behind it, his submachine gun firing across the deck as he fell. Osgood, who'd already been limping, was bleeding from the right leg, but started ahead at a run again, jumping over the dead man. Mulvaney dropped to one knee and grabbed the dead man's H&K submachine gun and spare magazine, then ran after Osgood.

He pulled the partially spent magazine, saw it contained fewer than five rounds, and tossed it, putting the full magazine up the well instead. With the submachine gun in his right hand and the revolver in his left, he kept moving.

They were well aft by now, and the man by the doorway was the first opposition they had encountered since leaving topside. Mulvaney was beginning to wonder if the bad guys really had put the bomb aft.

Osgood turned a corner in the corridor and then dropped back, shouting, "Look out!" A tongue of flame leaped out at them, hit the corridor wall, and fireballed outward from it. Osgood dropped flat, Mulvaney doing the same. The flames washed over them, not touching them. "Flamethrower!"

"No shit, John!"

Osgood started up, but Mulvaney pushed him down, went past him, and approached the corner again.

"Be careful, Ed!"

Mulvaney didn't dignify the remark with an answer. The smell of jellied gasoline was thick on the air. His eyes were tearing and his throat was closing. He stabbed the submachine gun around the corner and fired a half dozen rounds, then dived flat for cover. Another blast from the flamethrower almost cooked him. "John, can you double back, take that passage we crossed a minute ago, then work your way forward? I can hold 'em here and make 'em think we're still trying to figure out how to get past 'em."

"Good idea. Be careful."

"I was planning on it." Mulvaney edged toward the corner again, this time staying on knees and elbows. When he looked back, Osgood was already on his way. . . .

The passage led to the portside of the ship. There was no guarantee he would be able to do what Mulvaney had in mind, but they could not get past a flamethrower. They were neutralized, and time was running out.

At the end of the passageway, the corridor split two ways, fore and aft. Osgood started to go aft but stopped. If he went forward, he'd be able to get on deck again. If he could work his way aft topside, he might be able to get directly into the emergency center, where he hoped to find the bomb.

Osgood, his leg bleeding a little and his knee hurting worse than ever, started forward. When he reached the companionway steps, he started up along the left-hand side, hugging the bulkhead, the Uzi carbine in both hands.

The smell of cold sea air refreshed him, and the stinging feeling he'd experienced when the flamethrower was used partially left his eyes. He stopped, his head level with the deck, the Uzi's barrel protruding just ahead of him. He heard nothing. A little higher and he was able to see forward. The tarp covering a lifeboat moved, but not with the wind.

He realized that there was a man waiting inside the lifeboat, and that the Ketsumeidan were sufficiently dedicated to give up their lives in order to detonate the bomb. There were just too many of them here to pack aboard the helicopter that Osgood could just see on the pad toward the stern.

Osgood crept upward again, his right knee screaming in pain as he bent it. He brought the Uzi to his shoulder, ready. Using a knife would have been quieter, but riskier and slower. If he died later, then he died, but if he died now there was a substantial chance that neither Mulvaney nor Oglethorpe nor Kowalski, if those men yet lived, would be able to reach the bomb in time.

The tarp moved slightly again, and John Osgood fired a long semiautomatic burst upward, then downward, from the center of mass.

He was up then, his leg nearly buckling under him, but running aft, toward the helicopter.

Gunfire came at him from the helicopter control tower, and Osgood fired back. Bullets rippled across the deck plates, forcing him to take cover beside the accommodation ladder. Two men were near the helicopter, one of them firing toward him. Osgood put a fresh magazine into the Uzi's pistol grip and fired, emptying the magazine into the helicopter's gas tanks.

The helicopter exploded. The man who'd been firing at him pitched upward, and the second man rolled out of the fire, clothing and body aflame. Osgood put another magazine into the Uzi and fired toward the control tower. The flames were already spreading there on the wind.

Sporadic fire returned toward him. He fired again. This time there was no answering fire. Flames rolled across the control tower overhead, consuming the VHF mast.

Osgood was on his feet, running toward the companionway leading below.

Mulvaney fired out the H&K submachine gun and threw it down as he ran back.

Another blast came from the flamethrower, but it was a waste of jellied gasoline because the corridor bulkheads were already aflame, and the fire was spreading.

Mulvaney, the revolver in his left fist, found the first cabin door and opened it. What he saw made him vomit all over the floor.

It was a hospital ward room with four beds. Two of the beds were occupied, but by dead bodies, their throats slit.

"Motherfuckers!" Mulvaney started toward the porthole, trying to gauge its diameter against his shoulders and hips. As Andy told him, he was buttless, but his shoulders were broad. If he went out head first, got one shoulder and his head through and then wriggled the other shoulder out, there was a chance he'd make it.

Osgood moved down the companionway steps. The fumes from the jellied gasoline were intense here, and smoke billowed past him, swirling around him. The flamethrower had done its work, at least in part. The hospital ship was on fire.

Osgood kept close to the bulkhead as he reached the base of the steps. His palms were sweating, and his leg ached.

He saw a sign through the smoke, written in English, French and Japanese: Emergency.

John Osgood started toward it, realizing full well that if men waited here to die for their cause they would be inside this area, waiting for him, too.

He collapsed the stock on the Uzi carbine, making certain he had a fresh magazine loaded. He shifted the gun for a moment to his left hand, drew the P-38K from his shoulder holster, then switched hands again. The P-38K was in his left hand, the Uzi in his right.

Osgood took a step back from the door and kicked with his left foot, his right leg nearly buckling under his weight. The door slammed inward with a crunch, and Osgood dived through. He had to get inside or he was dead anyway. He hit the floor on his side and rolled to cover, as bullets tore into the floor and into the bulkhead, shattering cabinets and bottles.

Osgood returned fire with both weapons, firing through the interior bulkhead separating this area from the examining rooms beyond. There was a gurney near him, lashed to the bulkhead. Osgood decocked and changed magazines in the P-38K. Stuffing the pistol into his trouser band, he released the gurney, released the brake on the wheel near him, and turned the gurney around. Osgood shoved the gurney toward the double swinging doors leading to the examining rooms. The gurney punched through, and Osgood fired the Uzi as he ran through after it.

There were two Japanese with submachine guns, one of them already bleeding, dying. Osgood fired as they fired. A bullet skimmed his left hip, and another grazed his right forearm. Both men went down under the muzzle of his gun.

Silence.

Osgood turned around. Where was Takeuchi?

He changed magazines for the Uzi. Where was the decompression chamber?

There was a doorway to his left. He started toward it. And

the silence ended. It was replaced by laughter. "Is that you, Osgood-san?"

John Osgood, the Uzi tight in his right fist, pushed open the door.

Takeuchi Arisato was sitting in a chair. Wires ran from his hand to a stack of brown cardboard boxes marked "Plasma," which were stacked beside a medical decompression chamber. There was a large porthole at the front of the huge khaki-colored chamber, but Osgood didn't have to look through to know that the atomic bomb he searched for was inside.

Takeuchi laughed again and put his pipe between his teeth. He lit it, using only his right hand. His left hand held some sort of trigger switch. "You have lost, Osgood-san."

"It's hard to consider you a winner, either, Takeuchi-san."

"If I release the pressure of my hand on this switch which I hold, the explosives behind me in the boxes marked 'Plasma' will detonate. Perhaps with enough force to detonate the bomb. If you do not kill me, the bomb will detonate. I had originally left these explosives as a hidden device—"

"A booby trap," Osgood supplied without thinking.

"Thank you, Osgood-san. A booby trap. But when you destroyed my helicopter, I was doomed. So I thought, why not enjoy myself? Here I am."

The smell of Takeuchi's pipe tobacco was strong.

Osgood set down the Uzi on an examining table. "Mind if I smoke?"

"Please, Osgood-san."

Osgood slowly took his cigarette case from his right hip pocket, opened it, tapped a cigarette against it, then pocketed the case. "You know, whatever misguided sense of patriotism you follow, you're wrong, Takeuchi. You're not a hero, just a mass murderer, killing or maiming hundreds of thousands of people, women, children, old people. If you give it up, you walk. I swear that."

Takeuchi laughed. Osgood meant the offer sincerely, but doubted that Takeuchi would accept. "We will all be dead, Osgood-san, in two minutes or less."

"Hmm." Osgood nodded. "Just in case I do defeat you, where might I find Gorchek? Or for that matter, Friedman and Naguchi?"

Takeuchi smiled wickedly. "Minoru-san felt that while these persons lived, there was a danger that they might confess their part in what will happen here. For that reason they do not live anymore."

"Mr. Mulvaney—he's alive, you know. What about Mr. Peterson of the well-known 486 SX chip?"

"He knows only Gorchek. If his involvement is discovered, it will only reinforce the idea that America detonated this bomb to kill thousands of Japanese." He smiled again.

Osgood was searching his right front trouser pocket for his lighter, even though it was in his left.

There was nothing else now but to try this and pray.

Osgood's right hand came out of his pocket, the fingers slightly curled, as if around his lighter. His hand snapped up toward the butt of the Special Dart hanging below his spare magazines under his right armpit. As he grabbed for it, he threw himself toward Takeuchi. Takeuchi's left hand started to open.

Osgood had the knife snapped free of its sheath and hammered it downward, not knowing if what he was doing would work at all. The knife went through the back of Takeuchi's hand like a spike, impaling it to the arm of the chair. Takeuchi screamed, and tried to throw himself from the chair and reach for Osgood's throat.

Takeuchi's right leg snapped upward. Osgood took a glancing blow to his crotch and fell back as he let go of the knife.

He heard glass smashing somewhere, but there was no time to look. Osgood hit the floor hard, his head cracking against it as he drew his pistol. He shook his head, tried to clear it, punched the Walther toward the glass at the front of the decompression chamber, and fired as fast as he could, emptying the gun.

Simultaneously there were pistol shots and there was a small explosion.

For a split second Osgood thought the bomb had detonated, or thought the explosives in the boxes marked "Plasma" had. But it was only the rush of air. The door of the decompression chamber buckled slightly.

Behind him, he heard the sound of metal scraping against something. He turned his head. One of the Ketsumeidan stood there, holding the flamethrower.

There were pistol shots again, and Osgood rolled across the floor for cover from the flamethrower.

As he looked up, the man with the flamethrower just stood there.

Osgood looked toward the direction from which the shots had come. Still impaled to the chair by Osgood's knife, Takeuchi Arisato hung forward, bloodstains across the back of his head, his pipe smoking on the floor. He saw Ed Mulvaney leaning in through the shattered porthole. Mulvaney's right hand held a semiautomatic pistol.

Osgood looked back toward the doorway.

The man holding the flamethrower dropped to his knees, his eyes wide open. His head slammed against the doorjamb, but the flamethrower wedged his body there so it couldn't fall any farther.

"I figured that guy was just trying to help you out with a light for that phony cigarette dodge of yours, Ozzie. Otherwise I woulda killed him sooner. Did we win?"

John Osgood looked at the decompression chamber. The pressure gauge on the outside showed one atmosphere, which meant the bomb shouldn't go off.

He looked again at Takeuchi Arisato.

Then he looked at Ed Mulvaney.

"Yes."

Chapter Twenty-nine

Happy New Year

For all the bad P.R. the Japanese were getting lately—buying up everything that wasn't nailed down, pumping their cars and their electronics into the American market while still restricting U.S. imports to Japan—Mulvaney had to hand it to them.

They were almost as good at a cover-up as the folks in Washington, or even the folks in Chicago.

The bomb was quietly returned to the United States government.

The hospital ship, which was burning out of control and had nothing but dead people aboard (aside from Mulvaney, Osgood, Oglethorpe, and Kowalski), was scuttled, then blown up to clear the harbor. It was "a terrible disaster as the result of faulty electrical wiring aboard the ship, which will be investigated by several maritime commissions."

The deaths at the site of the Friedman-Naguchi Expedition were still being worked on, but nothing concerning them leaked yet to the press. Mulvaney, however, had confidence that the most devious minds in Tokyo and Washington would come up with something that would make everyone happy. It might even make Friedman and Naguchi get the Nobel prize, or something. Posthumously, of course.

Edith was on an extended vacation, paid for by Uncle Sam—a two-year cruise of the world to help her forget. If she didn't come back with a man after that, she wasn't really trying.

Rather than a reprimand—which Osgood had told Mulvaney was the least to expect—Osgood was quietly offered a medal by the Japanese government. Osgood—what a guy!—said he'd refuse it unless his friend—" without whom the job never would have been done, without whom Japan would have suffered a terrible disaster"—got one, too.

Andy had the medal now. Mulvaney had Fed Ex-ed it to her.

There were two things pressing at the moment. One of them was to get home by New Year's Eve. They'd gotten their medals presented to them on Christmas Day. Andy had presents for everybody—"Even got one for your pal Osgood, although it's probably not classy enough for him!" There was going to be a party, a New Year's Eve party. Lew was just out of the hospital and feeling pretty good, according to what Andy said over the telephone. Lew and his wife were going to be there.

As they drove through the swirling snow, Osgood said, "I really feel like I'll be imposing, Ed."

"Nonsense, John, unless you've got some wild gig goin' with all sorts of movie stars and models and shit."

"No. I was just planning, well, at the stroke of midnight I was planning on listening to an old Guy Lombardo record. You know the one."

"You're jivin' me, right?" Mulvaney laughed. He lit a cigarette. Osgood didn't say a word. Mulvaney said, "Then it's settled, man. Once we're through with this, we drive home together. We take it easy, and if the snow doesn't get too bad, we'll be home in plenty of time for the party. Andy's even lined up a girl for you."

"Ed, really, uhh—"

"Look, I know this blind date stuff can be a pain, but she's pretty, Andy tells me, and she's smart, so Andy figured you'd like her for sure."

"Thank you."

The second matter to be taken care of was coming up.

Osgood stopped the rented Jaguar at the curb.

Mulvaney looked at him. "Wanna flip for it?"

"Ed, I have a bit more chance of getting away with it than you do. If I'm caught, that is."

"Yeah, but I should do it."

"No."

Mulvaney lit a cigarette "Come on."

"There's only one gun, Ed, and it's my gun."

"You gonna be that way about it? I mean, like since it's your gun you're gonna make the rules and everything? What you gonna do if I don't go along with ya? Take your gun and go home?"

Osgood shook his head, his smile visible in the green light from the dashboard. "Really, Ed." Osgood took a cigarette from his fancy silver case and lit it with his fancy lighter.

"We both go in, we can let Peterson decide who kills him," Ed Mulvaney suggested.

"That's a little tacky, Ed."

Mulvaney grinned. "I knew you'd like it."